Synchronicity

Synchronicity

Two Hearts, One Spirit, a Forbidden Love

A Novel

Patricia Ann Chaffee

Book Design by Robert Harrison of Seneca Author Services
Cover Photography by Patricia Ann Chaffee
Author photo by Julia Manners Photography

Paperback ISBN: 979-8-9929847-0-5
E-Book ISBN: 979-8-9929847-1-2

Dedication

To my lifelong muses, Adam and Joshua, for all the ways you inspire me and make me proud to be your Mom. For reminding me, as I have taught you, that there are no limits to what we can accomplish. And those crack-of-dawn conversations that make me laugh til I cry.

To the angels who call me Grandma Patty...
Noah, Octavian, Aurelia, and Lucius.
I love you.

With Gratitude

To my brilliant itty bitty writing group, the two best cheerleaders on the face of the earth. Authors Hillary Oat and Dr. Joanne Moore, for their friendship, patience, encouragement, and relentless pursuit of the rest of the story.

To Dave Smith, former editor of Sun Publishing for believing in me, and giving my writing a platform to take off way back when. For his kindness, skill, and affirmation in the final editing of Synchronicity.

To weaver, writer, and photographer Grace Farell, for creating an opportunity for me to develop Seth and Anna's story during her fabulous writing groups in Rhode Island.

To Julia Manners for her miraculous photography skills, encouragement, and friendship.

To Robert Harrison for his exceptional interior layout and cover design and most of all his endless patience.

To my friend John Urbanski for his seminary mischief that inspired parts of Synchronicity.

To my partner Jim, for tolerating my absence while sequestered in my studio/sanctuary for countless hours of research, writing, and editing.

And to the Roman Catholic Church for giving me so much material to work with. So much to question, to challenge, to admire, and ultimately to love.

Thank you, Patty

Chapter One

"Let them run free," I whisper.

I've been told that you have to be extraordinarily clumsy to fall off a docked sailboat. Especially a 35' sloop. I don't know if that's true, but it felt true enough, especially after my prince jumped in to rescue me as if I were a drowning maiden. I know he was just trying to help, but I'm more than capable of saving myself, as I've done most of my life. I didn't need his help or anyone else's. Yet there I was, in the chilled September waters of Cape Cod Bay, wrapped in the arms of a handsome stranger who was about to change my life forever. In as unlikely a situation as can exist, more than I could ever know, we climb aboard the Synchronicity.

I'd had enough and knew it was time for a respite, a break, maybe an escape, whatever you want to call it. I arrive for an early autumn retreat, desperately needing to get away from Connecticut. I'm headed to Gram's quirky old cottage for a month. One quiet, solitary, shoulder season month, and then, who knows? Back home, I guess. Reluctantly. Gram left her old beach cottage to me when she passed earlier this year and I haven't been there since. I still think of it as hers, but couldn't bring myself to go to the place that held so many precious memories. I miss her so much.

I hold my breath refusing to blink, as I cross over the all-too-narrow Bourne Bridge spanning the Cape Cod Canal. It's the first landmark that makes me feel like I'm on the Cape. Heading out Route 6, I notice sand on the side of the road, and the scrub pines. I'm almost there. My home away from home. Another 15 or 20 minutes and I'll be in South Yarmouth. I take that exit and realize I'm just not ready, and instead of turning left toward 28 I go right and detour toward Route 6A.

September didn't used to be very busy, but folks have caught on to the spectacular shoulder seasons of the Cape. So, it's still pretty busy, although not nearly as bad as in the summer months. Beaches are packed. Restaurants have lines out the door, and you can't get a reservation. There is no place to park with main roads bumper to bumper. After Labor Day, droves of people leave who have been here all summer. Kids go back to school. And the tranquil beauty of this special place returns. That's the Cape Cod I love. And the one I'm looking for on this trip. Silence. Solitude. Sanctuary.

Cruising along the picturesque 6A I don't know where I'm going or why, when I spot the Lemon Tree Village in Brewster and pull in. I guess I'm just killing time, but that's okay. I have no place to be and no one to answer to. This place has been here for as long as I can remember. Gram used to bring me here to get an ice cream cone with colored sprinkles. The memory makes me smile. I give a nod to the Zen Frog, St. Francis, and laughing Buddha statues out front and find a parking spot. This marketplace is one of my favorite spots on the Cape. There are shops to get something to eat, find souvenirs, and buy everything from Adirondack chairs to jewelry to pots and pans. There is even a yoga studio where you can get a massage, do some energy work, or visit a salt cabin, which I'm thinking of trying during my stay. I meander mindlessly through the various shops picking up a gray sweatshirt with Brewster printed across the front. I select a jar of chocolates at the candy store that look exactly like real shells. I save pottery for last.

Lemon Tree Pottery is filled with hand-crafted treasures and yes, more pottery than I've ever seen in one place. I do love pottery. Just the idea that anyone can take a lump of clay and craft it into something functional and beautiful astonishes me. It's a true art. Venturing inside, I can't take in the sights fast enough. There is so much to see, each piece more beautiful than the last. I know I'm acting like a tourist but I don't care. I've missed it. I haven't been to the Cape in a few years except for Gram's funeral and that was a short, sad trip. I wish I'd made more time to visit with her. Isn't that always the way?

I select a hand-thrown coffee mug from the dozens on display, each one unique. It has a roomy handle and wavy colors blending dark blues, grays, and greens reminding me of Nantucket Sound. I look it over holding it with both hands assessing its weight, feeling its energy, running my fingers over the smooth finish, deciding that's the one. I set it on the counter while I continue looking around. I spot a wall of plaques by the talented Sarah Rubin. Some hang on leather cords, and others are stacked on a shelf beneath. Each has an inspirational word, phrase, or symbol in the design reflecting Christian, Judaic, or other faith traditions. I step back and look at the whole display, marveling at the craftsmanship. There are words like, "Namaste, Peace, Shalom, Cead Mile Failte, All Shall Be Well, Rejoice, Be Still," and many others. But there is one, in colors similar to the mug that I chose. It speaks to my heart, reading, "Serenity, Courage, Wisdom." I can use all three. The trinity of attributes I would greatly appreciate right about now. I add it to my selections on the counter, pay with cash, and set my things safely in the car. By now I'm hungry and grab a bottle of iced green tea, and a ham and cheese sandwich on a croissant from the deli shop and continue along 6A.

Heading back toward Yarmouth I notice the sign for Sesuit Harbor and turn toward another familiar spot. As I pull into the near-empty parking lot, I'm delighted that no attendant is stopping me. September is a magnificent time to enjoy Cape Cod because while most of the summer people have disappeared, seasonal rules and fees went with them. I just love the tranquility I experience at the Cape, though I admit I appreciate it more off-season.

I gather up my makeshift picnic, the beach quilt I always keep in the car, and an L.L. Bean tote. Armed with sunscreen, a journal, a hat, a kite, and whatever I'm reading, off I go. Visitors and residents of any shoreline should always have four things with them: protection from the sun, a book to read, a book to write in, and nourishment for the body and spirit. Through the sandy path between the dunes, I unceremoniously plod toward the beach and the spectacular beauty of Cape Cod Bay. When I decide on a spot at the base of the dunes, I drop my gear and pause long enough to close my eyes, take in a deep breath of the rich salty air, and let it seep into my body and soul. It feels good to be here.

My personality is very solitary and I prefer to keep it that way. Choosing a profession as a writer only perpetuates that lifestyle. I'm a firm believer that I write best based on my experiences in life, and if there are no new experiences to write about...well, I have to find some...or create some. But as I open the blanket and set up my little camp, I'm pondering this fact and don't feel like I want anything but to be left alone right now. Alone with my thoughts, my tea, my ham and Swiss, and my grief. I settle onto the old patchwork quilt and hide behind sunglasses and under a straw hat, hoping to be left alone.

There are a few people around but not many. An older couple strolls along the water's edge, holding hands, giving each other an occasional glance of appreciation, and a smile. I wonder what is their secret. A woman walks with her head down, stopping occasionally to pick up a shell, a stone, or a piece of sea glass, lost in her thoughts. In the distance is a younger couple with two little toddlers stuffed in a red buggy with big wide wheels traversing the sandy terrain. Both vying to escape containment. "Let them run free," I whisper.

I unwrap my sandwich and enjoy lunch, flavored by the salty air. Everything tastes better by the beach. I'm trying to savor this moment before I have to get back to reality. I've yet to process Gram being gone as well as other people who are no longer a part of my life. Some are easier to let go of than others. Gram was like a mother to me, far more than my own. We had a connection. A spiritual one. A creative one. In some ways, I'm not anxious to get to the cottage she called home.

The wind has picked up, and with procrastination high on my priority list, rather than packing up and getting on the road, I spot my kite sticking out of the beach tote. I always have it with me as you never know when the opportunity might arise to use it. I hate to miss a chance to play. So, it lives in my car year-round. I'm on Sesuit Beach with its wide-open expanse of sand, and few people around, so why not? I launch, and the next thing I know I find myself wrangling my kite, taking my mind off what lies ahead… for the moment. A momentary reprieve from life.

I love kite flying. But I especially love the freedom of it darting in and out, pulling on the string reaching so high in the sky and then coming close, daring to dip its nose into the Bay and out again. It's like it has a feisty personality. I'm admiring its tenacity with my nose to the sky when I realize I'm no longer alone. From the direction of the marina, some guy comes walking toward me and plunks himself onto the sand, not 10 feet from my blanket. Like there's a whole beach available. Why is he parking himself near me, I wonder? Give a girl a little space, eh? I return my focus to the kite, which is appropriately named, Wendy. Rainbow bright stripes in ripstop nylon fabric with a fluorescent green neon tail fly high above the cool grainy sand. My visitor doesn't say a word but sits in silence watching me, watching Wendy, barefoot, on the now deserted September beach.

Just about mid-day, the weather is gorgeous and I'm feeling particularly carefree and oblivious, yes, that's the word. I get so caught up sometimes that the rest of the world just...slips away. Normally I might have been concerned about this stranger, getting comfortable and enjoying my show, but I wasn't, not at all. From the corner of my eye, I notice he is tall, maybe 5'10" or even six feet, with a tanned, fit appearance although not in a building contractor kind of way. He's wearing khaki shorts and a navy Cape Cod sweatshirt with white, collegiate-style lettering across the front, similar to the one I just bought. That makes me pretty sure he is not from around here. Locals never wear Cape Cod sweatshirts. He seems unconcerned about his wavy and unruly, dark brown hair, as it blows in the very wind that is keeping my kite from crashing to the ground. We make brief eye contact and he smiles as I continue with my piloting. Yeah, he was an attractive guy, sitting there entertaining himself, watching me fly my kite. Strange, I thought.

I'd no sooner flashed him a smile laced with uncertainty when a gust of wind came along sending Wendy crashing to the ground. She is now entangled in a crooked piece of gray weathered fence, leaning toward the base of the dunes. I walk in that direction looping my kite string around and around its purple, plastic spool. As I get closer, I stand with one hand on my denim-clad hip looking at the tangled mess. I strain to reach over the fence to disentangle her and am lost in the situation when I feel a presence. My audience appears right behind me, apparently ready to assist.

"Hi there," he says with a confident voice that exudes a surprising gentleness. "Can I give you a hand?"

He doesn't wait for my response. I turn and look at him instantly becoming aware of …oooh yeah, you guessed it… the scent of Coppertone. Umm, my favorite. "Uh, yeah, sure, thanks," I stutter, trying not to appear too moved by his size or his scent, but I'm a sucker for sun safety. He had taken off his sweatshirt revealing a dark blue T-shirt and two somewhat muscular, suntanned arms. I notice the blue of the shirt brings out the intense ocean blue of his eyes. Eyes that hold me spellbound, for a moment. Intense. Dark. Mysterious. And his arms weren't bulging but arms that move with certainty. I step aside to allow my hero to rescue Wendy from her entanglement. He easily reaches beyond the fence and has it back in my hands within moments.

"Here you go," he says as he hands my treasure back to me. "I'm Seth," offering his hand, waiting for me to introduce myself.

"Nice to meet you Seth, I'm Anna." Our hands touch and a chill runs through me as he hesitates the slightest extra moment before letting me go. Did I imagine that? Yeah, probably, just my overactive imagination running away without me… or maybe not.

"Do you mind if I give it a try?" he asks.

I couldn't even imagine this guy wanting to fly my kite, but there he was, inviting himself into my reverie. "Of course. Enjoy!" I say, returning my kite to his seemingly capable hands.

I'm intrigued by this man who so unexpectedly entered my story, if only for these few moments. As I go over to my blanket and plunk down to watch, I consider the situation. That's what writers do. We consider any experience, to be fodder for the next piece just waiting to be written. We wonder and contemplate and imagine and sometimes do everything but fully experience the moment ourselves. We live vicariously through the characters we create, and the people we interview. I'm trying to change this and am reminded why I am here. To get real. To be me, in all my imperfect, messy splendor. To get in touch with the woman my God has created me to be.

I think we spend the first half of life being told we are not good enough, not pretty enough, not rich enough. Until it is so deeply embedded in our psyche, that it takes the second half of life to recover. It is then, that we discover the gift of our beauty, brilliance, and authenticity, who we truly are, and what is real for us. It takes that connection for us to allow ourselves to honor our truth and integrity through our creativity, in how we love, and in how we live our lives. I'm mulling this over when I hear a muffled crunch and an, "Uh, oh," coming from the direction of my new acquaintance. It seems my kite has taken a dive around the curve where the long stone jetty sticks out just before the Marina. And Seth has taken off after it.

Chapter Two

"Aw, come on, I'm harmless. I promise."

I wander off in the direction of my kite to investigate. As I round the bend and get closer, I observe the situation, witnessing an unbelievable sight, to say the least. Having given my kite a whole lotta line, Seth has entangled Wendy in the rigging near the bow, of one of the few sailboats still docked at the marina. I look around to see if anyone is watching as he approaches the boat with reckless abandon.

I yell out to him, "Hey! You can't do that!"

"Really? And why is that?" he asks calmly.

"That's someone's boat! You're trespassing."

By now my 5'6" frame has made its way to the dock at the crash site. Although no one would call me delicate, and I'm always struggling to lose some unwanted weight, I can make my way on a sandy beach in quick time. I arrive to debate with this stranger about the appropriateness of being on someone's boat without permission. Okay, so I'm one of those people who always does the "right thing."

Doing the right thing is being questioned at this moment as I watch this exceptionally handsome man attempt to free my kite. And it's all his fault.

I notice a handful of boats of assorted shapes and sizes are still in the water despite the peak season being over. The wind blows in my direction and I can smell his Coppertone again. I swear the stuff is an aphrodisiac. When I recover from the waft that has made me just a little dizzy, I realize he has retrieved my kite from the rigging unharmed. I am in shock. I can not believe his nerve trespassing onto someone's boat without hesitation, and I decide to tell him so.

"I can't believe you did that!"

"Well, uh, I'm sorry but it's not damaged or anything. The wind just took off with it," he says defensively.

"I don't mean that. I can't believe you just waltzed onto someone's boat as if you own it."

"Well, I do, at least it's mine for now, anyway," he says amused, clearly in control of the situation.

And happy no doubt, to make me squirm after my assumptions were wrong. Feeling like a fool and completely embarrassed I don't know what to say although it is clear he is enjoying the situation immensely.

"Would you like to come aboard?" he asks, grinning from ear to ear.

"Well, actually, I ought to be getting back to... uh."

"Your kite flying?" he asks, continuing to wind kite string around the spool. "Are you on a schedule? Where are you from anyway? I ought to know something about you before I bring a stranger on board," pointing toward the vessel.

"I'm from Connecticut. Mystic," I stammer, trying to regain my composure.

"Well, please come aboard Anna from Connecticut."

I look at the gentle stranger still near the bow, winding kite string, and take the giant step necessary to reach the deck of the boat that just won't hold still. The wind that was so adept at keeping my kite in action, is also keeping Seth's boat rocking. As I reach the deck and head toward the bow, a particularly strong breeze tosses the boat just enough to make me lose my balance. I lunge full throttle into him. I'm thoroughly embarrassed and I back away apologizing for the mishap. Creating some space between us, I don't watch where I'm stepping, careening backward off the boat and into the seasonably cool water. Spending as much time around the ocean as I have all my life, I, fortunately, know how to swim. But my knight doesn't stop to notice before jumping in to rescue me. I was attempting to swim over to the ladder on the starboard side, when, I was accosted by my rescuer, attempting to save me from some alleged drowning. I'm inclined to smack him away and rescue myself as I have done for as long as I can remember. But I don't. Before I know it, his arm is around my waist, our wet bodies facing each other as we reach the ladder. With one hand on the steps, we hold each other's eyes for just a moment … and the water doesn't feel so cold anymore.

"Ladies first," he says.

Paralyzed by his gaze I don't think to climb up the ladder. His invitation snaps me back to reality. The last thing I want is to have him underneath me as I climb the narrow ladder, but he gives me no choice and I just want to get out of the water. He follows so quickly I thought he must have hurled himself over the side like a gymnast on a saddle horse.

And here we are, Seth in his khakis and Coppertone, and, hey, where did his shirt go? He must have yanked it off before he jumped in. And me dripping in my denim shorts and bright green tee-shirt, leaving little or nothing to the imagination. The breeze that sent me flying, adds to the detail. I quickly cross my arms, attempting to cover up, shivering from the breeze as well as from this man who has taken me completely off guard. There is nothing good about this situation and I feel completely self-conscious, with a body that features curves in all the wrong places. That's how I feel most of the time. Especially when I notice the slightest suggestion of a grin being restrained by my knight. When he looks away, I'm guessing he's as embarrassed as I am. Mumbling something about a towel, he disappears into the cabin below. I attempt to regain composure, as he quickly returns with an oversized, fluffy white towel.

"Here you go. This should warm you up a bit."

I gratefully accept and stand there shivering in the wind. "Thank you... f-f-f-for everything," I stutter. "I think I should go now." Reaching out to hand the towel back I notice an imprint on it below a sailboat logo. It reads, *Synchronicity*.

"I'm sorry, but I can't let you do that," Seth tells me in his most authoritative tone, which I notice he does very well. Chills run up my spine. Because of the chill in the air or because of Seth's tone? I'm not sure, perhaps both.

"I feel terrible," he continues. "You're standing there

shivering. I can't very well let you go off to catch pneumonia, can I? I have some dry things you can change into, Anna."

I shiver again, the sound of my name coming from his lips makes my stomach flutter. *What is going on here? I'm a total wreck just being in this guy's presence. And now he's offering me clothes. Probably leftovers from the last woman he seduced into his lair.*

"I really ought to get going," I argue. "Lots to do, places to go, people to see…" Anything to get away from here, I'm thinking.

"Aw, come on, I'm harmless. I promise," he says with a grin. "Just offering some assistance to a very wet friend." *When did we become friends, I wonder?*

"All right, I guess that would be fine," I respond, remembering I have clothes in the car, although it is quite a ways away.

"Great!" Seth booms, and hurries down the stairs into the cabin, calling for me to follow. I'm swaying from the combined wake of his energy, the scent of his Coppertone, and the movement of the boat. I enjoy boats mostly from dry land. A sailboat like this is completely foreign to me. I finally go below after managing the ladder-like steps. My hero is rummaging through a cranberry-red duffle bag perched on a bed in an alcove on the opposite end of the boat. Passing by me to get to where he is going, he puts both hands on my shoulders as he squeezes through en route to a cupboard. Our bodies touch for the briefest moment, but Seth is on a mission and hardly notices. I, on the other hand, am still frazzled when he returns with his find. I take in my surroundings and wonder how I got into this situation. Seth holds out a handful of items.

"I'll leave you to change, just let me know if you need anything else." And he disappears up the stairs before I can say, "Thanks."

Looking around, I notice the galley, a small eating area, and a large bed. The bed has crisp white sheets peeking out from under a navy-blue duvet with *Synchronicity*, and the logo printed on the center, just like the towel. There is even a tiny bathroom. Very close quarters but also very tastefully appointed. The cabin has a masculine, nautical décor, with rich teak finishes everywhere. On two benches are solid blue cushions, and narrow long oval windows run along the top of the walls. Pinstripe curtains hang from pewter rods. On the table, I notice a small cedar candle holder. A gold crucifix is attached above a red votive glass, and a Bible marked *NRSV– Catholic Edition*, rests next to it. A very worn book with a black leather binding that reads *Liturgy of the Hours* perches next to the Bible. A rainbow of frayed ribbons dangles from the pages. I lean to look closer and hear Seth moving around.

Everything is small, close, and carefully secured. Everything but Seth. He isn't small at all. I'm taking in my surroundings and contemplating where I can change my clothes when I realize there is no place to go. The bathroom is barely big enough to sit down much less change. And the *bedroom* is more like a cupboard with a wall-to-wall mattress filling it. I reluctantly decide I have no choice but to change right there. Still dripping wet and shivering, I quickly remove my wet things. Unfolding the clothes he handed me, I realize I am holding a pair of men's plaid boxers and a crisp, white long sleeve, dress shirt…about two sizes too big. Before I can get the dry clothes on, I hear his voice calling from the top of the stairs.

"How ya doing down there? Need any help?"

"No! No, I'm fine. I'll be right up," I yell, trying to hide the panic in my voice at the thought of Seth bounding down the stairs right now.

The shirt is tailored and reaches just above my knees covering most of the shorts. I roll my sleeves up, muster some attitude, and return to the deck, delighted to find the sun strong and warm. And the wind has weakened, not unlike my knees. Feeling the warmth of the sun on me I take a deep breath of that salty air and evaluate my next move. While I'm evaluating mine, apparently Seth is evaluating his, by taking in the sight of his new *friend* on his old deck.

"Anna," he says in a slow deliberate tone, "you look absolutely…refreshed. How was your swim?" I could swear he was going to say something else, but "refreshed" is what came out. And I'm not sure which would have been worse…a compliment on how great I look in his shorts, or an antagonistic one about falling off his boat. I decide the latter is the better choice. Deciding to play it casually, I attempt to appear unscathed by the event.

"I feel very refreshed thank you. Nothing like a little dip in the September waters of Sesuit Harbor," I respond, trying to feign ego and pride intact.

He watches me closely, his gaze never faltering as if he'll miss something if he looks away. He listens well I notice and isn't bothered by the silence between us. But I am. In my nervousness, I decide to turn this around.

"It occurs to me that I don't know anything about you," I say, "other than the fact that you like to fly other people's kites."

"And rescue drowning maidens don't forget," he adds with a grin, that I already find unnerving.

"So, tell me about yourself. I'm standing here in *your* clothes, on *your* boat and I know nothing about you. Most folks would not say this is an ideal scenario."

"How about if I tell you all you want to know over dinner?" he suggests.

I'm torn between the logic of promising to return his clothes and getting out of there while I still have some dignity left and the undeniable attraction I'm feeling. It makes it hard to pull myself away. This is the part of the story where I'm likely to start fumbling all over my words as I figure out my next move. I feel safe with him despite the adventures of the day. And I don't feel safe with anyone. Trust is not my strength. Trusting people is not my strength. Yet he doesn't feel threatening at all. But I still need to keep my guard up, I remind myself. Always have to keep my guard up. Why the suit of armor? To avoid getting hurt, right? Will Seth hurt me if I let him get close? Like Ethan did? Like grieving the loss of Gram did? Like everyone I've ever loved has? I know I'm getting ahead of myself but that's what I do. I envision a cataclysmic ending and call it a day. My Mayday radar has been activated.

Oh, right, he's waiting to know if I'll have dinner, while I deliberate his intentions and life's big questions. I can't help myself. I'm willing to take the risk.

"Sure, dinner would be nice," I say with absolute uncertainty. I see that intoxicating grin of his, and look away, afraid to be affected any more than I already am. I think he wonders if I am gonna bolt right then and there. I thought about it. And I don't know what kept me from doing just that.

"Wonderful!" he says.

"Where shall we meet?" I ask.

"Meet?" he asks with a puzzled expression. "Why don't I pick you up…say around 7:00? Where are you staying? Or do you live here?"

"Ummm…Uhhh, I am in a cottage in Bass River," I respond with hesitation and give him the address. "It's right off South Shore Drive."

"Sure, I know the area well. And I know a great place for dinner. You'll just love it. They have the best food on the Cape. It's casual… so I'll pick you up about 7:00."

Standing there, holding a rainbow-colored kite, in boxers, and a man's dress shirt, with very little dignity left, I agree to have dinner with a handsome stranger. After all, I have to return his clothes.

Chapter Three

A white weathered sign hung just below its gable, that read Magic Cottage.

B y the time Anna gathers her things on the beach, gets back to her car, and across the Cape to Gram's cottage, she knows she won't have a whole lot of time to unpack or get settled before Seth arrives. She also wonders what she was thinking when she agreed to have dinner with him. For God's sake, she just met the man, and she came to the Cape to get away from one, not find another.

Anna is feeling emptiness, loss, longing, and a million other things. Not just because of losing Gram, who had been her shining light, no matter what was going on in her life. And not because of leaving Connecticut where she lived all her life. And not because of dumping Ethan who betrayed her in the worst way. Or that her life as a writer was so uncertain. There is much to grieve. What is she doing with Seth, who has no idea what she is going through? She is feeling sorry for herself and while she knows she needs time alone, she thinks the distraction of another human being will be nice. Perhaps, dare she hope, a kind human being.

But, nobody wants to be with a 45-year-old woman in the middle of a mid-life crisis, thought Anna. And I don't want to go home. I don't have to go home. This is my home now. I can write from here. I can finish my book. I can even get a freelance assignment or two if I want. I don't need to rush back to Connecticut. There is nothing there for me anymore.

Anna accepted Ethan's proposal three years ago and for the life of her, she didn't know why. She'd mistakenly allowed him to put that wretched marquise diamond set in yellow gold on her finger. He was quite impressed with his choice. Ethan is one of those "great on paper" guys. But at the heart of it, he had no interest in settling down. They were both independent and successful although in very different ways. He thought he could control her. Like she would be a *proper* wife for him to parade around at his investment firm events. Create a home to show off, a wife to show off. He was always nudging her to lose some weight and work out, and although she wanted to, she didn't need him reminding her. He didn't truly care about her. He was more interested in his money and how much he could accumulate. Stocks and trades and 12-hour work-days were of no interest to Anna. She appreciated a simple life more than anything and saw such beauty in that simplicity. Ethan raised all kinds of red flags and his arachnophobia was the least of them. That was a sight to behold when certain situations arose.

And even though she had just met him, Seth seemed like someone who genuinely cared about people. She wasn't sure how she knew that. She just did. She could feel it. Ethan doesn't care about anyone but himself and his money, money he didn't share too readily, at least not with her, except for that hideous diamond. She doesn't know what she ever saw in him. There were so many unanswered questions, evasiveness, and that ever-present arrogance. Those things were bad enough but that final straw prompted her to dig deep and make a decision.

Just a couple of weeks ago, while at his place, she had searched for something to wear for lunch. She only had a handful of clothes at Ethan's massive, upscale, uber-contemporary condo in Stamford. It was cold and unwelcoming, lacking character, not unlike Ethan she thought. Anna glanced at the clock and realized she'd better get moving if she was going to meet him on time at the Bull and Bear. That was a favorite of Wall Street types and so of course his favorite. She had agreed to meet him but intended to break off their engagement before she left for the Cape. Looking at a three-quarter sleeve, satin tea-length black dress, she returned to the moment. Grabbed a pair of black strappy sandals and went into the bedroom to get dressed.

Floor-to-ceiling windows lined one wall with views of the Rippowam River. Ethan's bed was an Alaskan king and she marveled at the size of it. At home, she has a queen which is plenty big enough for her but crowded when he was there. He liked staying at his place better anyway. Today will be the last of that, she thought. Their relationship was comfortable but dry and she thought of it like an Arizona desert. Pretty, but generally lifeless. She is an ocean girl and is nourished by that environment, by water, not the desert sun. She is rarely in his condo alone but feels a sense of curiosity and strolls around his massive place opening a drawer here and a closet door there, not finding anything out of the ordinary. She isn't usually one to snoop. It went against her character to even open his datebook, much less wander into his office. He always kept that door closed and she never crossed the threshold. Ethan Taylor Banks isn't the most trusting individual, not even with her.

They met when she was freelancing for Entrepreneur Magazine and she was assigned to interview a financial analyst. Not usually a topic of interest to her whatsoever, but it paid the bills. Usually unimpressed by either celebrity or high-powered business execs, there was something different about Ethan that initially intrigued her. He had an unearned arrogance about him that stirred up her reporter's itch. The more she learned about him the curiouser and curiouser she got. And he wasn't half bad-looking himself. Unfortunately, he would heartily agree.

Bringing herself back to brighter things, Anna pulls into the crushed shell driveway of the gray-weathered cottage. Periwinkle blue shutters with sea star cutouts adorn each of the windows. She just sat there for a moment taking in the view of Nantucket Sound at the end of the lane. A worn stockade fence flanked the opposite side of the road where the small houses were, sheltering much larger waterfront homes on the other side. Gram's cottage, now her cottage, was third in from the beach, close enough to smell the salt air and sometimes feel the sea spray when the water was rough and at high tide. She steps out of her silver vintage Volvo and stands looking at the little structure that hasn't changed much over the years.

A white weathered sign hangs just below its gable, that reads *Magic Cottage*. It had been the sanctuary where Grandma Iris lived year-round since Anna was in her late teens. Her name originated from the Greek word meaning rainbow. Although the iris flower was considered a symbol of power and majesty, it was often associated in the Christian faith tradition with the Passion of Christ and the Resurrection. Gram had been proud of her name. The cottage was a magical place in many ways as Anna would soon find out. For Iris, it represents a feeling of being carefree, where anything is possible and the sea breeze off Nantucket Sound was ever-present.

Anna wished there was some touching tale about the cottage being in the family for generations as was true for so many cottages on the Cape. The story is told that when Grandma Iris's name came up after several years on a lengthy wait list for low-income senior housing, something happened, something very big.

Iris had gathered at her best friend Harriet's house to celebrate her 60th birthday with friends on a typical winter Sunday. It was January, as she was a New Year baby, and there wasn't much in New England colder than January on Cape Cod. The fire was crackling, the smell of bourbon-spiked cider loomed in the air, the carrot cake with her favorite buttercream frosting was waiting to be cut and candles in the shape of a six and a zero were poised to be lit.

Iris opened cards as all her friends looked on. They had long ago agreed not to give gifts because they had everything they needed or wanted, for the most part anyway. Harry saved his card for last. He was a dear friend who had been wooing her for what seemed like forever, even proposed a time or two, unsuccessfully. But she just wasn't interested in him that way. Iris treasured her independence and he was a good friend. That was enough.

Harry was a large, robust fellow with a kind and generous nature to him. He loved to smile and was one of those people who made others smile too, just to be in his presence. Tucked in Harry's card, Iris discovered six lottery tickets, each one to represent a decade of her life, he told her. Iris loved his thoughtfulness and loved the idea of possibilities even more. And although she wasn't much of a risk-taker herself, she thought it would be fun to scratch the Frosty the Doughman, million-dollar instant lottery tickets. These things were always intriguing she thought, but rarely amounted to much more than a trip to Dairy Queen or a drive through Wendy's for a spicy chicken sandwich she mused. With a side order of Tums of course.

She scratched and scratched, first one, then two, then three, while the others looked on anxiously. Then four, five, "There's the chicken sandwich," she thought and continued scratching. Then with anticipation, wrestling with disappointment, she was about to scratch number six when she looked up at Harry. He was towering over her as she sat on the green velvet couch and said with a twinkle in her eye, "This one feels lucky." Everyone looked on with bated breath, as she sat poised with her lucky nickel, and scratched the ticket clean. And then... looking up at him, she calmly whispered in disbelief, "I won!"

Harry couldn't believe it and grabbed the ticket from her hand to see for himself. He'd no sooner grabbed and confirmed she was right, when he got down on one knee in front of Iris, and she was sure he was going to propose again. But instead, he started clutching his heart, and his six-foot bulk slithered to the floor with the grace of a melting snowman. They all started scrambling, one on the phone to 911, another, who was a retired paramedic started performing CPR, while a couple of others clutched their rosary beads and began praying. Iris sat there speechless while chaos happened around her. The ambulance arrived but it was too late and Harry was gone. But Frosty the Doughman remained and made Iris a very wealthy woman. And that's where the Magic Cottage came from.

Anna opens the old-fashioned aluminum screen door stepping into the enclosed porch, and puts the brass key in the lock. She takes a deep breath, turns the key, and pauses before crossing the threshold. Her heart is pounding and she doesn't know why. She'd been here dozens of times over the years. But this time, it is hers. Her life was about to change, and she had no idea how. The thought made her anxious. Excited, but anxious. She makes a bee-line to the thermostat to take off the chill in the air and can hear the familiar "tap, tap tap" of the baseboard radiators coming on. She can feel her grandmother's energy in the air and notices that familiar closed-up cottage smell, but she doesn't mind at all. Anna takes in the love and joy of the cottage that for now, she will call home. She has all the time in the world to work on her novel and write some poetry. That's exactly what she plans to do, knowing some-how, in some way, Gram will be guiding her.

Anna unloads the rest of her things from her car and puts the boxes and bags in their respective rooms. She hates to be unprepared, but at the same time is a fanatic about keeping things simple, two ideas that often wrestle with each other. She brought enough things for her Autumn stay, as a sort of retreat/escape. With all Gram's things still in the house, there isn't a whole lot she needs except her computer, camera, clothes, books, food, and journal. With those things, she can work from anywhere, including Cape Cod. She also benefitted from the wise investments her grandmother made with her lottery winnings after she bought the cottage. That set Anna up for a very long time. She no longer needed to write for anyone but herself.

Anna walks around the adorable little space, savoring the moment, taking in every knotty pine-covered nook and cranny she has always held so dear. She takes some time to unpack a few boxes and begins with her favorite books. Shelves are built around the fireplace as well as in a nook under the stairs that lead to the loft. Gram's books and inspirational tchotchkes fill those shelves, so Anna begins clearing one to make room for some of her books. She realizes the shelves of books are two rows deep. She chooses one shelf to start with, clearing the first row, and then clearing the second as she peruses each title, noticing how much of Gram's little library consisted of spiritual books, poetry, and contemporary romance. Over the years she never took the time to explore the inner depths of her grandmother's home. But on this day, while removing books from that back row, she came across a journal. Dark brown soft pliable leather with ties that wrap around it, secure deckle-edged pages. When Anna read the cover, imprinted in gold script, she gasped out loud. *"For Anna,"* it read. She had no idea Gram journaled or wrote anything at all, other than writing a check to pay a bill. As much as she wanted to curl up and see what treasures the journal held, she knew Seth would be there soon and she needed to get ready. She gently set the journal back in the precise location she found it, honoring the last place Gram had placed it. Anxious to learn more, she pulled herself away for now. She knew she had to deal with going through Gram's things, but she would get to that in time. That was one of the drawbacks of being an only child. No siblings to assist in a time like this, but also no siblings to negotiate with. She appreciated that.

Anna undressed and slipped into a hot shower, that felt so good after her earlier adventures on the Synchronicity. It was such a peculiar day. Not strange in a bizarre or worrisome way, but strange in an interesting, and intriguing way. A way that makes you want to know more. Anna is a curious sort, which helps make her a great reporter and a great writer. She thinks about the stranger who would be arriving shortly to pick her up for dinner and still can't believe she agreed. It's not her nature at all. Generally, she is not a particularly trusting individual, even more so now that Ethan has given her reason to be that way. She'd rather be alone than be with the wrong person. But with Seth, there was just something about him that gave her no cause for alarm. He has a confident yet gentle presence about him. She wonders how he feels about spiders.

Chapter Four

Anna was "starving" as she often is, but not always sure it is for food.

Anna rummages through her duffle bags to find something suitable for this impromptu dinner. When she packed for a lazy autumn on the Cape, she only brought casual clothes. She pulls on her favorite jeans, and a teal, embroidered cotton tunic with bell sleeves. Her brown Birkenstocks completed the quasi-bohemian look....which ought to be interesting with the J. Crew thing Seth has going on. Just as she was giving her lips a kiss of Burt's Bees for color, the bronze ship's bell clanged, that hung inside the enclosed porch next to the front door. A small plaque underneath it read, *Ring loudly to celebrate your arrival*. Lost in her thoughts, she was startled by it but made him wait a minute while she took one last look at herself in the mirror. Not bad, she decides, taking a few deep breaths, and making a faithful Catholic sign of the cross for good measure. She tries to establish a nonchalant attitude wondering why she is acting this way, feeling nervous. She recalls that her senses are always more alive near the ocean. She is more alive. It's always been that way since she was young. Eventually, she concedes that she has to let him in and goes to the door. She peeks beyond the blue and white checked curtains, through the panes of glass, and sees that friendly, self-assured grin.

Opening the door, she notices he's changed into jeans and a black polo, and is sporting boat shoes with no socks. He wears the look well, with his tanned arms, and his short-sleeved shirt tucked into his jeans showing off his perfectly toned body.

"Uh, hi, come on in," says Anna, trying to hide the nervousness in her voice as she takes a step back. My god, he's handsome, is all she can think. And that confidence, so unnerving!

"Are you ready?" he asks.

"Sure," she answers, without a crumb of certainty. She grabs her purse and they head out the door. Parked in front of the *Magic Cottage* is a deep dark blue Audi looking fresh off a showroom floor.

"Hop in," he says as he gets in the driver's seat.

No need to open doors, I guess, thinks Anna.

Buckled up and ready to go, Seth is rambling on about something while Anna stands there in silence looking at him. He realizes his mistake, gets out, comes around to the other side, and opens her door with a grand sweeping gesture of his arm.

"Here you go, milady," says her knight with an attempt at an English accent and that grin from ear to ear. "Sorry about that. I'm usually alone."

"I wasn't waiting for you to open my door," says Anna.

I don't suppose it hurt him, as old-fashioned as that may sound, she thinks, always a sucker for chivalry.

He revs up the engine, takes another look at her as if to make sure she hasn't changed her mind, and they're off. They ride in comfortable silence for what feels like an eternity, following the winding water's edge before Seth pulls across Route 28 heading back toward 6A.

"I thought you said you knew a great place close by?" she asks annoyed with herself for being in this position. She came here to get some peace and quiet, and to sort things out, not get seduced by the charms of some Adonis. This wasn't in her plans but there she was.

"Well, it is close by," says Seth, that boyish grin on his face. "It's only about 20 minutes away. That's not long. Are you in a hurry? Do you have a hot date? Every time I see you, you're in a rush." Her mouth gapes open and she gives him, the *look*. The one that silently says, Did you seriously just say that?

Unwilling to enter into a debate about what might be considered "close by," she settles into her seat and breathes in the subtle aroma of leather, soap, and shampoo she can't quite identify. He must have washed off the Coppertone and she closes her eyes to immerse herself in the moment. Soon, he pulls into the gravel parking lot of a smallish building with a sign lit up with twinkle lights that reads, The Naked Seahorse. Seth glances over at Anna to see her expressionless face.

Like much of Cape Cod, it's a single-story structure with gray weathered shingles and this one has the front and trim painted red. She never understood why anyone would paint over the beautiful, organic look of the gray-weathered shingles. The building has a chimney on one end and several Hydrangeas still in bloom with their huge blue and purple blossoms. There is nothing noteworthy about it, thought Anna, except for the name. She wondered who thought that up. *The Naked Seahorse*. It seems redundant, her writer self thought. Aren't they all naked? Walking up the path from the parking lot, Seth holds the door for her.

"I've never been here before," she says, stepping into the restaurant. The food smells delicious and she hadn't realized how hungry she was. She's always hungry.

"Seth, how nice to see you again."

"How are you, Anthony?" Seth says shaking his hand and putting the other on his shoulder. "It's been a while, hasn't it?"

As they are shown to a table in one of several cozy nooks off the larger dining area, Anthony whispers, "A quiet table just as you like."

"Thank you, Anthony," replies Seth.

"So, you come here often I gather?" noticing how comfortable the host was seating them.

"Well, often enough when I'm on the Cape. They have great food and I don't run into a lot of people I know. I like my privacy."

He was just too handsome not to be noticed, Anna thought. "You don't strike me as someone who likes to be alone."

"Not true. I enjoy solitude, but I also enjoy the company of good friends, when time allows." Opening the menu he asks, "What looks good to you?"

Anna looks at him and smiles, then realizes he's talking about the menu. She is often "starving," but not always sure it is for food. Cooperating, she picks up the menu, while looking around the dark and dimly lit room. Every table has a candle in the center and pressed linens. There are little alcoves everywhere with pine paneling, exuding not only classic Cape Cod charm, but a romantic ambiance she hadn't anticipated. A raised hearth fireplace crackles, just beyond their table casting a glow around the room. Warmed by the fire, she looks into Seth's eyes, smiles, and takes a deep breath. Shifting in her seat, uncomfortable with the whole situation, she decides on a cup of French onion soup and grilled swordfish.

"I don't care for seafood much but I do love swordfish. I love the smell of seafood. I just don't eat it," she says realizing she's rambling, not to mention insulting his choice of restaurants. Anna wonders what she was thinking ordering French onion soup, the messiest, time-consuming, labor-intensive soup in existence. Well, it's not like this is a date she reminds herself wondering how in God's name she's going to keep from spilling it on her blouse. It always drips. It is inevitable.

"I'm sorry. We could have gone somewhere else," says Seth. He brought her to The Naked Seahorse because they respected his privacy and didn't make a big deal. He appreciates that immensely.

"No, no, that's okay," she says. "This is nice. I do love swordfish once in a while," remembering when a friend grilled it with pesto that was out of this world. This also brought up a memory of breaking out in hives from one accidental bite of calamari when it got mixed up with an onion ring but decided not to share that with Seth.

"Well, I think I'm going to have the Lobster. I don't

indulge in that often but tonight's special," he says with that grin.

"Why is that?" asks Anna casually, trying not to be impressed by his charms.

"Well, I have a special guest with me." She looks around at first, noticing it doesn't seem to be very busy. "That would be you," he clarifies, thinking she didn't know who he was talking about.

Relieved that he ordered something equally messy as her soup, she can relax a little into the dark wood of the captain's chair positioned at the thick lacquered table. A votive candle flickers in a small dish of sea glass, warm and comforting. Facing each other, Anna, finds herself holding her breath. She often has to remind herself to breathe in uncomfortable situations. This was one of those and she wonders yet again, why she said, "Yes."

A waitress, Anna guessed to be in her 30s, whose name tag read, "Brittany," couldn't take her eyes off Seth. She stood at the table taking their orders and never once looked away from him. While Seth could hardly take his eyes off Anna. But as was his nature he was cordial to Brittany, but not encouraging.

"I'd like a glass of *Ballet of Angels* if you have it," says Anna.

"I'll have a glass as well," adds Seth, hoping to make Anna more comfortable. With their orders out of the way, she isn't sure what to say.

Anna was engaged to Ethan for the past three years and hasn't been on a "date" since long before that. She is an introvert by nature and just prefers time alone, or one-on-one with friends, not one to party in crowds, or go out much. She is a homebody by choice and as she thought about it, Ethan was always pushing her to attend dinners with his colleagues. He insisted that he needed her there as a show of stability as he climbed his delusional ladder to success. She hated doing that but he was relentless and she always gave in, as he knew she would. He made no effort to really know her better after all those years.

"Anna? I thought I lost you," says Seth, jerking her back to reality. She shakes her head and smiles at him.

"So, Seth, tell me a little about yourself," says Anna kicking into her familiar interview mode. She zips right into the reporter zone when she wants to take the focus off her and learn more about someone else. Very good at getting others to share their stories, and very bad at sharing her own. And that's just the way she likes it, maintaining her guard. Imagine 16th-century knights with their suits of armor. That's Anna, especially tonight.

In her early days, she did more work for magazines and newspapers, eventually being offered a full-time position as a reporter, writing lifestyle features. She worked with an amazing editor who was the first to recognize her gifts and give her a chance, and she ran with it. She always thought that new writers just needed someone to believe in them and give them the opportunity and space to shine. Scot did just that. Giving her the freedom to generate story ideas, creative directions for the paper, and even judging the local photo contest. The day she started at the paper, she summoned the nerve to ask if he had any interest in her writing a weekly column. I mean why not? His response was unforgettable. "Absofreakinlutely!" That was a definitive, "Yes!" She never missed a deadline, he knew he could count on her, and she was loyal to a fault. Until, they were both laid off as the paper downsized, as so many do these days.

But despite doing hundreds of interviews over the years, her inclination to avoid crowds never wavered. She enjoys being home, reading, meditating, attending Catholic Mass, writing poetry, making art, and working on her novel. She loves being by the ocean and moved to the Connecticut shoreline to embrace the inspiration of it and take her writing more seriously.

Brittany returns with their soup and salad and Anna is grateful for the distraction as she begins to maneuver through the mouth-watering, molten Gruyere topping her French onion soup. Seth bows his head a moment in silence and seeing that, Anna sets her spoon down to follow. He works on his salad but hardly takes his attention off her. He seems amused watching her attempt to be elegant with the succulent but sloppy soup as it inevitably dribbles onto her shirt. She is mortified and cringing, forcing a smile and trying to make light of it. A gulp of her wine helps and she is glad she thought to order it.

Seth didn't reveal much about himself but did tell her how he grew up in Middletown, Connecticut, and spent summers on the Cape at his grandparent's cottage in Brewster. His older brother Jacob, and his family, live there now year-round.

"Do you stay with them when you come to the Cape?" asks Anna.

"Uh no, actually I have a friend who invited me to use their accommodations when I'm here. That's why I was on the boat. It belongs to a friend. I'm just staying there a few nights before their guest cottage becomes available. Then I'll be there for a while. I'm on a little vacation. And what about you Anna? What brings you to Cape Cod in September?"

She looks at him, wipes her mouth, hoping there is no cheese stuck in her teeth, and proceeds to choose her words carefully. Just as she is deliberating what those words might be, Brittany returns with her swordfish and Seth's lobster. The woman flirts mercilessly, while generously offering to help Seth with a disposable lobster bib, which he declines. Twice. Brittany retreats and Anna is happy to transition to a fork and knife. Seth dives into his lobster with a flourish, while still keeping his attention on her. He is a great listener she notices again, once she begins sharing.

"My grandmother passed away earlier this year. She left me her cottage and I came to tend to her things and move in some of my own. To see what it needs, you know?"

"Oh Anna, I'm so sorry to hear that," he says setting down a claw. "Were you close?"

"We were actually. She was more like a mother to me than my own. We were spiritually and creatively connected in a very special way," says Anna, immediately regretting having shared something so personal. She wipes away a tear, realizing he is very easy to talk to. She feels safe with him for no justifiable reason. Straightening in her seat to regain her composure, she squeezes a lemon over the swordfish and takes a bite, surprise on her face at how delicious it is.

He smiles, thrilled that she is enjoying her meal. He doesn't go to restaurants often back home, although he rarely cooks for himself. So it is a real treat to share this meal with a new friend. One who doesn't want anything from him. He enjoys his meal as well, and their conversation continues, each sharing carefully curated tidbits about themselves. They are both skilled at getting the other to talk. When they are through, Anna realizes she hasn't learned a whole lot about the man who has somehow managed to get her to lower her guard. She breathes into the moment as they walk out into the night air and back to his car. This time he opens the door for her right away.

Chapter Five

Not wanting to miss an opportunity, he slept naked to enjoy the full luxury Egyptian cotton sheet experience, while the goose-down comforter kept him warm.

I t is early when Seth drops Anna off. She doesn't invite him in but thanks him for a lovely dinner. He is used to people wanting to prolong their time together but understands they just met. Seth walks a few steps to her door and watches as she goes in. Then he drives away, pausing at the stop sign trying to decide which way to go. His life has presented this question often lately. Which way to go? Which path to follow? It was early yet, almost 9:00, and the sky over the ocean was already brilliant with stars. He wished he was looking at them with Anna. Enjoying her company, he loves just looking at her, feeling very alive in her presence. This is new for him. He tries to shake off the thought and crosses the Cape toward Route 6A one last time.

He pulls into a pub he discovered when he first arrived in early September. Monk's Tavern is a place of refuge, rest, and a cold brew. It is only a short distance to the marina where *his* boat is moored. Monk's is small, and dark and has a mahogany bar and maybe a dozen square tables. It has a rustic, nautical theme and on weekends, musicians play acoustic guitar. A quiet, relaxing place to have a drink, order a light lunch or dinner, and not be alone.

Contrary to what one might think, it isn't named for an atmosphere that could suggest a monastery. Monk is the owner. Francesco Monkanelli, is a friendly, older gentleman who opened the place after he retired and was looking for something interesting to do besides playing golf every day. When he saw this boarded-up little place on 6A, with a *For Sale* sign on the door, he decided to give it a go. He came in, patched it up and it's been thriving ever since.

Seth spends a lot of time either alone or the focus of attention, and there isn't a whole lot of time spent in between. Monk's Tavern, like The Naked Seahorse, is a place where he can be around other people and not be the center of attention. He appreciates the anonymity very much. There is a seat at the end of the bar and he is happy to claim it, resting his boat shoes on the brass rail below. Seth orders a beer on tap and Monk greets him with a warm smile. "Good to see you again. Can I get you something to eat?"

"No, I'm all set, just the beer is good."

Monk goes about greeting his other patrons and checking tables to make sure everyone is enjoying their food. The smell of clam chowder, lobster, Fish and Chips, and traditional bar food hung in the air. Roni, Monk's wife/bartender keeps an eye on him as she waits on others. There is something about him that makes her curious. She can't quite put her finger on it. He is all charm and personality and people always gravitate toward him to strike up a conversation. He seems to enjoy it though. Shrugging off her curiosity, she figures some people are just like that. Nursing his beer as long as he can, with conversations coming to a close, and the bar now half empty, he decides to call it a night. He waves to Roni and Monk and heads toward the marina and Synchronicity for the night.

Although the accommodations are very elegant, for a sailboat, Seth is looking forward to sleeping on terra firma soon. He was grateful that Preston offered him accommodations during his time at the Cape. He is a good friend among other things, and his family spends the summer here. Now they are back in Beacon Hill, and their "regular" life. Preston's guest cottage, where Seth is going to stay, is occupied for another couple of days, by Preston's sister-in-law Brenda.

So many people summer on the Cape, just like Seth and Jacob had, when they were kids. Each year as soon as school got out, their mother would fill the wood-paneled station wagon with their suitcases and enough stuff to keep them clothed and busy for the entire summer. She would drive them to their grandparent's home in Brewster. They didn't usually see their mother again until Labor Day when she came to pick them up. He always wondered what she did all summer long, without them.

Back on board the *Synchronicity*, Seth gets ready for bed. He recites Evening Prayer from the Liturgy of the Hours, asking for guidance on his journey, and lifting up Anna on hers. He slides between the softest sheets he ever met, knowing he will miss them when he leaves, and slips away effortlessly into a dream state, unlike anything he's had before. And Anna is the star.

Next thing he knows daylight is shining through the little windows below deck, and he hears a woman's voice barking out, "Hello? Anybody home?" As he hears the voice coming closer, Seth jumps out of the berth and pulls on a pair of shorts before whoever it is, decides to come looking for him. Not wanting to miss an opportunity, he slept naked to enjoy the full luxury Egyptian cotton sheet experience, while the goose-down comforter kept him warm.

"Just a minute, I'll be right up," he shouts while scrambling around for a T-shirt. He scales the steeply angled ladder in quick time to reach the deck, where he is instantly reminded it is September. Shorts and a T-shirt aren't cutting it at that hour. It is cloudy and has begun to drizzle. Anxious to get more clothes on, he asks, "Can I help you?" The brazen stranger, already on the deck of the boat, walks toward him. She is almost as tall as he is, medium build, with a head full of curly dyed-blonde hair. She wears a Pepto Bismol pink outfit that looks like she might be on her way to a yoga class, yet he notices the smell of alcohol on her breath, even from a distance. He doesn't have to wonder what she had for breakfast.

"I think you can," drawls the woman. "Are you Seth Alexander?"

"I am. And you are…?"

"Brenda… Lizzie's sister." He stands there trying to make the connection when it dawns on him.

"Oh, Elizabeth's sister, okay, right. You are the one

41

getting ready to leave Preston's guest house. Nice to meet you," he says offering her a hand. "How can I help you?"

"Well. You've got that partially correct. I was *supposed* to leave the guest house tomorrow," says Brenda with a hiccup. She leers at him, giving him the once-over. "But I've run into a bit of a snag and won't be leaving just yet. However, if you'd care to join me, there is plenty of room for both of us."

"I thought it was a one-bedroom cottage," he says.

"Well yes, but as I said, there is plenty of room for both of us."

Chills run up his spine and Seth has all he can do not to show the look of horror he is feeling. "Any idea when you will be leaving?" he asks, not liking where this is going.

"Well, it's kind of uncertain at this time. I'm sure you know, the main house has been winterized for the season, so that's not available. I just thought I'd let you know in case you were planning on coming by later with your things. Let me know if you plan to join me."

She waltzes off the boat, leaving Seth speechless in her wake, a waft of alcohol lingering in the air, and his mouth hanging open. What is he going to do now? The marina will be closing for the season and *Synchronicity* is one of the last vessels still in the water.

Chapter Six

Once a priest, always a priest?

After getting warmer clothes on, Seth drives over to Divine Mercy Chapel. Pulling on the huge ornately carved doors, they give way to his urgency. Entering the narthex, he takes in the scents of the sacred space he knows so well. In the sanctuary, he dips his fingers in the holy water font, "In the name of the Father, and of the Son, and of the Holy Spirit. Amen." Always with great reverence, he approaches the altar. Breathing in the ever-present smell of incense, he sees the flickering of votive candles that people have lit in prayer for someone. He wonders if perhaps he should light one for himself. He sees the door in the chancel area with the sign that reads, *Private-No Entry.* The church is at once both open and closed, not unlike him. He is open to where God might lead him and closed to where he feels he no longer belongs.

As Seth discerns his ongoing call to the priesthood after all this time, he can't help but feel like even asking the question, is creating some feeling of loss. Arriving on the

Cape for a three-month sabbatical leaves him with too much time to think. Too much time to question. Yet that is exactly why he is there. To question. To discern. He knew he wanted to be a priest, ever since he graduated from Middletown High School and was certain he would apply to seminary. Where had that certainty gone? Why, 25 years later, is his vocation coming into question? He loves his parishioners and being a part of their lives. And he loves God even more. And yet, he isn't sure he can bear the loneliness another day, much less for the rest of his life. Yet serving God *is* his life. How can he possibly consider walking away from it? His heart aches to stay and it aches to leave. He hopes that a sign might appear to give him direction. He isn't really one to believe in signs. But he does believe in God's grace, God's miracles, God's way of inviting us in one direction or another. Guiding us on this journey we call life. If we are open to the possibilities. Is he? He wonders. He has had enough loss in life and doesn't want to dwell on this loss any longer.

He looks up at the life-size, alabaster statue of St. Joseph to his left and Mary mounted high up on the right. He's always been close to her and often wonders if it has anything to do with his own mother dying so young. Seth looks at Mary's face hoping she might give him some insight. The church is empty. He genuflects and slides into a pew in front of her, dropping the padded kneeler to the floor with a gentle thud. He kneels, hands folded in prayer, head bowed, and closes his eyes.

It isn't long before he hears shuffling of feet and someone clearing their throat. Seth looks up to see Father Alfred looking back.

"To what do I owe this pleasure, my dear Seth? I heard you would be out this way, and wondered when you'd be stopping by."

"Oh, Alfred," says Seth rising to greet the old man. "How are you? It's so good to see you. I've been attending early morning Mass, but you weren't there. I wondered if we might connect. I'm here for a few months. Provided I find a place to stay. I had one set up but it's looking a little iffy now. Anyway, how are you doing old friend?"

"Who are you calling old?" asks the 82-year-old priest, laughing. Seth smiles at him, appreciating the exchange with his mentor. They go way back, meeting when Seth finished seminary and Alfred was the parish priest, where Seth was first assigned.

Seth Alexander was a handsome one right out of the gate. His sparkling blue eyes and smile lit up the dark confessional and even through the heavily screened window, made him a favorite of many parishioners. His chestnut brown, somewhat untamed hair, gives him that devil may care look, even though he tries endlessly to tame it. A look his female, and sometimes male parishioners, swoon over. Standing nearly six feet tall, he is very fit, after all those hours working out in the rectory attic, where he'd set up a gym for himself. He works out in bike shorts and one of his ancient seminary T-shirts. He's usually dressed in black with that Roman collar, or he's all decked out in a cassock or colorful vestments while celebrating Mass. Seth enjoys socializing with parishioners but also likes to be alone with his God. At heart, he has many monastic inclinations and often wonders if that was his calling rather than a parish priest.

He usually prefers one-on-one conversations or a small group, versus a crowd, There is depth and substance to this priest who enjoys getting to know people on a deeper level. The whole outgoing priest thing comes easily, but there is a part of him that enjoys retreating to his own space. Well-loved within his parish, he does his ministry with grace and ease. He genuinely cares for his parishioners. They vie for his attention, readily donate to favorite fundraisers, invite him to dinners, volunteer for any event in hopes of being in his holy presence, and are very generous with their gifts. Even the men enjoy him, particularly some men. He loves them all and he loves being a priest, serving at St. Ignatius of Loyola in New Canaan, Connecticut, where he has served with Father Harold for the past 12 years. Originally assigned for six years, his very affluent, generous, and vocal parishioners did what they could to keep him there.

Seth and Alfred kept in touch over the years so it is especially serendipitous that Alfred is now retired, filling in to celebrate Mass occasionally while living on the Cape.

"Do you know why I'm here?" asks Seth.

"I have an idea," replies Alfred, joining him in the pew. "Why don't you tell me about it."

Seth fills his old friend in, sharing how much he loves the church and God. He is struggling with some of the teachings of the church, which are painstakingly slow to evolve in a world that desperately needs evolution. A church that has tolerated, even hidden some abhorrent behaviors within its own family, while judging and condemning others. The message of Jesus to love one another has somehow gotten lost.

"It makes me wonder what I stand for as a parish

priest," says Seth. "And Alfred, after all these years, I've kept busy, insanely busy. Now, for some reason, I'm realizing just how alone I feel, even amid a huge parish. I'm just not certain I want to spend the rest of my life feeling that way. The longing I have for a real connection with someone, besides my God, is palpable. And I don't know what to do about it." Seth pauses to think about what he will share next, as Alfred listens. "And to make matters worse, I'd only been here a short time when I met this woman on the beach. She's not like anyone I've met. I find her captivating. She's so wonderfully smart and unassuming. She has no interest in wealth, fame, or fortune. She's a writer, guarded and so cautious. She makes me think of myself in that way. We only went out for dinner. In this short time, she has made me feel very, very...*Alive!*" Pausing again he asks, "Alfred, have you ever felt this way? Questioning your call? Questioning if maybe God might be done with you? If maybe your time in ministry is over? If maybe, our God has something else in mind? I know taking vows to become a priest is a commitment forever. I never expected to feel this way. To question my calling."

Seth catches his breath giving Alfred a chance to catch his and wonders if he's said too much. Some fresh air might be a good idea. Maybe a walk on the beach might clear his head. But it feels so good to say the words that he'd been thinking and feeling but had no one to share them with. He never said them out loud before, not even to himself, even though they'd been stirring around within him for a while.

Alfred looks up at his young friend, with wisdom in his soulful, and compassionate eyes, telling Seth all he needs to know. Answers to all his questions can only come from his Source, in time, and Seth will need to go within to find them.

"Only you can know the answer to your life's deepest questions," says Alfred. "I understand your quandary all too well my friend. One day you are going about your business celebrating Mass, officiating funerals, weddings, and baptisms. Growing in relationship with your parish members, being a part of their lives, and truly caring about them. One day, you want to go home, wherever that is, and you realize there is no one to go home to. I mean, we love Jesus of course, and are filled with the Holy Spirit, and that never changes. In that way, we are truly never alone. But all of a sudden out of nowhere, that's not enough. The loneliness grabs hold of us like a viper. And what can we do?"

Seth appreciates the sage wisdom of his friend who has been a priest for more than 50 years. Through the sacrament of Holy Orders, a seminarian commits his soul to Jesus Christ for life. Once a priest, always a priest, thought Seth, wondering if that was his truth.

Anxious to leave the church before anyone else recognizes him and puts him to work, Seth is in dire need of coffee. He heads toward the Brewster General Store. Route 6A is scenic, meandering 62-plus miles that run the length of the Cape from Bourne to Provincetown. On it, there is a variety of small villages and a plethora of restaurants, services, galleries, and quirky little shops to cater to every need. The general store is just one of those places oozing nostalgia with an assortment of peculiar items that all had a purpose in some era. Of course, they have tourist treasures and practical things as well. It is early in the day, but the lights beam through the tall wavy window panes inviting him in. He loves the vintage New England charm of the old building that was built as a church in 1852 and converted to a general store in 1866.

As a child, Seth and his brother rode bikes there from their grandparents' house to buy penny candy in search of his favorites like Laffy Taffy Ropes, Reed's Root Beer candy rolls, and York Peppermint Patties. Then they would go over to the Stony Brook Grist Mill, a historic place built in the late 1800s, where they would chase each other, run around throwing stones in the stream, and fish in the pond. Though neither of them ever caught a thing. Having worked up an appetite, they would stop by the Jolly Whaler and get pizza for lunch and sometimes ice cream. Then they would venture on to Paine's Creek Beach, where they spent the rest of their day. That was back when kids could disappear for the day and no one thought anything of it. Today, there would be an Amber Alert in quick time. But back then, they just did what kids do, enjoy the outdoors, play, and have fun without a care in the world.

Seth hasn't been there in years and finds that the store still has jars of penny candy although it's certainly no longer a penny. Old church pews flank each side of the ancient door that creaks when you open it and is outfitted with a bell that jangles announcing every arrival and departure. There is a chill in the air, made more noticeable by the warmth of a wood stove in the old shop. The crooked floorboards creak as Seth takes a morning newspaper from the stack.

"Mornin," says a welcoming face behind the counter. "Come on in." Seth smiles back and inhales the aroma of coffee and freshly baked something. "We have cranberry almond scones this morning and blueberry muffins if you're interested," says the voice who sees his interest piqued. Seth looks at the middle-aged woman behind the counter and then around the store in search of the coffee. "It's right over here," she says knowing what he is looking for.

"Thanks. Smells delicious. I'll take a couple of scones too."

"Comin' right up." Barbara puts them in a bag while Seth fixes his coffee. He meanders over to a bulletin board with hand-written notices, flyers for upcoming community events, and classified ads. One catches his attention for a house-sitter and while he doesn't need a job, he does need somewhere to stay. That might be perfect. He jots down the phone number and stuffs the scrap of paper in his pocket. He grabs a handful of caramel creams for nostalgia's sake from one of the candy jars and tosses them on the counter.

"Where you headed this early hour?" she asks, not caring if she is being nosey. There are few secrets in a small town like Brewster.

Seth offers her that brilliant smile and says, "Oh, nowhere special. Thanks," grabbing his coffee, caramels, and cranberry scones, and leaves a $20 bill on the counter. Before he gets out the door, Barbara calls after him that the house-sitting gig is just down the road. No privacy, none at all.

Seth attends Mass every day even though he is on sabbatical. Still, he lays low so that he won't be recognized. He does appreciate not having to deal with parish administration tasks, celebrating Mass himself, or listening to Mildred Montowese tell him about the bunion she had removed from her left foot. They seem to leave nothing to the imagination, his beloved parishioners. He adores them and truly cares for them, some more than others, but he doesn't miss them. Not now. Sabbatical is his time. And in his case, time for discernment. He can't imagine life as anything other than a priest. Although Anna has certainly helped stretch his imagination…just a little. Maybe a lot.

Seth's time on sabbatical is helping him to realize the less-than-admirable character traits within himself. The attraction to material things, brought on by his life as a parish priest in a wealthy, affluent Connecticut community, is in opposition to the reason he chose to be a priest. Twenty-five years later he knows he has grown fond of a life filled with generous, thoughtful, well-meaning parishioners. Too fond of the lifestyle he never intended. Was the son of God a whim of fate for him? He wonders. Or are his promises of celibacy and obedience something he can continue to stay committed to for the rest of his life? As well as his own desire to lead a simple life. He needs to know. He hops into the Audi and heads back to the marina with his coffee and scones, considering how grateful he is for this simple breakfast while driving a very pricey car to get it. He wonders where he is going to stay when any day now, that luxurious *Synchronicity,* will no longer be an option.

Chapter Seven

A Magic Cottage by the sea.

Though next morning Anna is still recovering from the unexpectedly lovely dinner with Seth the night before. She stands at the bedroom window as rain pours down in buckets, but she can still appreciate a view of Nantucket Sound. The ocean is usually a balm for whatever is bothering her, even when it is as unsettled as she is. Clarity eludes her in many ways at the moment, and their whole exchange last night creates more questions than answers. There is so much more she wants to know about him. The journalistic sleuth in her kicks in and she thinks maybe she'll do some research about Seth Alexander to see what she might find. But that will have to wait. Now, looking out the window she alternates between anger at Ethan, heartbreak from losing Gram, curiosity about Seth, and feeling very alone with it all. That isn't usually like her. She knows she should just sit in prayer, with gratitude for its lessons, for the memories, for everything. Her life is so blessed. Tears stream down her cheeks, mirroring the rain cascading down the window panes.

Gram often said to her, 'My dear, what is it you plan to do with your one wild and precious life?" quoting Mary Oliver in her famous poem *The Summer Day*. There is a framed print of it, hanging on the wall in the living room that has been there for years. Looking at it now, Anna realizes that was the question that plagued her. Even more so since having dinner with Seth. He listened in such a way that made her feel genuinely heard. He asked questions about her that made her feel like he was actually interested in what she had to say. Not just going through the motions. She noticed he wasn't so forthcoming about himself though, and wondered what secrets he had hidden.

She is comfortable wearing a pair of plaid flannel pajama pants and a long-sleeve T-shirt. It is printed with Eyeore's silly yet profound wisdom that reads, *I was so upset I forgot to be happy.* They are her favorites. But she doesn't realize the irony of his message at the moment as she contemplates all she is feeling. There is a chill in the air as she relocates to the oak chair that was hand-crafted by Gram's friend Harry before he passed away. She glances at the fireplace deciding that building a fire will be too much work, opting instead to wrap herself in one of Gram's cozy, well-worn patchwork quilts that still smelled like her. The faintest scent of Donna Karan's Cashmere Mist, Gram's favorite, and a little of that closed-up cottage by the sea smell. She loves it all. Gram made her quilts with all kinds of random fabrics left over from other projects, creating a rainbow of color and texture with no rhyme or reason to the design. But guaranteed comfort, handcrafted skill, and coziness, perfect for contemplating the big question that will shape her future. What *does* she want to do with her one wild and precious life?

Anna considers there are few times in life when one realizes their life can be whatever they want it to be. It's an actual epiphany. She wants to take her writing career in a new direction. Of that, she is certain. Anna is tired of being a feature writer for her local newspaper and even more tired of the freelance gigs where she has to hound editors to get paid. She is tired of hunting down assignments. She has books she's started and not finished because she spends all her time writing other people's stories instead of her own. That plagues her. She won a few journalism awards but she wants more from her writing life. She wants to finish the novel she started over a decade earlier. She also loves to write poetry and has published a few. And until now, she didn't have the nerve to break free of the endless cycle of newsroom nonsense, and the risk involved in leaving. But Gram's passing is both a heart-wrenching reality, as she already missed her so much, and also liberating because Gram left her estate to Anna. How can she feel so blessed and so devastated at the same time, she wonders?

Anna remembers the journal she found earlier and takes it out of its *hidden* location on the shelf. She curls up on the couch, and with great admiration for her beloved Gram, she opens the soft leather cover. What did her grandmother have in mind when she started this, she wonders, hoping to find out. Flipping through the pages she sees that the journal is mostly blank, as if it began with great intention as these things sometimes do, but never finished. She decides she will appreciate Gram's efforts regardless of how many entries there are. She is surprised to have found this journal at all.

Dear Anna,

One night while at my Magic Cottage on Cape Cod, I stood outside and took in the beauty of its gray weathered shingles, periwinkle blue shutters, and fairy tale peaked roof. Two window boxes were filled with flowers year-round and a tiny white picket fence stuck in the ground pretending to protect the miniature garden, just below one of several multi-paned windows. Most of them opened inward like a ship's porthole when you lift the latch. Everything there was miniature except for the massive oak tree in the front yard, which towered over the cottage and made its already small size appear Lilliputian. A path of crushed shells wove its way to the tiny house.

Looking up into the night sky, among the stars and wafting clouds I saw a rainbow moon. Blinking my eyes I rubbed them the way people do when they aren't sure of what they've seen. I needed to clarify what I thought I might not be seeing. But in the land of a Magic Cottage, why wouldn't one see a rainbow moon? A giant full moon surrounded by a rainbow hovered luminously over Nantucket Sound shining down upon my enchanted home. I found its unique presence a statement of my life and God's blessings.

For me, that rainbow was a symbol of healing and movement, openness and freedom, childlike wonder and simplicity. Representing the many parts of each one of us.

The unique, diverse, original way that we become more authentic and more fully who we are. What a gift to be permitted to be who we are and to have the ability to embrace that truth.

Anna, it came at a time in my life when I was ready to move on, step in new directions, embrace the future, and be released from the bondage of the past. That full moon invited me to embrace my truth with reckless abandon. Open arms and an open mind, to say yes to the invitation that had called to me for so long, an extraordinary gift from an extraordinary Spirit. And it was there, in front of a Magic Cottage only a short walk from the ocean's shore, that I realized I had a story to tell. A story of a journey and enlightenment. A guide on one path toward a life overflowing with spiritual intensity, childlike simplicity, and abundant creative energy, leading me toward my passionate sacred destiny.

As we grow and nurture our inner children and outer adults, we may find that while one way works for a time, another path may speak to us differently at another time. Embrace those differences.

When I began writing this for you, my only grand-child, I accepted I'm getting on in years and never a day goes by when I don't express gratitude for my Magic Cottage. Many tears were shed there. Tears of joy as well as sadness. When we met, it was worn and tired with just a spark of light left in it. With more love, gratitude, and attention than I thought I had in me, it was transformed, as was I, after all, isn't that what love does…transform us? And with that transformation comes renewal.

On these pages discern with love and wisdom, which

of these reflections speak to you, which challenge you, and which, for now, you need to pass by. These experiences and insights are the things I have learned on my journey and, things which I hope you find helpful on yours. May this special little place be one of renewal for you and those you choose to share it with.

All My Love, Gram

Anna closed the book and looked around the cottage as if seeing it for the first time. There are so many wonderful memories. Reading her grandmother's words, written just for her, she sits wrapped in the quilt made by her hands and cries and cries. And when she didn't think she had any tears left, she cried some more and listened to the rain as her heart swelled with gratitude. She strolls around peering over the blue and white checked curtains that cover the bottom half of the windows, looking at the water view.

She remembered that Gram's friend Adele custom-made them for all the windows of the cottage. Several pieces of furniture were still wearing "protective" sheets thrown over them by the caretaker after Grams' funeral. One by one, Anna began uncovering them, each piece revealing another memory. Gram had such a vibrant spirit about her and a story for just about everything. Some of which she repeated multiple times during a visit. But Anna didn't mind. When she pulled the cover off the couch, she remembered curling up next to her to watch movies with a bowl of popcorn they shared. They loved watching *Jaws* together each summer and more than once the popcorn she made in the old air popper, would go flying into the air with the next terrifying scene, even though they knew it was coming.

She opened a window a crack just to let in some salt air and whipped off another sheet putting some of her anger at Ethan into the unveiling. In some ways, she was as disgusted with herself as she was with him. Upon reflection, she could hardly believe the time she wasted with him. They had nothing in common. She had a passion for simplicity, for the things in life that have meaning. She knew so many people trapped by their possessions, living for the acquisition of the next big thing. They wanted the next luxury car, vacation house, or climb up the corporate ladder. Anna wanted nothing to do with any of that. She realizes she is being judgmental, but also believes that her life is beginning to take shape. What that meant to her was having a simple life, opportunities to write and create near the ocean, in a small, safe place to call home. She values a few close friends, a growing devotion to the Blessed Mother Mary, and a beautiful relationship with her God. With the ability to celebrate life on her terms, that meant freedom. Ethan had no interest in any of that. Not one little bit. He was bound by his next quest which she eventually realized, was her. But even she was not enough evidently, as she discovered the last time she saw him.

One thing she hopes for in coming to South Yarmouth is to work on her book without interruption. As someone who craves comfort and familiarity, she plans to set up a space in the cottage where she might be a magnet for inspiration. A space to finish her book, write poetry, or whatever she feels called to. She stares at the threshold of the tiny first-floor room that Gram used as her bedroom. Anna hadn't entered this space yet since she arrived, but it was time. It was a simple space with two double-hung windows with a glimpse of water view and walls covered in knotty pine. There is a vintage white iron bed with one of Grams' quilts on it. She had so many talents, thought Anna. A gold crucifix hangs over the headboard. The bed appears well-loved and there is a three-drawer antique oak dresser with statues of Mary and Jesus with a votive candle in a red glass holder in between, situated on a lace doily. She remembers seeing a candle just like that below deck on Seth's boat. A box of wooden matches nearby read, *"Keep a little fire burning; however small, however, hidden."* - Cormac McCarthy. Anna picks up the little box with the big message and wonders if Gram had any little fires hidden.

A painted navy-colored desk and pecan wood chair are placed at the window with a banker's lamp and green glass shade. A candlestick table next to the bed holds a stained glass lamp with colors of the ocean blues and a pull chain. The room is unimpressive but simple and cozy like the rest of the cottage. She loves it. Anna gently sets her laptop on the desk and runs her hand over its cool gray surface fondly. She and Itzer, as she calls him, have been together a very long time. He is the second half of the Pulitzer she aspires to receive one day. Anna knows she should probably replace him with an updated version but they have been through a lot together and she can't bring herself to let him go. Maybe soon.

She tucks her backpack with notes for her novel and a draft of early chapters on the floor next to the desk. Her book was slow going but she hopes her time on the Cape will be well spent. Gram always encouraged her writing career and was so proud of her. She always introduced Anna to friends and neighbors as, "my granddaughter, the award-winning writer." Anna can feel her spirit still there. She looks around the room as if she might see her, takes a deep breath, and closes the door as she leaves.

When the tea kettle in the kitchen whistles Anna realizes she'll need to get to the grocery store sooner rather than later. She hasn't gone shopping yet since her arrival, but there are still a few staples in the cottage. She finds mint chamomile tea bags in the pottery canister, some honey, and that curious mug she often used when she visited. Gram told her each mug in the cupboard had a story. Her life was so very rich with meaning, so much so, that even a mug warranted a story. She should have been a writer, Anna thought. She pours the hot water from the vintage-style stainless steel kettle. Gram talked about finding it on a weekend road trip with a friend to the Vermont Country Store. She wonders if that friend was Harry. Anna gazes into the white and black *Tuesdays at Ten*" mug, and watches the steam rise, wondering what was happening on *Tuesdays at Ten*. Adding honey, she stirs, allowing her mind to drift to the night before at *The Naked Seahorse*. She had an ever so brief vision of a nice romantic dinner for two. It was just a thought. Moving into her "Eyeore spirit," she decides to let it pass like a Cape Cod fog, unwilling to be too hopeful.

She returns to the couch and her comfy quilt and sips her tea, bouncing the tea bag up and down, savoring the scent of the mint and chamomile, with just the right amount of honey. Anna knows she needs to do something rather than sit there and contemplate the unsettled nature of her life. She doesn't know what to do next. She came to the Cape for some deeply reflective soul-searching and to get some writing done. She wants unencumbered, uninterrupted, peaceful, quiet time in a place where few know her and anonymity would feel delicious. To disappear into the landscape of Cape Cod, the place that settles her body, mind, and spirit in a way no other place has. The cottage, especially, has always been a magical place for her. And now it's all hers and she can stay as long as she wants to. Settling into a reality that makes her smile.

Once upon a time…they lived happily ever after. That was all Anna ever hoped for. She was a strong, smart, independent woman, but she also thought it might be nice to meet Prince Charming. Can't a girl want both? She imagines Seth probably isn't her Prince Charming as most princes would open the car door when they pick you up. But in recent events with Ethan, she had become a realist, no longer the romantic she once was.

She is a writer, she reminds herself, deciding to focus on that. The room is silent except for the rain. She savors the sound and takes another sip of her tea, peering over the *Tuesdays at Ten* mug hoping that whatever is happening on *Tuesdays at Ten*, is fabulous. She wonders if she'll ever find out. She gets up, walks again toward the closed door, and places her hand on the crystal knob, noticing the creaking of the old wood floorboards as she walks in. Setting her tea on the desk, next to Itzer, she eyes the antique side chair and its cane seating. Sitting down cautiously, hoping she doesn't break the petite little thing, she hesitates further, because of what the action means. She opens her laptop and waits as it boots up, thinking just maybe this is the dream. Maybe writing her book is her happily ever after. Why not? She opens that Word document that she's opened a hundred, maybe a thousand times before. She takes a deep breath to steady herself, poises her fingers over the keys, and the brass ship's bell clangs announcing someone's arrival. "You've got to be kidding," Anna says out loud to no one.

Chapter Eight

"Excuse me missy, but aren't you engaged?"

Walking toward the door she peers over the curtains to see Zoe standing on the enclosed porch as the rain pours outside. She flings open the door and nearly knocks her friend over with her embrace. Anna is beyond happy to see the familiar face. "Come in, come in," says Anna moving aside to welcome her. Zoe hands over a creamsicle colored box and a small bag of provisions, hanging her wet coat on the rack by the door.

"I thought you might not have had a chance to get groceries yet so I figured I'd stop by with a few things. Here are a few grocery staples and a welcome home treat from *Tokens of My Confections*, over near my shop. This bakery just opened a month or so ago and Peyton, the owner, makes the best croissants, cranberry scones, cinnamon Danish, and Bundtinis you've ever had in your life."

"Thank you so much Zoe," says Anna, grateful for her friend's impromptu visit. "What a nice surprise."

"I love what you've done with the place," says Zoe, noticing the sheets still covering some of the furniture. Anna looks down and realizes she is still in her pajamas and feels compelled to apologize.

"I wasn't expecting anyone today. I'm still trying to figure out what to do next I guess."

"Hey, it's me, Zoe, remember? No apologies are needed. I just wanted to check in on you and see how you're doing and wondered what your plans are?"

Always one to make herself at home, she walks toward the kitchen. "I'll fix some coffee and get out some plates and we can dig into those pastries and catch up. The thing I love best about that new bakery is that they make minia-tures of everything. Tokens of My Confections. Get it? I love it! The tiny size almost makes you forget the carbs and calories. Maybe that's the idea. I don't know."

Zoe fixes coffee for herself while Anna retrieves her tea, and puts the pastries on a plate for them. Anna puts away the bag of groceries her friend was kind enough to bring.

Sitting across the table from each other, Anna breaks down in tears. She isn't even sure why. Maybe it's a little bit of everything from Ethan's betrayal to losing Gram, to the hopefulness of meeting Seth and then the joy of Zoe's arrival. She just isn't sure. But she knows she is grateful for the company, for Zoe's thoughtfulness, and caring. Zoe gets up to hug her friend before sitting down again and digging into the tasty treats. Anna laughs at her own tears and joins in.

"So I know you just arrived yesterday. Have you had any fun yet?"

Anna wonders if she should share about her dinner

with Seth and decides she wants to say, "yes" to a whole lot more than she usually would. Especially after reading Gram's journal entry. At that moment she decides she is going to live a little more authentically, a lot more vibrantly, and not hold back on joy. Why not? She has nothing to lose. Anna tells Zoe all about running into Seth on the beach, the "incident" on the boat, and their wonderful dinner together.

Looking a crumb uncertain, Zoe clears her throat, normally a huge advocate for living with passion, and says, "Excuse me missy, but aren't you engaged?"

"Not anymore. I had enough. Something happened before I left, and I broke it off. I was going to anyway." Zoe leaned close to avoid missing a word while munching on a raspberry cheese Danish.

"I had a dream Zoe, so real and so vivid it woke me up. My heart was pounding and I was in a sweat. I was in my Volvo, on a bridge on the way to visit a friend when the pavement beneath me began to shake. Heavy ominous clouds hovered above and a noise so loud it was beyond my imagining roared, as huge cracks in the pavement took shape before me. The surface began to give way... Ethan was snoring next to me. I slipped out from under the covers, slid my feet into my fuzzy-lined Crocs, and wrapped myself in a fleece robe. I headed for the kitchen to make coffee. The night before we had dinner at the Savory Oyster and just before dessert arrived, Ethan excused himself from the table to take yet another business call and stepped outside. Leaving me alone, again, in a restaurant I don't like. Ethan knows I don't like Seafood but he is clueless about my needs nine-tenths of the time. He just doesn't care. I wondered how long he'd be, as he never unplugs from his work ever. I thought about that dream and about what my life with Ethan would look like. We've been engaged for three years, and to be honest, I don't know why. He was staying over at my place for the weekend, and the next day it was pouring rain.

"What an awful day," he said looking out the window after finally rising from a lazy Saturday morning sleep.

"Oh, it's just raining," I said. "Let's go for a walk in the rain!" I ran into my bedroom and pulled on a pair of shorts, wearing Ethan's wrinkled "I'd rather be trading" T-shirt I slept in. I swapped my Crocs for a pair of bright yellow rubber gardening boots I kept near the door, and asked him, "Aren't you coming with me? Let's go walk in the rain!"

Ethan stood there looking at me like I had two heads, alternately while glancing out the window. "It's raining buckets out there," he complained.

"I know, isn't it great? Maybe we can find some seriously deep puddles. Come on!" I grabbed my raincoat off the rack stopping with one arm in the sleeve and looked at him. "Come on, it'll be fun," I said trying to convince him.

"No that's okay. All I have with me are my Gucci loafers and I assure you, they've never seen a puddle, deep or otherwise."

"While my playful spirit was fading fast, I responded to him in a cynical tone and already resented how he was trying to ruin our day and my mood. "Do you hover over them?" I ask."

"Hover? Over what?" "He looked confused. I shook my head, pulled my slicker on the rest of the way, and with somewhat dashed hope for a fun day, ran to the elevator. Ethan was alone at the window, contemplating his relationship with his safe, dry, Gucci loafers. What I saw in the financial analyst I had been engaged to for too long I do not know. Sometimes he dampens my vibrant spirit for life. I know this. You know Zoe, Ethan had played the role of the perfect gentleman, bringing flowers on our first date, opening doors, and surprising me with gifts. That Tiffany tennis bracelet was particularly nice, but not my thing. He doesn't listen and he doesn't know me and makes no effort to know me. But I do listen and have been paying close attention, noticing Ethan's lack of transparency, deceptions, and half-truths. I looked the other way. It was easier."

Zoe nodded understanding and perused the plate to choose another decadent morsel, this time one with chocolate while hanging on every word. She is a good listener and a good friend. Anna continues.

"The next morning, I woke early and was sitting at the table spreading raspberry preserves on toast and thinking about my fiancé, and what it was like to share breakfast with someone. I fixed a pot of coffee, and when I heard him stirring, began preparing scrambled eggs. He didn't eat breakfast during the week, but on weekends he wanted a hearty breakfast and expected me to make it. At first, I was flattered that someone appreciated my cooking, which was simple at best. But that got old quickly. Sometimes we would walk over to the Whispering Wind B&B where they had a little café that was open to the public, and if the weather was nice, we could sit on the porch and eat. They have sumptuous omelets, Belgian waffles topped with berries, real Maple Syrup, and a bottomless cup of coffee.

Ethan always ordered the same thing, a swiss cheese omelet, turkey sausage, and grilled bran muffin. He definitely needed more bran. But that morning, I wanted to finish packing and load my car to leave the next day for the Cape, so I decided to whip up breakfast myself. The smell of scrambled eggs and bacon permeated the air in the apartment. The hazelnut coffee gurgled, reminding me of another thing I do for him. In truth, I don't even like hazelnut coffee. I enjoy taking care of him, but lately, I realize, I like the idea that someone might want to take care of me, too. A reciprocal thing. There's a novel idea. I filled two small glasses with orange juice no-pulp, cause that's the way Ethan liked it. Thinking of him, I flipped the bacon and wondered how something so bad, could possibly be any good. Maybe it wasn't.

We ate breakfast together, Zoe, with minimal appreciation or conversation, with Ethan's mind appearing to be elsewhere. I assumed it must be about work. Ethan lived and breathed work. We parted ways, planning to see each other when I returned from the Cape. He said he'd be too swamped at work to make time before I left. To push through my thoughts about whether being engaged to him was a good idea, I thought I'd surprise him later and so I did. I drove down to Stamford, knocked, and stood at his front door waiting. He never had given me a key to his place, even though we were engaged. You'd think a key would be an appropriate next step. Eventually, he opened the door, looking startled to see me.

"Hey, I thought I'd surprise you," I said to him, holding up a brown-handled bag from Pasta Vita. "I brought dinner."

"Uh, tonight's not good," he said, continuing to block the door. I pushed past him wondering why he was acting weird, placing the bag on the counter and taking off my coat."

"What are you up to? Is someone here?" I asked hearing a noise from the bedroom.

"Anna, now isn't a good time. I have some work to do. Maybe later."

"I headed toward the bedroom and opening the door, gasped at the sight of a naked woman in his giant bed. The bed we shared. I grabbed my jacket and holding back tears, had only one thing to say…*"We're so done!"* I pulled the hideous gold ring off my finger and sent it flying in his direction where it flew past him into the kitchen sink and down the garbage disposal trap.

Ethan stood there in shock as if watching it in slow motion before chasing after it, shouting, "What the fuck! That's two carats." I looked at him with disgust, grabbed my Pasta Vita bag, 'cause I sure wasn't leaving it for him, and stormed out the door."

"Oh Anna," said Zoe sitting there with rapt attention, her mouth gaping open as the story unfolded. "I don't know what to say. I'm so sorry."

"Don't be. I'm just glad I found out about him now and not later…so in answer to your question, no I'm no longer engaged and feel perfectly fine going out for dinner with someone I just met. I'm here now and in no hurry to go back. Now, if you don't mind, I'll have one of those teeny pastries, maybe two, maybe three."

Chapter Nine

It smells like cookies and coffee and a
slight scent of smoldering ashes
in the fireplace.

Seth walks onto the porch of his old summer sanctuary, the house where he spent every summer when he was young. Like so many Cape Cod homes, it has gray weathered shingles and white painted trim with varied rooflines where additions were added over time. The porch ceiling is covered in wainscoting stained a rich mahogany and nautical-style lanterns hang on each side of the front door. Years ago, when his brother Jacob met Grace, they decided to make Brewster their home full-time. When they had the chance to buy his grandparent's big old cottage they couldn't pass up the opportunity. Seth hasn't been there in a couple of years and can see that the place needs a little attention but is well-loved. The porch swing he used as a child still hangs in the same place. The wood is weathered and perhaps the ropes and cushions have been replaced, but the memories are fresh enough. He imagines Jacob's two kids enjoying it as much as he did. A couple of green porch rockers have been added with a small wicker table in between. Flower boxes hang off the porch railings filled with bright autumn mums, and a bristled doormat, worn over time, welcomes visitors even with its faded message "*We're Happy You're Here.*"

Jacob opens the door when he hears Seth's footsteps on the porch. "Well look who's here. It's Father Seth! To what do we owe this great honor?"

"Knock it off, Jacob. Where's Grace and the kids?"

"She ran to the store for a few things and promised the kids they could go, too. She'll be back soon. Come on in," he said welcoming him.

Seth steps into the familiar space and notices that the old-fashioned beach cottage smell he knew from so many summers past, isn't there. It smells like cookies and coffee and a slight scent of smoldering ashes in the fireplace. He looks around taking it all in before giving his brother a warm hug.

"What brings you to the Cape," asks Jacob, thrilled to see his brother.

"Oh, just taking a little time off," says Seth evasively.

"Oh, really?" Jacob questions skeptically. "My brother the priest, who never takes a vacation and never has time to visit family is just taking a little time off? What gives?"

Seth ignores the question. "Remember how at night the animals came out of the woods?" Seth asks looking out the window into the backyard. "They looked like animals anyway, when you're eight years old."

"I remember," says Jacob. "We used to play well into the night, all summer long. Gram and Gramp sat on the front porch with their gin and tonics, and friends. There were always friends and neighbors stopping by to visit. The oak forest in the back, with its scrub pines and line of juniper bushes, created a great place to hide as our imaginations went wild. Hiding from each other we pretended to be bobcats, bears, and whatever else we could dream up until Gram summoned us in with the clang of the metal triangle."

"I see it's still there," says Seth smiling that brilliant grin Jacob knows so well. But Seth isn't going to tell his brother everything. Not yet. He hears footsteps coming up the front stairs and the screen door opens and slams shut. Grace and the kids are back.

"Gracie, how are you?" asks Seth getting up to help her with her bags.

He tries to give her one of his one-armed "parishioner" greetings, but she says, "Oh no you don't," and grabs him, wrapping her arms around him to give him a big hug. "What a wonderful surprise! What brings you out here? Are you staying with us? How long are you here for?" peppering him with questions.

"Geez Grace, give him a chance to answer," says Jacob. The kids keep their distance, a bit shy because they haven't spent a whole lot of time with Uncle Seth and don't know him that well. His friendly personality makes it easy to overcome that though. Their son Brady is 10, named after Tom Brady of football fame and Jacob's favorite quarterback of all time. He's even forgiven him for leaving the Patriots to head south to Tampa Bay before retiring to sportscasting. Caia, whose name means "one who rejoices," is exactly that. At 12 years old she keeps a close eye on Brady and takes care of him like any big sister would. She is a bright light in the Alexander household and is curious about Uncle Seth. But Grace asks Caia to put away the few groceries she brought in and shoos Brady away so she and Jacob can talk with him. They haven't seen him in so long there is lots of catching up to do and she hopes they will have the opportunity to do that.

They relocate to the back deck so that Jacob can throw some burgers and hot dogs on the grill, and Grace gathers the rest of an early dinner for them to eat outside. Sitting with Gin and tonics, made with their favorite Highclere Castle Gin, and a twist of lime, they relax a little as they share what's been going on in their lives.

"I'm still teaching science at the middle school and I love lobstering on weekends. In the summer I take tourists out on our lobster boat to fish, and once in a while, we'll venture out to Stellwagen Bank for some whale watching. Caia has a real interest in whales and can tell you all about them."

Grace jumps in with a summary about life on Cape Cod year-round. She works at the Chamber of Commerce, welcoming visitors, providing dining materials, maps, brochures, etc, and suggestions for what to do and where to stay.

"Cape Cod has become a year-round destination, not just June through August," she says, clearly passionate about her Cape Cod. She was born on the Cape, not just a summer resident.

Seth shares that he is taking a three-month sabbatical as most priests do after 25 years of service. "It's a chance to refresh and recharge our batteries," he says smiling. They wait to hear more…but the burgers need flipping, the kids come running in looking for dinner and Uncle Seth is very grateful for the interruption. He said all he wants to say.

A couple of hours later, with a full stomach and surrounded by love, he makes his departure, promising to return soon. He realizes they have a busy home and a busy life and staying in their guest room would not be the setting he needs right now, although he knows he would be welcome. He needs time alone. He reaches into his pocket for his key and finds the scrap of paper with the house-sitting phone number on it. Seth wonders if that just might be the answer to his prayers.

Heading back toward the marina, he pulls into one of the near-empty beach parking lots overlooking Cape Cod Bay. He says a prayer for guidance and punches in the phone number. He knows nothing about it, except that it is a house-sitting opportunity. "I can do that," he says to himself as the phone rings.

"Good afternoon, Honey-Do Farm," sings the voice into the phone, "How may I help ewe?"

"Well, I'm not sure if I have the right number, but I saw a posting for a house-sitter at the Brewster General Store. I wanted to get more information."

"Oh honey, you've got it right. Come on down and we can meet you and you can meet us and we'll see what we see. We're right down off 6A. I can text you the exact address. Just look for the sign that says, "Honey-Do Farm." Can you come in an hour? Hold on…" He screams bloody murder into the phone, "Honey, someone wants to come in an hour to meet us. Is that good with you?"

He's so loud Seth has to pull the phone away from his ear.

"Oh sorry about that. My Honey has a hearing problem." Now I do too, Seth thinks. "We'll see you soon." And the voice hangs up. Seth holds the phone out and looks at it, unsure what to make of the situation. This feels like a lot of work already.

Seth stops by the marina for a quick change of clothes and heads over to meet the owners of Honey-Do Farm, wondering what in God's name he was thinking. He pulls the Audi into the gravel driveway, gets out, and looks over the situation. There is a charming old cottage in Cape Cod's requisite gray weathered shingles. A rainbow flag flies in front of the house and highlights the colorful autumn gardens and landscaping. There is a barn in the distance and there are a few different paddocks enclosed with wood and wire fencing although he doesn't see any animals. He notices a huge RV parked next to the barn. The property is meticulously cared for. It's set off the main road and is very private.

Before he has a chance to use the brass door knocker in the shape of an anchor, he is on the Cape after all, he hears the voice from the phone heading toward him, inviting him in.

"You must be Seth," says the man dressed in jeans, sneakers, and a bright pink polo. "I'm Travis and this is my wife, Toni. They shake hands and he is led into their living room which is very casual and cozy and like the grounds, everything is immaculate. The couple are friendly and welcoming. Seth imagines they are both in their late 60s or so and is curious why they need a housesitter. He doesn't have to ask, and with no time to waste, Travis gets right to the point. Toni fills in details here and there but could hardly get a word in as Travis is quite the talker.

As it turns out, the couple was about to head out in their RV for a little cross-country adventure. A new grandchild is about to be born in San Diego. The person they had lined up to house-sit had a personal emergency and had to cancel last minute.

"We're supposed to leave in two days and have no one to watch over things," says Toni.

"If you don't mind me asking, exactly what needs to be watched over? It seems like a very quiet, peaceful place," says Seth.

Toni looks at Travis as if trying to decide how much she should tell their guest. They desperately want to leave as scheduled, but also want to make sure their property is in good hands. Travis takes over the conversation with enthusiastic, but carefully curated, details about the task.

"We'll give you a tour if you're interested, but our cottage has five bedrooms, two on the first floor and three on the second, each with its own bath. There's a kitchen, living room, den, and a small library. We have someone come in a few times a week to clean and help out with laundry, etc. She also does a little baking in case we have guests. A landscaping company maintains the grounds, and we're hoping you would be able to tend to the care and feeding of our pets. We have just a few. And we would need you to oversee things in general, keeping everything impeccable, managing any unexpected issues, that kind of thing. We will be back by the end of November before the snow falls. We don't want to be traveling in the RV in the winter weather. We can pay you $700 a week for the 10-week period we'll be gone. Just to be clear, we need you to stay here. Some people inquired who just wanted to check on the place, but we want someone who will be on site. So, if you're interested, we would love to hear more about you."

"Well, what would you like to know?" asks Seth. "I am currently visiting the Cape for a few months and had plans to stay at a friend's house. And like yours, something came up and plans changed, so now I'm looking for a situation where I can be of use and also have some solitude. No loud parties, just peace and quiet. This sounds like it might be the perfect situation for us both," says Seth.

Travis and Toni look at each other as if they just found gold. They can tell Seth is someone they can trust. They can feel it.

"We will pay you half of the salary up front and the balance when we return. Are you able to commit for the whole 10 weeks, through the end of November?" asks Travis.

"I can," says Seth. Although he didn't need the money, and after seeing Jacob and Grace, he already knew where he was going to use it.

"We have occasional guests visiting. Are you able to be a good host and cater to their needs?" asks Toni.

"I don't see why not. How often are your guests here? You have guests coming to visit even in your absence?" asks Seth curious about this.

"Yes, we have guests here year-round. But not many. We will leave you all the details of what to do regarding guests, as well as taking care of our pets. We have a complete binder with all the information you will need. Lastly, can you start in two days?" asks Toni.

She looks at her husband who nods and they agree that Seth will work out fine. With his agreement, Travis offers to show him around the house. It sounds like just what he needs.

It is a typical old Cape cottage with all its additions, built-in nooks and crannies, and loads of character and charm. It is obvious the couple loves this place and has put much effort into updating it and keeping it pristine, keeping in mind the imperfections of antique charm. The décor is comfortable farmhouse chic with whispers of nautical flair and symbols of their Christian faith here and there. The land consists of about seven acres of pasture and woods, with three small paddocks for the "pets," which turn out to be 12 Katahdin Sheep and a flock of chickens.

Honey-Do is a "hobby" farm, and they have the sheep simply for their love of them. The Katahdin breed, named after Mt. Katahdin in Maine, is very friendly and docile and requires less care than most, not needing to be sheared.

"They just need to be fed and watered, although they partially feed themselves eating pasture grass. Anyway, easy breezy, it will all be in the Honey-Do binder for you. The chickens are great for the eggs obviously. Sound good?" Travis asks, hoping to wrap this up before Seth changes his mind. "If you have any questions, you can always give us a call."

Seth leaves there feeling good about the meeting, and his plans to stay at the Honey-Do Farm for the rest of his sabbatical. He isn't sure about caring for sheep, but perhaps being there might not be much different than what he did at St. Ignatius, he mused. Nurturing his flock.

With concern about where he is going to stay out of the way, he hopes it isn't too late to call Anna. He is anxious to see her again and hopes she might feel the same way. Back on the *Synchronicity*, and tucked into the cabin for the night, he dials her number. While he waits for her to pick up, he thinks about the meaning of *Synchronicity* and how the boat brought him and Anna together.

"Hello?" says Anna, hesitant to answer a call from a number she didn't recognize.

Hearing her voice was like a breath of fresh air to him. "Hi Anna, it's Seth. I hope I'm not calling too late. How are you?"

"I'm great," she says unable to keep from smiling at the sound of his voice. "It's nice to hear from you. It's not too late."

"I wondered if you might like to do something, maybe tomorrow? We can take Wendy out for a spin, somewhere with plenty of space, no fences, no boats. Or we can go to a movie or dinner or both? What would you like to do?" This conversation, this asking a woman out on a date, is so foreign to him. Was this a date? *No, it's not a date*, he tells himself. Of course, he's been out for dinner. Of course, he's been to the movies. Of course, he's been out with men and women. But not *this* woman. He can't even identify why it feels different. Maybe it's the magical energy of Cape Cod, he thinks. The salt air, the anonymity, and the freedom that brings. He isn't sure. He just knows he wants to spend more time with her.

"Dinner would be great," she says. "There is actually a restaurant right near my cottage that overlooks Nantucket Sound. Would you like to go there?"

"That sounds good. I'll pick you up at seven. And Anna… I look forward to seeing you," and he hangs up.

Chapter Ten

Our Sacred Destiny

Anna gets chills just hearing him say her name. She wonders what she will wear and goes to work to finish unpacking her bags and setting up her bedroom which she hadn't done yet. She planned to stay a month but with no reason to return to Connecticut, she has every reason to stay on the Cape as long as she wants. Eventually, she will have to decide if she is going to keep her apartment in Mystic, but there is no hurry. Today's issues are of more interest to her, like what will she wear and what will she order for dinner tomorrow. She always struggled with food issues. So she makes it a point to decide what she will order before she goes to any restaurant, so she will hopefully be making a reasonably healthy choice when she gets there. Otherwise, left to her own impromptu devices, who knows what ridiculous thing she might order.

Her food issues go way back to when she was a child and continued through her young adult years, and even now, to some extent she supposed. Thanks to her control-ling mother, whose size and shape were in direct contrast to Anna's, who had a more substantial build, shall we say. Especially when she was younger. Nowadays, she can handle a few petit fours or a cupcake with no problem. But back then, she would have devoured the whole box. Her parents lived in a mansion in Newport, Rhode Island and for them, everything was about appearances. Anna's appear-ance was never perfect enough. She hated this about them and in defiance she learned to create a life oozing simplic-ity. That's the life she wants for herself, not Newport Mansions. Not presumptuous presentations. Just a simple, beautiful life.

Anna was an only child and they expected much of her, even sending her off to camp as a young adult to lose weight. She was shanghaied by their driver James one day, and dropped off in the middle of the woods, under the guise of being sent for a week to a world-class spa as a birthday gift. Her bag was packed, with another in the trunk that her mother had smuggled in. If only she had known what they had planned she would have made herself scarce that Sunday. She would have gone to church and then meandered over coffee and goodies in the dining hall, chatting with friends, and then off to the Diner for brunch. Instead, she found herself on the way to a "Spa," with someone she thought she could trust. The memory is vivid…

Three hours later, James pulled up in front of the Calvin Woods Retreat Center, a.k.a. Starvation Station. He lifted her bags out of the trunk, looked at her apologeti-cally, and said, "I'm sorry, Anna. I'll be back to get you in six weeks. Have fun," and drove away as fast as he could, kicking up dirt as he flew through the timber gates.

"The bastard!" I said out loud watching the dust cloud settle. This didn't look like any spa I'd ever been to. A young woman with a glowing smile bounced over in my direction as if she were walking on air.

"Hi there, I'm Lilliana. You must be Anna. We've been expecting you."

"My "retreat" started with a stalk of celery for dinner. A six-week retreat I didn't sign up for, called *How Skinny Are We When We Are Carbohydrate Free?* I'm repulsed by the notion. Lilliana, all 100 pounds of her, tells our group of eight equally indignant, plus-sized young adults to middle-aged women, "The first week will be fasting, to cleanse our bodies of toxins. Tonight's menu," she announces, "is vegetarian broth and green tea." Her concession to those who want real food is celery sticks. We groan in unison. After dinner, we have a yoga class at Insight Hall. More groaning follows as we all just want to get to bed.

Calvin Woods Retreat Center is deep in the woods of the Berkshire Mountains in Massachusetts. So deep, we couldn't escape if we tried, with a mixture of staff who are all very suspect. All tree-hugging, gluten-free, vegetarians with a bounce in their step, an ever-present smile on their face, and the perfect answer to every question. They have perfect complexions, perfect shapes, and effervescent energy. It's nauseating. I don't think Illiana has struggled with body issues a day in her life. How can she know what it's like to have celery and broth for dinner when you crave a burger and fries?

What seemed like a month rather than a week later, I

entered the dining hall and saw Illiana waving frantically, for me to join their group. At 18 I appeared to be the youngest of the suffering souls. I headed toward the food line, alone, as everyone else already had their meals and were sitting down. I was thinking about how hungry I was after the introductory seven-day fast we endured. Welcome to "starvation station." I didn't care about being skinny back then. At 195 pounds that was probably a hopeless endeavor. I loved my parents but hated them at the same time. Then camp got interesting.

I met him in the rain that Friday afternoon when we were on day eight and real food was just moments away. He smiled and held the door for me when I entered the hall. Then he was gone. As I stood in line with the drab brown tray in the huge dining hall with its giant vaulted ceiling and columns made of logs, I looked around wondering where he went. The standard soup and salad bar was in place as I'd come to view it every day on the way to our "special" dining room. But that day lunch was to be enjoyed, likely even celebrated in the main dining hall with everyone else.

There were just three people ahead of me and I was honestly salivating at the thought of some real food. Three people between me and something I could chew. I could smell all the luscious goodness of whatever it was being offered. I saw the steam rising from the silver pans filled with options, and couldn't look away as if taking my eyes off might make it disappear. Then, it was my turn. I was hungrier than I ever imagined possible. I scooted my tray along the rails effortlessly as I perused the offerings. Then, I looked up and there he was, all brown eyes and a big smile looking right at me, poised with a serving spoon. His name tag read, *Robin. Shit!* I thought and maybe said it out loud, I'm not sure.

I looked at the delectable selection of foods to choose from, which right about then could have been anything. There was vegetable lasagna, chicken parmesan over whole wheat linguine, salmon and couscous, Brussel sprouts, (ugh!), and *oh my God*, cauliflower crust pizza! I figured they would have done something to "healthy" it up but I didn't care. Pizza was my "non-negotiable." I looked at him poised and ready to serve me *whatever I wanted*. I saw that smile and a twinkle in his eyes and spoke the most difficult words I'd ever uttered. "I'll have the fruit salad." My stomach winced, but just below it, was filled with possibilities.

The memory is still fresh but thank God those days are gone. But Anna still had to figure out what to order for dinner with Seth. She grabs a few things to go upstairs to the cottage loft and continues the task of settling in. She ruminates about what she might order at the restaurant, as she unpacks. Wanting to be more spontaneous, she is still compelled to carefully choose the outfit she will wear tomorrow for her date. The restaurant is a very casual seaside place and she doesn't want to overdress. Choosing a multi-colored broomstick skirt that hangs just above her ankles, a coordinating three-quarter sleeve tunic belted at the waist, and a pair of her favorite brown leather Birkenstocks sounds just about right. She adds a short denim jacket, in case it gets cool later. She stops to look at some of her grandmother's jewelry and chooses a fun, chunky short necklace in all the blue tones of Nantucket Sound. She remembers Gram telling her the piece was handmade and purchased at one of the Artist Shanties over in Hyannis. She loved to support the arts and Anna was happy to have a chance to wear that beautiful handcrafted piece.

The main level of the 650-square-foot cottage consists of the living room, kitchen, bathroom, bedroom, and enclosed front porch. Gram used the downstairs bedroom. The second floor is an open loft with two closets and a bathroom with a spacious walk-in shower. The ceiling is vaulted with exposed beams and both the ceiling and walls have a rustic whitewash finish as if Tom Sawyer himself might have painted it. The loft was always Anna's room when she visited and had the best view of the ocean. It is only natural that she would make it hers now.

There is a queen-sized sleigh bed, an antique oak dresser with a mirror, and a small pine trunk near the window with a white wicker chair and navy cushion. A pair of narrow, ornately carved 1920s nightstands painted a light aqua flanked each side of the white bed, and a lamp of stacked stones shaped like a cairn stood on one. Between the white bed, the oak dresser, the pine trunk, and the nightstands, it was quite a mish-mosh of furniture, gathered from various places over the years. It was cottage furniture. But to Anna, it was home. Gram's quilts were on the bed, a throw tossed over the chair, and an extra in the trunk. Shells and sea glass she'd picked up on previous visits over the years gathered in a mason jar. A photo of her and her beloved Gram when she was younger in front of the cottage, rested on the dresser next to a turquoise clock.

She can hear the tick tock, tick tock. No matter what happens in life, time moves on. It used to lull her to sleep.

Now it reminds her that time never stops. Blue and white toile curtains cover white blinds that block out the sun when she awakes each morning. And upon rising she immediately goes to the window to see the ocean, as if making sure it is still there and not just a dream. The ocean speaks to her for reasons she will never understand. She finishes unpacking her clothes, sets aside the outfit for tomorrow, and looking around satisfied, goes downstairs to read another journal entry. She likes to read just one at a time and savor the gift her grandmother left her. Talks they never had, but wisdom she wanted to convey.

My Dearest Anna,   Our Sacred Destiny

I believe Passion is a desire within our souls, placed there by God and the reason for getting out of bed in the morning. Passion defined by the American Heritage Dictionary (1985 Houghton Mifflin), is, among other things, "A powerful emotion or appetite... boundless enthusiasm," so isn't unearthing our passion, what life is all about? Our purpose for living and breathing on this earth is more than attempting to embrace the monotony of nine-hour days in lifeless environments, rather we are called to reach beyond what is comfortable and seek out that which speaks to us on a most individual and intimate level.

For most of my life, I was challenged to find what gave me life. It changes over time and evolves as we do. But on a universal level, I know I am here to make a difference. That difference comes through my writing, through poetry. I didn't always know this though and spent the better part of my younger years, raising your mom, living my days within the boundaries of an unhappy marriage, and performing the whole archetypal version of myself that was on this earth for the sake of others. To serve and nurture and to serve some more. Well, I was always a free spirit and never got myself too attached to the men who came in and out of my life after your grandad passed. There was one special one that I fell so deeply for that no other could break through the fortress of my heart. But he was not mine to have in the end. That's why when Harry came along we just stayed good friends and no more. My heart belonged to someone else.

I've been a seeker for years, growing in my relationship with a God who my Catholic upbringing taught was very serious, very much into accountability, and very, very far away. This didn't seem right to me and I have long since developed a very close and intimate relationship with a God who I consider to be my best friend and the love of my life, rather than the vengeful, punisher I was told about so long ago. At some point, I came to know a God who loved me beyond measure, forgives endlessly and is not far away but deep within me and made present with every breath I take. I hope you know him too Anna. It is this image that guides me to discern what gives me joy and happiness and what I find to be most fulfilling in life.

It is so easy to be swept along on another's path or to choose in favor of the "responsible" thing, the path offering the most "security." But what is "security" anyway? Security is an illusion, Anna.

What if the world was full of people doing exactly

what they were called to do? What if they were fulfilled by their jobs and vocations and looked forward to going to work every day? Can you imagine it? And what if because they chose to do what they love, they were really good at it? And when we are really good at something we are usually rewarded for it in one way or another. And what if, the whole world was all of a sudden doing what they love and reaping the rewards of their labor, ingenuity, creativity...and what if we had a whole world full of happy, joy-filled people? We might just have a happy, joy-filled humanity, all giving each other the very best they have to offer. Love would abound as would success and abundance and good health and service and, and, and...

All My Love, Gram

Chapter Eleven

"Anna," he whispers. "I don't know if I can
do this."

The moment Seth entered the room, Anna gasped, catching her breath at the sight of him. He wears a tux as Anna stands at the threshold of the French doors leading out to a flagstone terrace overlooking Cape Cod Bay. He is gorgeous, tall, handsome, and all mine thinks Anna. Their eyes meet and she feels a little self-conscious dressed in her grandmother's white satin gown. So formal and traditional, not like her at all. But the sentimentality of wearing Grandma Iris's gown won over her design choice. The justice of the peace clears her throat. Priscilla is an old friend who has been marrying people on the Cape for more than 40 years. Anna walks across the room to join Seth as close family and friends look on. There couldn't have been more than 20 people at the event, to help them celebrate their special day. When she reaches his side, he takes her hand in his and turns to face her with so much love in those expressive eyes.

"Anna," he whispers. "I don't know if I can do this."

She bolts upright on the couch where she was taking an afternoon nap. Shaking her head she wants to make the dream disappear like an Etch-A-Sketch erases an image. But she can't make the thought go away easily. What a strange dream, she thinks looking at the clock, realizing she'd better get dressed for their date.

Anna takes great care to get ready while simultaneously telling herself to relax, keep it simple, and stop fussing over every detail. This is just a quick dinner with a new friend. Right??? Right. They are going to Seastar Grille just a short walk from her cottage on South Shore Drive. She finds the name interesting because she loves seastars, or starfish, depending on what you want to call them. Mostly she is inspired by their tenacity. Many of the species have the miraculous ability to grow back an arm or several when they have but one left. They regenerate, re-invent, and renew themselves. She loves their strength and ability to do that. And finds herself doing that same thing, feeling stronger every day, and more empowered by life's events rather than feeling depleted by them. This is what she tells herself anyway. She checks the mirror and decides she is ready to see Seth again and is looking forward to it.

She hears a car pull onto the crushed shells in the driveway. Anna takes a deep breath hoping to calm her racing heart, and goes downstairs. The ship's bell clangs and she opens the door to see Seth's most fabulous smile awaiting her. She can't contain her own. She notices he is dressed again in jeans, this time with a Vineyard Vines pinstripe oxford, and navy sneakers with leather laces. No socks. She spots the tiny whale logo on the pocket, and the Audi in the driveway, observing that this man lives well. Perhaps with a spirit of playfulness, although she still hasn't learned how he makes a living. For the most part, she doesn't care. Or so she thinks. How could that possibly matter?

Anna not only admires a simple life but thrives in it. There is such beauty in minimalism and she has an appreciation for the simplest of things. She also appreciates the *quality* of fine things she admits, but favors one well-crafted, carefully chosen item over a bounty of others. She wonders what Seth might think of that, with his Audi, his sailboat, and preppy clothes. He's probably got a Rolex somewhere, she thinks, unconsciously touching the Timex on her wrist. She wrinkles her nose at her judgmental thought and welcomes him in.

"Just let me grab my bag and we can leave. The restaurant I told you about is just down the road. We can walk if you like. It's that close."

"Actually," says Seth, "I had an idea that I hoped you might enjoy. I've brought everything for a picnic dinner for us and thought you might like to eat on the beach. What do you think?"

Anna is taken off guard unaccustomed to spontaneity, as she doesn't usually care for surprises and she is all ready to order the *smart* thing at Seastar. She is quite proud of herself for being so prepared. But she is also desperately trying to be more spontaneous and live life more fully in each moment. She decides she can do this.

"Okay, that sounds great," she says, completely uncertain of her own words, but wanting to mean them. They stop at his car to pick up a picnic basket, and a large canvas tote bag filled with assorted things including a bag from Shaw's grocery store. Walking to the end of her street and down a few steps to the beach, they walk a bit to enjoy the still-warm early autumn evening and find the best spot for their picnic. The very idea of a picnic on the beach makes her stomach flutter. They come upon a quiet area, free of other people, and set their things down in the sand. The picnic basket is quite elaborate with everything they need but the food. Seth takes a large woven Mexican blanket out of the tote bag, unrolls it, and lays it out for them. He unpacks the basket with plates, silverware, napkins, corkscrew, and two wine glasses. He lays a large cutting board down between them to set the food on. Anna is both impressed and speechless watching him set up their dinner. First, pulling out a store-bought rotisserie chicken and removing the lid, a container of potato salad from the deli, and a small Ceasar salad with dressing, complete with tongs. Lastly, he removes a chilled bottle of Ballet of Angels from an insulated wine bag. This man knows how to do it, thought Anna, wondering how many times he's done this before, and with how many women. Further impressed by his attention to detail, she notices he has remembered the wine she ordered at the restaurant. She sits there grinning and he looks at her, waiting for her to say something.

"The only thing missing is the flowers," she says teasing him. He holds one finger up as if to say, "Wait a minute." From the picnic basket, he takes out a pair of scissors. Looking around, he gets up, walks over to the Rosa Rugosa bushes that border the beach, and snips a few blossoms, returning with the tiny bouquet for her. He pulls out a bottle of water from his tote bag, ceremoniously sticks the flowers inside, and sets it in the middle of the cutting board. He *has* thought of everything.

As soon as that thought surfaces, he says, "Oh shoot! I forgot a sharp knife to cut the chicken." She could tell he tried so hard to create this perfect experience. Contrary to her previous thought about him having a harem, she had a feeling he had not done this before. He feels bad about forgetting the tools to cut and serve the chicken. Anna spies the tongs he brought for the salad and tears into the chicken, pulling it apart easily. That is the great thing about rotisserie chickens. They're very cooperative and the meat just about falls off the bone, even on a beach. She serves him and helps herself to some chicken. He is thrilled to have that problem resolved after briefly envisioning them having to grab meat with their bare hands like cavemen. The tongs were much better. They each help themselves to the Ceasar and potato salads and with plates full, Seth offers her a glass of wine which she welcomes.

Then he does something that catches her off guard (even more than she already was). And she loves it. He reaches for her hands and bows his head as he offers a prayer to bless their food and the gift of their new friendship. And for a brief time, maybe only seconds, there is a reverent silence, broken only by the rush of the waves meeting the shore. They both look up into each other's eyes grateful for that shared moment and reluctantly let go. The feeling stays with her.

As Anna catches her breath, she notices they are both curious to learn more about the other, but are cautious about revealing too much of themselves. As they eat and talk, Anna asks a lot of questions, unconsciously finding herself in reporter mode. She learns a little more about his summers on the Cape with his grandparents. They both feel deeply connected to Cape Cod for its beauty, mystery, and endless ocean access. That's harder to come by in Connecticut with so much of its shoreline privately owned. She learns that Seth has recently found new accommodations, house-sitting for an older couple on a small farm, which he'll be moving into the next day. *Synchronicity* will be taken out of the water later in the week.

"I appreciate that she brought us together in some way," says Seth about the boat.

"Is that what you think?" asks Anna laughing. "It didn't have anything to do with you absconding with my kite, eh?"

Anna asks him about what he does for a living, and he is evasive, saying he takes care of people. He already knows that Anna is a writer, but asks about her grandmother and learns more about their relationship. They continue sharing controlled, tiny bits about themselves but nothing too earth-shattering.

Seth seems a little nervous, even fidgety looking around, down the beach and into the distance. He does this while alternately, paying attention to Anna as if she is the only other person on the planet. He is really good at that. When they are done with dinner, and the sun begins to set, Seth pulls out a small copper lantern from what seems like the bottomless carpet bag of Mary Poppins. From the picnic basket, he retrieves huge strawberries and a container of chocolate hummus. He offers her both, along with more wine to finish the bottle. How does he know? she wonders. That is one of her favorite desserts. They both enjoy the treat made more special with the glow of the lantern, the sound of the waves, and the taste of the wine. For a short while they both stare out toward the horizon, each lost in their thoughts, until Seth asks if she wants to walk.

"I'd like that," is her quick response. She doesn't even need to think about it. They gather everything up, from what Anna is sure was the most romantic beach picnic ever. Then, they slowly meander along the shoreline back toward her cottage and the setting sun. Stealing sideways glances their conversation comes easily and they know each other a little better, but are certain they want to know more.

When they arrive at her cottage, Seth loads all his picnic gear in the car, asking if she wants to keep the strawberries and hummus. Anna readily accepts the offering setting them aside. Standing inches from him, she looks up into those gorgeous blue eyes, and ever-present smile.

"Thank you so much for a lovely evening. It was… just… wonderful," she says unable to find more accurate words. She is a writer, surely she can do better than that, she thinks. *Magical,* would have been good. *Transcendent,* would have been great. Then she remembers…

"Oh wait!" She leaves him standing there as she runs into the house. He notices the neighbor's curtains move and knows they are being watched, though the woman wouldn't see much in the dark. Anna returns with his clothes from when she was on the boat.

"I forgot to give you these the other night. I put them in the washer. Thank you for loaning them to me." She gives him a quick unexpected hug. Seth holds on just long enough to breathe in the smell of her coconut shampoo before she scoots away into the house with her strawberries and hummus.

Seth gets back in the Audi and somewhat reluctantly

drives back to *Synchronicity…* alone. He didn't expect anything other than that. Did he? But his *awareness* of how he feels about it seems to be changing. He has to pack up his things on the boat to relocate to Honey-Do Farm tomorrow. But tonight, his thoughts are with Anna, and if he's smart, with his God.

Seth struggles with sleep that night, unable to get his time with Anna out of his thoughts. It was just having dinner with a new friend, he tells himself. Yet it feels like so much more. He is glad he Googled, *How to make the perfect beach picnic for a woman you just met.* There were several listings and he chose one and followed the suggestions. He can't remember having such a wonderful time with someone. He loves getting to know Anna and her questions about him are probing, which is both annoying and endearing. He is going to have to tell her soon. It's unfair not to. He is enjoying this new friendship and he doesn't want it to end.

Inside the cottage, Anna curls up on the couch to relive the magic of the evening and eventually opens Gram's journal.

My Dearest Anna   The Lies We Tell

When we think about lies or half-truths, I wonder if lying to ourselves counts. Unconscious. Unaware. How often do we feign understanding or direction? How often do we embrace the silence, digging deep enough to mine the real treasure within our hearts?

Exterior forces and interior restlessness, create human beings that…instead of becoming healthy, strong lives reaching for their dreams, become enslaved to sound, activity, and a constant array of stimulation that binds rather than sets us free.

Freedom comes from the awareness and expression of our gifts and the wisdom and willingness to feel that which we are afraid to feel. To move past the agonizing discomfort of intense awareness that is made manifest only through silent discovery into the subterranean portals of the human condition.

A profound movement in our society toward simplicity prompts me to reassess what is essential. To truthfully evaluate what I need and want and critically determine the difference. For me, Anna less is more… much more.

Like you, I find fulfillment and an unassuming clarity, not in the presence of bigger, better, best, but in the presence of an empty stillness. Being a huge proponent of silence with inclinations not unlike a monastic or hermit, I am drained and the very life siphoned out of me in the presence of noise and excess, longing instead for the silent reflection that I know will ultimately bring me closer to the place where lies are not told, not even to myself. Be true to yourself little one. Be true.

All My Love, Gram

Anna looks at the following pages to find them blank and the date on the last entry told her that Gram died just days after she wrote it. She wondered how many other messages for living Gram had for her but never got to write down. She will never know. With that realization, wrapped in her grandmother's quilt, she cried until she had no more tears left…for tonight.

Chapter Twelve

He was expecting peace and quiet, but began to wonder if he would find either at the Honey-Do Farm.

Early the next morning with his limited possessions from the boat packed into the Audi, Seth heads over to the DMC (Divine Mercy Chapel) for Mass. Even though he is on a sabbatical, he still can't keep away and attends Mass most days, not because he is required to but because he *needs* to. There aren't a lot of people there at 7 a.m., and he appreciates the anonymity that quiet provides. Seth has the spirit of a monk seizing every opportunity for prayer, retreats, or any time alone with his God.

But there is a playful side of him that ministry keeps at bay and Cape Cod makes him recognize, perhaps for the first time in a long time. Father Alfred wasn't celebrating Mass which he was kind of grateful for, feeling just a little guilty about dinner with Anna. He doesn't know why. It was just dinner on the beach. He has dinner with parishioners all the time. They are forever inviting him to their homes, their events, their celebrations. He is a part of their lives in a multitude of ways.

But being with Anna feels different. Following Mass, he heads over to Honey-Do Farm, his home for the next 10 weeks. But when he arrives, the huge RV that was parked by the barn is gone. There is no sign of life anywhere except for the sheep moving toward him in the paddock. Walking over to the house he finds a note taped to the door.

Dear Seth,

The baby came early and Toni and I couldn't wait another minute to get on our way to San Diego to be with the family. We left the binder on the kitchen table with all the information you might need and stocked the refrigerator. I'll handle all the finances from here so don't worry about a thing. The key is under the mat. You have our number if you have any questions. Good luck, God Bless, and we'll see you at the end of November. ~ Travis

Hmph, thought Seth looking around as if he was on Candid Camera. He bends over to lift the doormat and sure enough, there is the key. He looks at it as if there is some mystery to this undertaking that he has yet to discover. He turns the key in the lock, opens the door, and enters the house with no idea how his time there just might change his life forever. Gathering the rest of his belongings and depositing them in the foyer, he settles down at the kitchen table and opens the binder that Travis promises will have all the information he needs. How hard could it be to tend a few sheep, thinks Seth.

The black three-ring binder that reminds him of seminary, is divided into numerous sections including contact numbers, sheep, chickens, property maintenance, daily schedule, recipes, and most noteworthy, reservations. "Reservations..." he says out loud. He is having a few of those himself. He was told there might be a guest or two, but reservations? He closes the binder and looks again at the cover wondering if he has the right book. Under the words *Honey-Do Farm*, in minuscule print, are the startling words *Bed & Breakfast*. Seth doesn't know the first thing about operating a B&B. He has stayed at them on occasion, but staying at one and running one, are two very different things. He was expecting peace and quiet, but began to wonder if he would find either at the Honey-Do Farm.

He no sooner had the thought, when the phone rang. It was a yellow wall-mount phone with a curly cord and push buttons. It hung just above a small counter area set up like a workspace in the corner of the kitchen. It rang again, that jarring shrill he remembers from when he was young. He didn't think they even made those phones anymore. He lifts the receiver to his ear looking at it curiously and finally says, "Hello?"

"Hi there. Is this the Honey-Do B&B? "asks the caller.

"I guess so," says Seth, looking around incredulously.

"My name is Emily. I'm on my way, driving in from Rochester, and Toni and Travis usually have space for us at the Inn. Er...rather me, it's just me this time. Are they there?"

"Actually, they are gone," says Seth. "They left yesterday to visit family out west. I'm house-sitting while they're gone. When did you plan to arrive Emily?"

"I'm about 20 minutes away, just crossed over the bridge."

Seth raises his eyebrows and flips through the binder while she is talking. In the reservations section, he doesn't see any notes about her coming, but he does see that others are. What has he gotten himself into? Seth does not like this, not one little bit. He sits down at the kitchen table and rests his forehead in his hand. Maybe it won't be so bad. It might take his mind off, well... everything else.

"I guess I'll see you soon, Emily," he says hanging up.

It isn't long before he hears the door knocker banging. He reluctantly gets up and walks over to the front door, takes a deep steadying breath, and opens it. He isn't sure what to expect, but standing in front of him is a woman, about 65 or so he speculates, wearing jeans, a blue oxford shirt (untucked), and hiking shoes. She has short blonde hair, appears pretty fit, and has a sweet smile. He senses she is upset about something. Seth offers to help with her luggage and invites her in. She stretches a bit from her long drive, before taking a seat on the couch across from him, looks Seth straight in the eyes, and begins to cry. These weren't little tears but rather a river of tears that streamed down her cheeks with reckless abandon.

"I'm so sorry. I just couldn't contain myself another minute," she choked out. "It was such a long drive, and I'm usually here with my husband Bert, but, but, but he didn't come this time because he left me." Sobbing, she went on. "We were packed and ready to leave for our annual trip to the Poconos in Pennsylvania and he told me he didn't want to do this anymore. I thought he meant he didn't want to go to the Poconos. But he meant he didn't want to be married…to me. We've been together 35 years." More tears. "He said he met someone else, someone from the gym where he works out. As if that wasn't bad enough, their name is Benjamin. Benji! He calls him Benji!" Emily spits out, clearly both angry, shocked, and heartbroken all at once.

Seth listens somewhat amused by how she tells the story, but also filled with empathy. He brings her Kleenex and sits there listening, encouraging her to go on. He is a great listener with a lot of experience in that area. Emily shares that the Honey-Do Farm has always been a sanctuary for her, a retreat, and it makes sense that she would make a beeline there when her life was in turmoil. Travis and Toni always welcome her, as Seth is doing just then. He remembered his hosting duties and when the time was right, asked if she might like a cup of tea. He heads toward the kitchen leaving his guest to collect her thoughts.

Seth searches out everything he needs to make tea and puts the pot of hot water on the stove. He finds oatmeal raisin cookies in a container that looks like they were made fresh that day and puts some on a plate. Waiting for the water to boil, he leans against the counter and prays for Emily. To the only One who can help her in her sorrow. He hadn't heard her whole story, yet, but he heard enough to know that a prayer won't hurt. Prayer never hurts. Serving trays are plentiful in the pantry and he fills one with tea and cookies. He has been a keen observer, all the numerous times he was waited on over the years, enough to have learned how to be a good host. He hasn't done much of it himself, but he certainly knew how. His time at Honey-Do would put him to the test. He returns to the living room with the tray and learns more about Emily and her story.

With perfect timing, he asks, "So Emily, how long are you planning to stay at Honey-Do?" Seth felt silly just saying the name, Honey-Do, but knew he better get used to it. Still sniffling and trying to hold back more tears over her mug of Tetley tea, she tells him she doesn't know but will decide soon. After a little small talk about the inn, Seth carries her bag as she directs him to the room she usually stays in with her husband. That just generates a new round of tears.

"Perhaps you'd like to stay in a different room?" offers Seth. She thinks a minute and says, "Maybe you're right. Let's do that." After getting her settled in alternate accommodations he returns to the kitchen to review the object he has quickly come to refer to as the "cursed binder."

Chapter Thirteen

**"Don't say it, don't say it, don't say it,"
he prays.**

All Anna wants is the rolling pin. She hides in the tiny pantry off the kitchen and wishes she had grabbed it before she ducked inside and shut the door. She just came into the kitchen with a couple of bags of groceries and set them down on the counter when she heard the front door open.

"Who's there?" she whispers, too terrified to speak louder. She isn't sure what to do and looks around for a weapon. There is a broom but that wouldn't do much damage she thinks. Three cast iron frying pans are stacked precariously on one of the open shelves. She grabs the small one and then changes her mind and replaces it with a larger one. She holds it out in case the intruder opens the door. The sun is just setting and the cottage is almost dark but for the glow of the sunset to the west. She thinks briefly about climbing out the pantry window but it is quite small. She isn't.

Her mind wanders back to her childhood when she hid

in the pantry to avoid her father during one of his unpredictable bad moods, which she later learned was associated with bipolar disorder. As a child his yelling and fits of rage made her feel threatened, even though he never hit her. It was terrifying nonetheless. The pantry with all its comfort foods, made her feel safe back then, but not so much at that moment. She wishes her grandmother was here now as she hears the footsteps, big, loud ominous footsteps, entering the kitchen. Her heart races with each step. The rolling pin would have been good. The glass doorknob begins to turn as time stands still and Anna holds her breath. Lifting the pan in the air she is poised to do some damage when looking down she sees that familiar Gucci loafer, making her even more inclined to swing that skillet. But she holds back screaming at Ethan.

"What are you doing here? You scared me half to death!" Walking out of the pantry and into the kitchen, Anna works unpacking her groceries. "What do you want Ethan? Why are you here?"

He steps toward her and she backs away, not wanting him anywhere near her.

"I wanted to see you. And tell you I'm sorry. Lindsey didn't mean anything to me. It was just a quick fling. You know," he says casually.

"No, I don't know Ethan, but as I said when I saw you last, we are through. Now get out!"

"Anna, give me another chance. We were great together."

"We weren't great together then, and we sure aren't great together now Ethan. I'm done," she says. "My only regret is that I didn't realize it sooner. You are so full of yourself. You don't care about me. You care about what you can accumulate, and how much money is in your portfolio. The illusion of wealth and prestige. It's all a façade. Add to that your lies and deceit, and now cheating? Really? Just go. I don't want anything to do with you. And I don't want to see you here again. Ever!"

"Oh, you know you don't mean that, sweetie. Give me another chance. I have this thing coming up at work for the holidays and I need you by my side. You know you love these events. I can't go alone. How would that look?"

"Seriously? You came all the way out here because you need me to attend a holiday party with you? And you actually think I enjoy them? And you actually think I would go with you? You've really lost your mind, Ethan."

"Anna, I get that your pissed and that you're trying to make a point of some kind. Just get your stuff and let's go. We can talk about it all the way home if you want. But I don't have time to deal with this right now. Just lock up the house and let's go."

Looking around at the humble space, he scrunched up his pointy nose. Then he remembered the location just steps from the beach and water views. He calculates the value of the property in his mind, and with the market such as it is, he thinks he can get a substantial price for it. He will broach the subject with Anna on their way home. She should sell.

The cupboard door slamming shut brings his attention back to Anna rather than dollar signs. With groceries put away, Anna glares at him and he realizes she is not going anywhere.

"Goodbye, Ethan."

"You know I haven't really seen this side of you before Anna. So strong, so decisive. It's kind of sexy. I like it," he says, inching toward her.

"*Get out!*" she shouts at him.

He can't remember Anna ever raising her voice before. He decides not to press his luck and to pursue this another time. Selling the house and the holiday party. Ethan backs out of the kitchen, not entirely sure that he hasn't provoked Anna to violence. He makes it out the front door, and gets into his car, peeling out of the sand-dusted lane.

Anna takes a deep breath, glad he is gone. The whole encounter with Ethan was unnerving, to say the least. But she felt good about herself for handling him the way she did. Where did she find the bravado, she wondered. Maybe it is Gram's strong, wise energy. She can feel her presence in the cottage at times.

Just as she is calming down and thinking about how much she misses her Grandmother, her phone rings, showing a number she doesn't recognize. She hesitates but decides to answer and smiles when she hears that deep sexy voice on the other end. She just can't help herself. It's Seth.

"How does a movie sound?" he asks.

They make plans for later that week. Seth picks her up at the cottage. She is a little anxious but also excited to see him. Anna isn't a big movie theater fan, but the thrill of being with him again is worth it. She has experienced one too many dilapidated old theaters that smelled like dirty gym lockers, and stale popcorn, with floors sticky with spilled soda. But she recently discovered the beauty of old theaters being rehabilitated with comfortable new reclining seats and wide aisles making for a very enjoyable experience.

They walked into the Cranberry Crescent Cinema in downtown Hyannis which was one of those wonderful revived theatres. It has been there as long as Anna can remember and she wondered if Seth went there as a child. She imagined that they might have been there at the same time way back when. The last time she saw a movie there, was the late 70's when John Travolta was doing disco in *Saturday Night Fever.* Like many others, it had been restored and didn't smell at all like a dirty gym locker, for which she was grateful. Cranberry Crescent showed older movies these days and they were going to see *When Harry Met Sally*, a classic from the 80's with Meg Ryan and Billy Crystal. Seth hasn't seen it, but it was one of Anna's favorites.

Seth knew that theater inside and out from the summers he spent on the Cape as a child. He and his brother used to love to go to Saturday matinees with double features that would keep them occupied for hours and scare the daylights out of them. The more frightening the better according to Jacob.

Anna chose a rom-com but that is fine with Seth. He just wants to spend time with her and thinks that is the perfect place to do it. And if he has to sit through *When Harry Met Sally*, that is fine with him. He'll enjoy every minute, just being next to her. She doesn't care much about the movie either but just wants to be with him again. Even though they haven't spent a lot of time together, she feels an attraction to him that she has not felt in a very long time. Ethan took up much of her energy and not in a good way. She also knows she is guarded, after her experience with him. She tells herself that Seth seems different, and she wants to believe that in the worst way.

They enter the theater and after getting their tickets, he asks if she wants popcorn. Who doesn't want popcorn at the movies, right? She thinks for a moment about the elegance of salty popcorn stuck in her teeth and declines.

"Well, how about we share one?" he asks not waiting for an answer. That makes her happy. They choose seats in the back of the theatre off to the side and notice there are not many people there. A few couples scattered about, and one rowdy group of older women can hardly contain themselves, even after the lights go down. Once they get past the previews of upcoming attractions, the group settles down immersed in the complicated story of a special friendship.

Seth places the bag of popcorn on his lap and the two munch away, enjoying the movie. At some point, Anna reaches into the bag at the same time as Seth. As their fingers touch, their eyes leave the big screen, instead focusing on each other. Neither one retreats. Until… a roar of laughter from the ladies' group startles them back to reality. Anna excuses herself to use the restroom and slips past him toward the aisle.

She stares at herself in the bathroom mirror and wonders what exactly she thinks she is doing. She has no interest in getting involved with another man now, or possibly ever, she tells herself. Shaking her head trying to clear whatever is going on between her and Seth, she washes her hands attempting to remove the feeling of his touch, and returns to the movie. This time, she plans to keep her hands in her lap. And she does. Until Seth reaches over to take her hand. Powerless, she gives in to him. They sit there like that for the rest of the movie, right up until Harry proposes, in the most awkward way possible of course. The credits roll, the lights come up, and as they get up to leave, standing right in front of him, is parishioner Millicent Wright. He drops Anna's hand as if it were hot charcoal burning frankincense and myrrh during Mass. Seth's palms get sweaty at the sight of the woman fearing what she might say.

"Don't say it, don't say it, don't say it," he prays. And sure enough, out it came. With all the finesse he would expect from her.

"Father Seth, how lovely to see you. What a surprise. Now who is your friend here?" she drawls, making sure to pronounce "Father" good and loud, and giving Anna the once over.

The woman is in her late 80's he guessed, with pitch-black hair, and penetrating eyes that saw everything, like a vulture waiting to swoop in for the kill. She is thin as a rail and loves to gossip. More importantly, she loves to get Father Seth's attention and hates it when anyone else has it. He turns toward Anna to introduce them and sees a look on her face he will never forget. When the older woman leaves them, "Please take me home," is all Anna can say.

Getting into his car, he turns to her. "Let me explain," he pleads. She won't even look at him. She *can't* ...even look at him. "Please take me home," she repeats softly.

Chapter Fourteen

*She knows something delicious is there,
but she can't quite get her hands on it.*

Seth awakes the next morning from a night of uneasy sleep, remembering a dream. He had transformed into a red cardinal. Feathers flapping, he didn't know what to make of it hovering over the goose-down comforter. He was frantic, looking down at his bed at the Honey-Do Farm, the bed Seth climbed into just hours before. Feeling small, trapped, and out of control the bird began flying around the bedroom and saw itself in the mirror over the dresser. It flew up close looking into those dark penetrating eyes he didn't recognize. He became increasingly agitated and flew at top speed into the mirror and fell to the dresser's top with a thud. When he awoke, Father Seth Alexander was safely tucked into his bed, alone. What a strange dream he thought.

Just then, the doorbell rings and he remembers where he is, caretaker of the Honey-Do Farm and Inn. "Ughh, now what?" is his response as he pulls on jeans and a T-shirt and runs down the stairs. With his hand on the doorknob, he closes his eyes a moment, makes the sign of the cross, pastes a smile on his face he isn't quite feeling, and opens the door. But no one is there. The smell of bacon and eggs is coming from the kitchen and something is baking in the oven. He remembers Emily is in residence and goes to investigate.

"Good morning, Seth. I hope you don't mind me getting things going this morning. Toni and Travis loved it when I would cook something up for everyone and greet the guests with fresh muffins or scones. Coffee is over here all ready for you," says Emily.

"But we have no guests," counters Seth.

"Oh, I know someone will be along. There are always guests. Looks like it's just the two of us this morning. How would you like your eggs?" The table was set and Seth had the feeling that he was home in the parsonage being waited on just like he was used to. It took him off guard just for a moment but he realizes that maybe cooking breakfast is helping Emily take her mind off her errant hubby and his Benji.

"You know you don't have to do this, right?" says Seth sitting down to devour her delicious offering. "I understand that someone comes in to cook and clean and shop, etc."

"Oh, I know someone will be along. I went out and got eggs from the chickens and I don't mind a bit," says Emily, sitting down to join him, grateful for the company. Seth listens as she tells him more about her life. People like to share their stories with him, and he is happy to listen.

Seth isn't the only one whose sleep is interrupted by dreams. Anna dreamt she was in church for her first Confession. She is eight years old and is the last one alone in the back of the church. She had shoulder-length dirty blonde hair back then and wore red pedal pushers and a blue and white striped T-shirt with an anchor on it. She sits in the pew and everyone else is gone except for Oliver Obermeyer who goes in just before her. She realizes she is holding her breath and takes a deep one as she holds her hands together wringing them nervously. When she hears the door open, she looks up to see awkward Oliver stumble out looking as if he'd seen a ghost. He makes the sign of the cross and kneels in a pew for at least a few *Our Fathers* and more *Hail Marys* she guesses. She knows it's her turn. She moves slowly toward the confessional, one foot in front of the other, each step deliberate yet cautious, toward the open door. Like everything in the church, it is dark. Stepping inside she bends down on the padded kneeler and hears the swoosh from the other side of the screen as it opens and the priest makes himself known. The familiar voice says, *"Hello my child, remember that God will always love you and always forgive you. Now what sins have you committed?"* Anna awakes, sitting straight up, gasping for air. The hair at the nape of her neck is damp and she struggles to catch her breath. Her heart is racing as she replays the voice in her dream. *"Hello, my child. What sins have you committed?"* It is Seth.

Anna's roots as a Catholic run deep making that dream jarring, to say the least. Thoughts of Seth had her tossing and turning all night. Until, she finally surrendered to her restlessness at about 4 a.m., throwing back the covers and sitting on the side of the bed. First, she'll make some breakfast and begin a bright new day. Then some fresh air will be in order. The antique white iron bed frame groans with every movement until she stands up and stretches, looking around at the cherished space that is now hers. She is beyond grateful. She misses Gram right now, especially after Seth's big reveal last night. Anna wishes she could talk with her about it. On to a new day, she thinks, trying to get Seth out of her mind, if not her heart.

She is trying to stay positive and let go of whatever angst might be creeping into her already wounded heart. She isn't sure if she is angry or hurt. Or both. She knew they'd only known each other a short time but he is so easy to fall for. She keeps telling herself this was just a friendship. She could really use a good friend right now. But those eyes, that smile, that voice, and he listened like no one she'd ever known, making her feel genuinely heard. That's so rare these days. He is sensitive and she could tell he was spiritual and that meant a lot to her. But she hadn't realized just how spiritual, as in *Father* Seth. Mostly, she decides, she is confused. What did he want with her when he committed his life to God through the priesthood? Why is he staying on a sailboat and why is he house-sitting? Why is he driving a seventy-thousand-dollar car? She knew that only because she had written a freelance piece for Luxury Car Magazine. None of it made any sense. She felt like a fool for spending time with him, trusting him for even a moment. Especially after the disaster with Ethan. Yet he was just being a friend, right? She wants answers and she wants them now.

Anna makes her way down the creaking stairs and into the kitchen foraging around for something to eat for breakfast. Anger made her hungry. The black wrought iron latch clicked softly with each cupboard closing. The hammered metal was bumpy yet cool and smooth to the touch. The latch secured the pantry door as well in the small but functional kitchen. The pantry is a huge bonus for storage, filled with shelves, drawers, and hooks for hanging. This reminds her how much she loves the quirky charm of the old cottage. The cabinets and interior doors of the house are all made of knotty pine and have that same vintage wrought iron hardware. There is something very nostalgic about both making her feel warm and safe. The fact that the house is quite small added to that cozy feeling. Or in Scandinavian terms, Hygge, an overall feeling of warmth, coziness, and well-being. She loves that Gram's cottage exuded all those things. It has everything she needs and is the perfect escape from what had become a life filled with stress and more drama than she cared to admit. And yet here she is looking for an escape, but finding more drama with Seth. Sometimes she thinks she is a magnet for questionable characters. She has a faulty *picker* she'd been told more than once. Although she still couldn't believe she had read Seth wrong. She didn't want to believe it, yet there it was. Truth.

She prepares coffee with the ancient white Mr. Coffee machine on the counter, chiding herself for not setting it up the night before. She is a woman who appreciates good planning and preparation. Yet to be fair she was a bit preoccupied. Two scoops Eight O'Clock Columbian, and two scoops New England Vanilla. Pushing the magic button she immediately hears that blessed gurgle and breathes in the aroma that soothes her soul and stirs her senses. Some people are tea people and some people are coffee people. She likes both. But mornings and being ready to take on a new day called for the sustenance only coffee can give. In

116

the same way coffee stirs her senses, so does Seth. How is that possible, she wonders. Getting her new pottery mug out of the cupboard, she shovels in a heaping scoop of sugar. "I like it sweet," she says out loud to herself as if to justify the act.

Opening the refrigerator, she takes out creamer, a carton of eggs, some shredded Swiss cheese, and a container of chopped green bell peppers. "Bliss," she says, wondering what Seth is doing. With a splash of extra virgin olive oil into the pan, she throws in a handful of peppers to saute, adding a dash of paprika, onion powder, and black pepper. When she hears a sizzle, she pours in her scrambled egg mixture. Anna prefers a messy scramble over a neatly formed omelet although the ingredients are the same. It tastes different. When the eggs are just about cooked, she sprinkles in shredded Swiss cheese until it melts out of sight. Kind of like Seth she thinks. She knows something delicious is there, but she can't quite get her hands on it. And with what she knows now, she wouldn't want to. *You don't mess with a priest.* She wonders if he *wants* to be messed with.

She finds utensils and a plate and pushes down a slice of 12-grain bread in the toaster trying to make healthier choices when she can. She dreams a moment about Zoe's Tokens of My Confections as she butters her 12-grain bread. The 12-grain is supposed to be a healthier choice despite it tasting like cardboard. She slathers on a little seedless raspberry Trappist jam to flavor up the cardboard. Nobody makes jam like those Trappist monks, she thinks, always looking for ways to support priests and those devoted to religious life. She has a very healthy respect and even reverence for those who commit their entire lives to God in such a complete way. Jesus deserves that kind of devotion she figures.

Before every breakfast, she lights a candle and says a prayer. For her loved ones, family and friends, artists and writers, priests, and religious communities, and for the world to get along in peace, understanding, love, and kindness toward each other. She doesn't think it should be that hard, although evidently, that isn't the case. That is her prayer every day. And with a God who can do absolutely anything, she believes it is a worthy one. Sitting down to her scrambled eggs, her prayer said, she sips her coffee and thinks about what the day might bring.

After enjoying her favorite meal of the day, and not quite ready to re-enter the world, she grabs her yoga mat and brings it out to the back deck. The sun is just starting to come up. She stretches her arms wide, breathing in the cool salty autumn air. Beach Plum bushes grow along the crooked split rail fence in the tiny backyard that separates her yard from others. She begins with a few minutes of sitting meditation. Then with an intention for greater understanding, she moves through simple actions like cobra pose, mountain pose, and downward dog. When she is through, she feels better. After a hot shower and getting dressed, she decides her picker has been faulty long enough. She wants answers from Seth and she is going to get them. She hops into her old Volvo and heads off in the direction of 6A and the Honey-Do Farm. But at the intersection of Route 28, she finds herself heading toward St. Anthony Church. St. Anthony of Padua is the patron saint of lost souls she remembers from her early catechism days. How symbolic that she feels called there. In some way, she feels like a lost soul. She wants answers but rather than get them from Seth, she feels called to get them from God, at the moment anyway. She turns left and heads toward the adoration chapel in the rear of the grounds. When she pulls in, there is only one other car in the big parking lot.

The chapel is a magnificent peaked stone structure with numerous stained-glass windows. It was built exclusively for Eucharistic Adoration which ideally would have someone present all hours it is open. Eucharistic Adoration is a practice of the Roman Catholic faith tradition. Anna often goes there just to enjoy the silence, and be in the presence of the Eucharist whenever she is on the Cape. She hasn't been there since Gram died and she misses it. Today, she has the desire to silence the raging thoughts in her mind and seeks answers from her God whom she realizes may not have them. Anna looks up at the stained-glass windows that each tell a story and wonders what her story might be. She kneels in one of the pews, closes her eyes, and listens, hoping something will make sense to her. She hears the only other person there leave and knows she is alone in the silence now, just her and her God. Feeling her whole body relax in that sacred space, Anna realizes she is crying, silent tears just trickling down her cheeks. Her heart is broken, for all she has been through in the last year. She is finally giving in to what she needs to do. Surrender..surrender to the grief, the sadness, the loss…maybe the love. She sits there alone and cries. Feeling empty, yet purified in some way, she prays to her infinitely loving God to guide her moving forward. She is open to whatever that means and as another person comes in, it is time for her to leave.

Still seeking answers, she decides to confront Seth. She drives across the Cape and shows up at the Honey-do Farm. Banging the door knocker, she waits for a response and is startled when she hears a sweet voice behind her.

"May I help you?" an older woman asks.

"I'm looking for Seth Alexander. He is supposed to be house-sitting here."

"Oh, he had to leave unexpectedly for a short trip north to help a friend. I expect him back tomorrow. I was just feeding the sheep and tending to the chickens. Can I help you with something? Would you like to come in? My name is Emily."

Anna looks at the older woman holding a basket of eggs and smiling at her. She wonders where that peace from the chapel has gone and feels annoyed and confused. She accepts the woman's invitation and follows her into the kitchen where she immediately notices the smell of freshly baked pastry. Emily seamlessly makes her way around, starting water for tea and putting out croissants with butter and honey. In no time she has gathered a couple of mismatched antique plates, tea cups, and silverware. She is the perfect hostess. When the tea is poured, she sits down across from Anna who went into her interview mode to learn why Emily is there. Without hesitation, Emily shared how her husband left her to go to the Poconos with a friend from the gym.

"I'm sure he will be back. He will come to his senses," she tells Anna, who isn't convinced. "He ran away with Benjamin. "Benji" he calls him. He will be back," she repeated sniffling and holding back tears.

"I'm so sorry," says Anna, thinking about the wretched Ethan.

"And when I got here Seth was so kind, welcoming me with open arms, and has been just delightful, making me feel at home and giving me the space I need. Honey-Do has always been like a retreat place for me, a haven in a troubled world. Usually, I'm here with Bert, but not this time. Then Seth got called away and asked me to tend to the sheep and chickens while he was gone, which I am more than happy to do, and off he went. How do you know Seth?" she asks.

Catching Anna off guard she isn't quite sure what to say but appreciates the chance to meet the woman and get to know her a little. After thinking about it, and about how kind Seth has been to Emily, she says, "Well, I guess we're friends," wondering if that could be true. Anna looks around noticing the sunlight streaming through the wavy glass of the old windows, the mismatched dishes, the smell of warm croissants, the smile on Emily's face at having someone to talk with. She reminds Anna just a little of Gram. It all felt so warm and inviting, even nurturing.

The feeling was interrupted when they heard someone coming in the front door. Emily was startled and Anna thought it might be Seth returning early. A tall young woman dressed in jeans, a T-shirt, and a plaid flannel shirt, sporting a brown ponytail came into the kitchen. Her smile beamed and she had a bucket of cleaning supplies and grocery bags with her.

"Hi there," she greeted them, unphased by strangers in the house. "I'm Mary. I've been helping out around the Inn for Toni and Travis. They told me they would be away and that someone was overseeing things. Are either of you the innkeeper?"

Emily and Anna looked at each other. "Uh, nope," answered Anna. "That would be Seth. He had to run an errand and will be back tomorrow. It's nice to meet you, Mary. This is Emily, she is a guest who has been coming here for years, right Emily? I'm surprised you haven't met."

"Oh, I've been around here just the past few months," says Mary putting her things down. "I came to the Cape for the summer and couldn't bring myself to leave. I love it here. I'm from Westport, Connecticut."

Anna eyed her suspiciously giving her the once over. She was young, fit, cute, and friendly. She wondered if Father Seth would agree, feeling just a little tug of jealousy.

"Anyway, if you don't mind, and I'm not interrupting anything, I'd like to get to work," says Mary. "I usually clean whatever needs attention, change sheets, refresh the rooms, etc. I deliver breakfast staples for the kitchen and bake something for the guests to enjoy. Toni and Travis usually prepare breakfast for their guests."

"I'm happy to help with that," Emily chimed in, happy to have something to keep her busy. "I love to cook and I'm pretty good at it." Anna affirmed this as she took a bite of one of Emily's croissants.

Chapter Fifteen

"If this is a pep-talk you need to work on your pastoral care skills."

Seth ends the call from his best friend and knows he needs to respond to the request. They are like brothers and met in seminary years back. Brandon just could not manage the vow of celibacy, getting caught in his room with the monsignor's niece one night. They were on a four-month assignment together in a local parish not far from where Seth grew up in central Connecticut. The seminary sent him packin' and he never really settled down after that. That was years ago, and tonight, Brandon was calling from the police station in Conway, New Hampshire, and needed to be bailed out... Again.

Getting off the phone with Brandon, he throws some things in a duffle bag and double-checks the Inn's calendar on his way out the door. From Yarmouth Port, it is going to take 3½ hours to Conway, in the White Mountains. What Brandon is doing there he had no idea and hadn't thought to ask, as Brandon's phone time was limited. He got on his way with no idea what he would do when he got there. Brandon was his Achilles heel. He had no other family and Seth was his dearest friend. He always felt like he needed to watch over him and so, whatever he needed, Seth would make it happen. But he couldn't make him straighten out his life. And here he is again, dropping what he's doing to run to his aid. Whatever Brandon did, he hoped it would be an easy fix, especially if a priest arrived to bail him out. For that reason, he wore his black shirt with the clerical collar, carefully concealing it from Emily as he left. It never hurts he thought. The drive is long and he can stay on I-95 until he gets to Portsmouth and Route 16 should take him right to Conway. He'll have to stay at Brandon's apartment wherever that is. Seth has no idea where he is living these days but assumes it is somewhere around Conway. Then he has to get back to Anna. And the Honey-Do Farm he remembers with a sigh. He left Emily in charge of things and hoped that was a good decision. He'd no sooner arrived at Honey-Do when Emily showed up and he was called away. He's waiting for the quiet reflective time he was hoping to have when he agreed to *house-sit*.

With a couple of stops on the way, Seth covers a good distance with Google Maps guiding him. He prays the rosary and listens to Melissa Etheridge, not at the same time. He stops at a diner off the highway in Portsmouth to get something to eat. People are usually very friendly and respectful when they see he is a priest, or depending on their personal experience might look at him with general contempt. It could go either way.

The Catholic church has been challenged with wide-spread sexual abuse as well as social and moral issues that make many people struggle. The sight of a priest might be a good thing or a bad thing, depending on who you talk to. For that reason, he meant to take off his collar before he went in and forgot. He ordered a burger and fries and got coffee to go. When he left the diner, he fired up the Libby app on his phone to listen to part of Thoreau's *Walden* the rest of the way. He'd read it before of course, but enjoyed the relaxed, calming nature of it. Despite appearances, he really does enjoy a simple life. A couple of hours there, and he'll be back at the inn before he knew it, he told himself. He could hardly believe he was *inn-sitting or farm-sitting*. But first… he had to deal with Brandon.

Arriving in Conway, with Melissa, the Blessed Mother, and Thoreau tucked away for now, his clerical collar in place, he enters the police station. It is late.

"Hello officer, I'm Father Seth Alexander, here to pick up Brandon Barlowe."

"Ah, yes. He told us you'd be coming but we weren't sure you were for real. Your friend is quite a piece of work."

"Yes, I suppose he can be," says Seth reading the name badge on the woman's uniform. "Officer Pendleton, can you tell me why he was arrested and what I need to do to get him out?"

"I'd be happy to. Buckle up," she says. "First, he got intoxicated at Johnny's Place and picked a fight with one of our locals after hitting on the guy's girlfriend. He then tried to get an Uber but his credit card was declined. Plus, it's nearly impossible to get an Uber around here at this hour, or any hour for that matter. We're still not sure how he got there. He had 23 cents on him and couldn't pay his bar tab. When we got the call and took him in, he proceeded to vomit all over the back seat of our cruiser. That really pissed us off. We are just holding him overnight so he can sleep it off. Johnny isn't pressing any charges if he pays his tab. You want to see him?"

"Yes, please." Seth follows her to the holding cell which appears empty... until they see two legs dangling from the HVAC vent in the ceiling. "What the hell?" she says talking into her radio to call for backup. Another officer, the one who was cleaning the vomit in the cruiser came running. The two of them grabbed Brandon's legs and got him down.

"I was just trying to get some air," says Brandon slurring every word.

"If you want to pay his tab you can take him now. We'd be *happy* for you to take him now, actually," says the officer.

Brandon catches sight of him and slurs in his direction, "Seth, what are you doing here? That's Father Seth" he tells them. "He's my best friend."

"Lucky you," says the officer. "If you want to come with me to pay his tab you can take him."

Seth follows her back to the desk, pays his bill, thanks her, and waits for Brandon to be released and turned over to him. When he comes out, Brandon looks like he hasn't shaved or bathed in several days. With dirty jeans, a plaid flannel shirt, and a jacket, he hangs his head and looks up at Seth with guilty eyes and not much to say. He follows Seth out the door to the Audi.

"Whoa, Father Seth. Things are going well, eh?" as he admires the car in the moonlight.

"Just get in," says Seth noticing the bar stench coming from his passenger seat. "Let's get you home and cleaned up. Where are you living these days? I haven't heard from you in a while."

"Well, uh, I don't actually have a place right now. I thought I had something lined up with this girl I was seeing but it didn't really work out. She wasn't quite my type." Seth gave him the side eye while Brandon went on. "You know the kind I like. European, thin, like a model, fit, and confident. Oh, and young, like late twenties. A little wealth behind her wouldn't hurt."

Seth looks at him again, still in the parking lot waiting for an address.

"Aren't we almost the same age? What does a fifty-year-old need with a twenty-year-old?"

"I said late twenties, maybe early thirties, " he adds after thinking a moment. "I'm not greedy you know."

"Are you telling me you don't have a place to live? More importantly, you don't have a place for us to stay tonight?"

"Well, that would be correct," he slurs.

"Do you know of a decent hotel around here? Never mind. I saw one when I came into town. We'll go there, and then...you can tell me all about why you have no place to live...again."

It was late when Seth checked them into the Conway Country Motel. After getting his overnight bag from the car, Seth realizes Brandon has no clothes with him. Brandon has nothing with him. Being prepared as was his nature, Seth brought extras just in case he needed them. They are both about the same size so what he brought will have to do until they get Brandon's things or get to a store. There is nothing open at that hour in the little country town.

The room was a typical New England motel, simple but clean and adequate for a quick overnight stay. Seth showered and when he came out, Brandon was sound asleep in his grungy clothes. Seth pulls a blanket up over him and realizes he'll have to wait until tomorrow to hear his story. He always has a story and he's rarely at fault, thought Seth. He turns off the lamp and crawls between the sheets of the other bed, comforted that he was able to help his dear friend. He is annoyed by his behavior and lifestyle, but also compassionate to a fault when it comes to Brandon. Seth is always willing to come to his aid like a big brother. He closed his eyes and with thoughts of Anna not far away, drifted off into a sound sleep.

The sunlight streamed through a break in the curtains waking Seth earlier than he would have liked. He turned over and saw Brandon still passed out on the other bed, sleeping like a rock. He pulled on some clothes and stepped outside with his Liturgy of the Hours to recite Morning Prayer. He never went anywhere without it. It was a comfort and connection to God that he never wanted to be without. There were two pumpkin-colored rocking chairs in front of each room with a table in between. At that hour, the silence of the fog lifting, interrupted only by two loons flying overhead, was just what he needed. Between the loons and the brilliant leaves covering the mountains in the distance, it was a beautiful autumn awakening.

When he was done with prayer, he walked over to the office to get coffee and some Advil and returned to their room to find Brandon sitting up on the side of his bed. He held out both, and Brandon welcomed them. Seth went through his bag to gather a few things for Brandon to wear so he could get cleaned up and dressed. He needed to get him settled wherever he was going so he could get back to the Honey-Do. Brandon came out, showered, and dressed looking good as new in Seth's clothes, though they were a little big on him.

"So, where do we go from here?" asks Seth sitting back with his patience of a priest look on his face, ready to listen, although the clerical collar was gone. "What's your story this time?"

"Thanks for the coffee...and Advil...and clothes...and rescue. I really, really didn't want to wake up in that cell today," Brandon says with a weak, apologetic grin on his face. Seth waits for him to go on. "It's no big deal. I was seeing this girl and she turned out to be a raving nutjob and accused me of cheating on her. I was working for her father at a local ski resort. They give staff a furnished studio to share and long story short, she threw me out, I lost my job and a place to live." More silence. "I can usually find a place to stay and I don't take up much space as I like to keep things loose and free, not tie myself down with possessions, you know?" More silence. "When she threw me out, after catching me charming one of the ski bunnies, she threw my duffle with everything I own into the bonfire. That's why I was at Johnny's."

Giving Brandon space to add anything else to the story, Seth remains silent. Nothing else came. Not even an apology for calling him to come all that way to save his sorry ass...again. He wonders if he will ever, ever get his act together. But instead of saying what he really thinks, he moves into priest mode. Kindness and compassion wash over him, against his better judgment.

"Would you like to come to the Cape? I'm on sabbatical from the church for a few months and house-sitting in Yarmouth Port, through November. There's room for you there. You could use the time to figure out what you want to do with your life, assuming it's not to continue on your current path. You could help out. We have some sheep and chickens.

"You want me to feed your chickens? And take care of sheep? Are you kidding?"

"Well, you could stay here. No clothes. No money, No home, No job. No ski bunny to play with. Or you might just want to think about what you want your life to look like moving forward. Maybe create a new one if the old one isn't serving you. Maybe if you can't stop drinking and abusing people who care about you, you might consider accepting that you just might need the help of some higher power, greater than your overindulgent, pleasure-seeking, penniless, alcoholic self. "

"If this is a pep-talk you need to work on your pastoral care skills," says Brandon, considering that it might just be a very, very long ride to the Cape. But he doesn't have any choice. Seth will get over it. He always does. He can't stay mad at him. Not at anyone. He has a built-in forgetter tool.

"I will go with you to the Cape. I'll feed your chickens and shear your sheep if you show me how. And tote that barge and lift that bale and anything else you want me to do. I'm ready for a change. Thanks, Seth. I owe you."

"The sheep are the Katahdin breed and don't need shearing. But they do enjoy company and being talked to. I'll let you do that," said Seth smiling. "And the eggs get collected daily so you can handle that as well. It's a small farm, without much activity. A quiet place to clear your head and see what God has in mind for you. Remember him? I'm gonna checkout. We'll stop at this great little diner I know on the way home for breakfast."

Chapter Sixteen

"What do I have to lose, right? My peace, my independence, my sanity?"

nna wakes up with surrender in her heart. With a white flag in hand, she realizes she has done enough plotting and planning of her own design and is ready to turn it all over to God. Her God, the God she was praying to in the Adoration Chapel. It's time, she thought. She's spent her life thinking she knew what to do, stumbling through, never quite getting it right. She is tired and ready for guidance from the God she has been developing a close relationship with since grammar school. They came to know each other and she relied on his presence to guide her, but rarely surrendered to that process, or trusted Him in the way she knew she could and should.

Gram was a devout Catholic, attending church every Sunday and Holy days, praying before meals, and giving something up each year for Lent. Her cottage reflected many symbols of her faith. Although Anna has been there a few weeks already, she still hasn't made many changes to the space to make it her own. She hasn't delved into each nook and cranny and there are many. It felt like changing anything at all might take away any remaining signs of the grandmother she loved so much.

Never far from a cup of something warm, she carries her tea with her as she strolls around the small space as if seeing it for the first time, hoping to learn something new. Led by curiosity, she meanders from one nook to the next, one bookshelf or cupboard to another. She opens the narrow coat closet, the pine door creaking and the cool touch of the black latch feeling so familiar. Gram's coats and jackets still hang there, her boots that withstood many a Cape Cod winter, standing at attention. Her purse hung on a wrought iron hook. Anna runs her hand over the multi-colored batik fabric attached to a silver frame with a single short handle. She lifts it off the hook and looks inside. She finds Gram's wallet, a small packet of Kleenex, burgundy lipstick, and a small spiral notebook with a seahorse on the cover. There is a pen from the Cooperative Bank of Cape Cod and a key on a brass ring with one piece of green sea glass dangling from it. The key appears to be old. As Anna runs her fingers over it, she wonders what it is for. More importantly, why was it in Gram's bag? That's usually a place where you keep things you use often. She hangs it on the brass anchor hook near the front door with her car key and makes a mental note to try to figure out what it might unlock. She wonders if Gram's attorney might know.

She continues her exploration of the little place she is calling home. A crucifix hangs on one wall, a picture of the Blessed Mother on another with rosary beads hanging from it. Anna peruses the books that she knows were Grams' favorites and ones that she read herself while spending time there over the years. *Gift From the Sea* by Anne Morrow Lindbergh, several of Nancy Thayer's novels set on Nantucket, Julia Camerons's classic *The Artist's Way*, and poetry by Mary Oliver to name a few. There are still some children's books too, like *The Velveteen Rabbit, The Snowy Day*, and Anna's favorite *Harold and the Purple Crayon*. She touches the smooth gray rock of the fireplace that towers up toward the ceiling. Anna finds the whole place so charming, that she can't hold back a smile, feeling Gram's spirit at that moment. A tear trickles down her cheek and somehow she knows everything is going to be okay. She feels like she is home.

Anna thinks about the women she met at the Honey-Do Farm the day before. They seem very nice. She wonders if Seth will be back today as expected because she still wants to talk with him. Although she admits she's had time to calm down since her original plan to confront him. There is something about Honey-Do that feels very special, very serene and inviting. She can't quite put her finger on it. She enjoyed meeting Emily and Mary, as unexpected as that was, but she was hoping to see Seth. She needs to see him.

Setting aside further exploration of the cottage for now, she showers, dresses, and gets ready for her day planning to go over to Zoe's art shop. She hasn't seen her friend since she showed up with a few kitchen basics and those delicious little pastries.

In the backyard shed, Gram has a couple of beach chairs, sand toys, a kite, a kayak, and her bicycle, a hot pink cruiser style that she could ride like the wind even as she got older. Anna thought about wrestling the bike free from all the other beach paraphernalia, but seeing the ominous sky, decided she better take the Volvo. A bike ride will have to wait. She grabs her neon green backpack and off she goes toward Hyannis. With windows down, Anna breathes in the salt-soaked autumn air. The roads are an easy, five-mile ride past cottages, motels, and even some cottage roses still in bloom here and there. It is a dream location for a writer or photographer, where inspiration awaits around every turn, especially off-season. The roads are nearly deserted.

It didn't take long before she arrived in Hyannis. The bells on the door of *Tokens of My Confections,* located right near Zoe's shop, jangled as she entered. She bought some sweet treats and two coffees and walked into the art supply shop Zoe aptly named *Inspirations.*

"Surprise!" says Anna, holding up her offerings. Zoe drops what she is doing with a customer and practically knocks the coffee out of Anna's hands as she hugs her. When Anna has a chance to set things down, she hugs her back.

"This is a surprise. How wonderful to see you!"

"Finish with your customer. I'll wait." Anna sits in one of the bright green mid-century modern chairs and sips her coffee. Then sticks her nose in the bakery bag, offers a quick silent prayer, and selects one of the delicate Danish. Everything there is nearly bite-sized so she pops it in her mouth with ease. "Mmm, mmm, mmm," she moans, savoring the teeny-tiny treat. It's as if all the flavor of a bear claw was packed into one little bite. Delish, she thought. Zoe wraps up with her customer and joins her.

"What are you doing here?" asked Zoe.

Still chewing, Anna pushes the bag toward her friend and hands her the other coffee wanting to share the goodies. Zoe doesn't hesitate.

"I can't believe you remembered," Zoe says.

"Remember what?" asks Anna.

"It's my birthday. I'm 67 years young," she reminds her friend, noticing one more ache than there was yesterday, as is often the case.

"Oh, I'm so sorry," says Anna. "I've been wrapped up in, well, a little bit of everything, and forgot all about it. How terrible of me."

Zoe hadn't wanted to open the shop at all that day. *Inspirations* is staffed with a little off-season help, but none of them are key holders. I'll have to change that, she decides. What she really wanted to do rather than spend a day surrounded by paintbrushes, palettes, and a plethora of other art supplies, was to spend the day at home, painting. But she did love helping people connect the natural world, and spirituality with their art.

"Spirit and creativity, are so interwoven, and often people just don't make that connection," she mused while lying in bed that morning, contemplating getting up. She rambled into the kitchen, stuck a pod in the coffee maker, set the brew-strength to bold, and tapped her fingers in the silence waiting for the gurgling to begin. It was her birthday and she wondered what her special day might be like.

"Are you planning anything special?" Anna asked.

"Well, I'm thinking about placing a personal ad," says Zoe out of the blue. Anna is shocked.

"I drafted something. Want to hear it?"

"Absolutely," said Anna, curious to see where this was going.

"It's just a draft. Writing a personal ad is more challenging than I thought. How's this? *67-year-old hot mama seeks a friend for endless hours of companionship, conversation, and creative unbridled passion. Shy person welcome, as I'll show you the way.*"

Anna's mouth drops open, not sure why she is so surprised by her friend's boldness. That's Zoe.

"I know it's a little forward but I don't want to waste any time. I live a fabulous life and I want to share it with someone. I've been alone a while and I love it, but also want to share my time with someone special."

Anna wondered if she would ever find her own *someone special.*

Zoe thought about the person who might respond to such an ad. Would they be curious? Would they be funny, kind, anxious, quiet, or adventurous? All kinds of possibilities popped into her mind. She never posted a personal ad before and she thought, brief and to the point was the way to go. She'd read other ads and it seemed like they were writing a bio. Good grief, she thought. Just put what you want out there. That's the way to do it. And skip the pic. No need.

Zoe straightened up the brushes in her display rack and

tidied up single sheets of Arches watercolor paper while she was talking with Anna. Her shop was empty at the moment which was often the case in the mornings off-season. Her clientele tended to meander in after noonish to pick up whatever supplies they needed for their latest project. *Inspirations* was the only art supply shop in Hyannis and the only one in the mid-Cape area.

Zoe enjoyed the freedom of being her own boss but during quiet times, she often reflected on what her life might have been like if she'd stayed in Vermont. She grew up living on Hemlock Lake and couldn't help falling in love with her high school sweetheart. Neither she nor Jeff had gone to college. Jeff worked at his family's hardware store in the center of Brattleboro. She worked at *The Common Loon*, a gallery that featured the work of local artisans. They didn't sell many paintings. But tourists appreciated the Vermont handcrafted items like pottery, hand-woven shawls and wall hangings, baskets, and maple syrup products. She enjoyed the creative atmosphere and loved to meet new people visiting the area. After 32 years of marriage, she thought she was happy. She thought *they* were happy. Then Jeff turned 52 and all hell broke loose in their very peaceful, steadfast, ordinary existence. He was handsome, built like a lumberjack, and he was all hers. Or so she thought. Then a mid-life crisis came to town in the shape of a dreamy, dyed blonde, leaf peeper tour guide, who wreaked havoc and changed their life.

What if she had stayed in Vermont? What if she had forgiven him? What might Zoe's life be like now? No, she did the right thing. Hyannis was her home and she loved her freedom and planned to keep it that way. For now.

"So, what's going on with you and the guy you met on the beach?" asks Zoe.

Anna looks down and smiles as she thinks about the time she and Seth have shared.

"From the look on your face, it's going well?" asks Zoe.

"It was going well. Really well. We went out a few times, had a nice romantic dinner on the beach, and had several long phone conversations. Then, we went to the movies and things got a little squirrely. Someone he knew approached him and greeted him as...Anna pauses hardly able to say the words. "Father Seth."

"*What???*" cried Zoe. "Are you kidding?"

"I wish I was," said Anna quietly. "I've just been trying to process it all. I really, really like this guy. I've run the gamut of emotions about it and even drove over to this farm he's staying at to talk about it, but he had left the state."

"I'll bet he did," says Zoe.

"No, it's not like that. He was called away to help a friend. He should be back today actually, according to the woman he left in charge. It's complicated. What about you Zoe? What have you been up to? Do you have birthday plans?"

"I did actually. Last night. I don't usually date, but I figured why not? What do I have to lose, right? My peace, my independence, my sanity? But my bright-eyed assistant offered to fix me up on a blind date and in a moment of weakness, I agreed. Jenny is a 21-year-old optimist who believes everyone should be in love. She told me her uncle's friend is visiting from Maine. I had visions of an old flannel-clad, suspender-wearing lobsterman, fresh off the docks. It's not a look I'm opposed to. But I was a little surprised when Danny stepped into the store. I was just closing up and she kind of caught me off guard. I thought she was a customer. She was quite charming and did indeed sport a flannel shirt, and jeans, sans the suspenders. She pulled off that L.L. Bean/Merrell look effortlessly. I tried not to be too taken in by her charms, but I actually liked her… a lot," says Zoe surprised by her own reaction. "She's a little younger than me. We went out for dinner down by the harbor and then sat on a bench and talked until the moon was high in the sky. We talked like we'd known each other for years. It was so comfortable. But hard for me to believe, too. Everyone can use a new friend though, right?"

Anna noticed Zoe was lost in her reverie.

"You deserve this Zoe. I'm so happy for you. Surprised maybe, but happy. Will you see her again?"

"I hope so," she says all dreamy-eyed. "This caught me completely off-guard. I'm not quite sure what to do with it."

Zoe heard another crack of thunder as the lights flickered and finally went out. She knew they would, as these shoreline storms often took the power out at her shop. *Inspirations Art Supply* is the go-to source for artists young and old, and she has been in the same Main Street, Hyannis location for 15 years. She is located just a stroll from the docks and artist shanties on the waterfront, offering opportunities for artists and craftspeople to sell their work. Some order their supplies online of course but going into the shop is an experience that many enjoy and make a part of their creative practice. She has no intention of retiring anytime soon, not her business or her social life.

Zoe loved meeting other creative souls and hearing about their work. She likes being able to support the creative life of aspiring artists as well as offer resources for them. Her shop is also a place to do her own creative work in the back studio when business is slow. Another crack of thunder brought her into the present moment. The power is out, and dark gray skies open up, pouring rain. The store is dark. Zoe suggests they wait it out as these storms often pass through quickly.

Anna excuses herself to use the facilities and just as Zoe is about to flip the *Closed* sign over, a woman runs up to the door, pushing it open. Zoe's face lights up when she sees Danny, and they both look at each other smiling. Saying nothing. Which was unusual for Zoe who is rarely speechless.

Anna returns, clearing her throat, hating to interrupt, as she watches the interaction between the two. Zoe introduces them and Anna makes a quick exit, wishing her a happy birthday one more time, especially so Danny would know in case Zoe hadn't mentioned it. She hugs her friend and is off, leaving them alone, and offering a silent birthday prayer. Zoe deserves someone wonderful in her life, and so does she.

Driving home she says aloud to herself, "In only a matter of weeks, I've broken off my engagement to Ethan, fallen in love with a Catholic Priest, and have not written so much as a chapter in my book. Did I just say love?"

She looks side to side as if making sure no one heard her, even in her solitude. But God heard her. What would He think of that, she wonders. Whenever she is feeling overwhelmed by life, she often finds a place to go on retreat if only for a weekend, to collect her thoughts, and process the things going on in her life. It was like a mini retreat to step into an empty chapel or church for the same thing. She used to run to the Cape when life got crazy in Mystic or at her parent's house in Newport.

The Cape was her safe space with the ocean just minutes away in any direction. Now she has her cottage within a stone's throw from the beach and she still feels a need to run. She wonders if she will ever settle down, ever be at peace in one place. Just as she is pulling into the cottage, her phone rings. Seth's photo pops up on her screen, minus the clerical collar. She hesitates to answer it. Anna thinks for just a moment about how Zoe and Danny were gazing at each other when she left them. Her heart aches for that same feeling with someone. Someone she can trust. She lets the call go to voicemail and goes inside.

Chapter Seventeen

Twelve apostles, a flock of chickens, and one sin of omission

Returning to the cottage Anna wonders if life will ever settle down long enough for her to finish her book. With everything else going on, she can't seem to get focused, but that has always been the case. There seems to be an endless array of things to pull her away from the very thing she feels compelled to do. Write. Yet here she is. So much has brought her to this place in time. Telling her editor she was leaving for the Cape for a few months. If Gram hadn't passed and left this space to her. If Ethan hadn't given her reason to leave. So many ifs. It feels like no one understands what it means to her to finish her novel. Maybe Gram did.

At this rate, I may never finish my book, thinks Anna. That manuscript sat in the bottom drawer, growing each year with so many new beginnings, still, it sits there, unfinished. But with each box unpacked in the tiny cottage more and more ideas for it are revealed. The vaulted ceiling in the loft lifted the roof off her self-imposed limitations. The peculiar windows provided insight into her intentions for the story. The creaky uneven wood floors invited acceptance of imperfections in herself and others. That cottage became a metaphor for her life. If she had never taken this step, her manuscript would still be in that deep dark bottom drawer along with her desire to complete it. She brought it with her to the Cape for a reason.

Her phone rings again. She takes a deep breath and looks at it. There he is again. Persistent.

"Hello."

"Anna, thank you for taking my call," says Seth. "I need to speak with you. I want to explain. It's not how it looks."

"On the contrary, I think it's exactly how it looks. How could it be anything else?" asks Anna feeling increasingly deceived with every word. "What do you want Seth, or should I say Father Seth?"

"Anna, you have every right to be angry."

She interrupts him with, "Ya think? Listen, I can't even imagine what you were trying to pull or why, but I don't have the time or energy for another lying, cheating man in my life. And certainly not a priest!"

"Anna, I know you don't owe me this, but please give me a chance to explain. Let me come over to talk with you and I promise I'll leave whenever you say."

"You're right I don't owe you this. Why should I invest another moment with you?"

"Because I'm so, so, so very sorry. And I just want to explain."

She finally agrees to see him but is still uncertain of what to say. Or why she should give him the time of day. With reservations, she tells him he can come over to the cottage. When she hears his car pull in, she idly fluffs the pillows on the couch. She checks herself in the mirror out of habit and considers, ever so briefly, heading out the back door. The ship's bell rings so loud it announces visitors to the whole neighborhood, both welcome and unwelcome. She isn't sure which Seth is, but she is prepared to find out. She opens the door and the draft from the October air makes the candle flame on the coffee table dance.

She looks at Seth and simultaneously feels hurt, and aches for his arms to be around her. How could she feel both she wonders? How is that possible? He steps into the cottage and doesn't even attempt to touch her.

"Have a seat," Anna says trying not to sound emotional in any way. He sits on the couch hoping she will join him. But he knows better. She stands looking at him, keeping her guard up, with an awkward silence between them.

"Can I get you anything?" she asks trying to fill the quiet.

"I'm fine thanks. Listen, Anna, I was going to tell you. I'm sorry you heard about it this way. I never meant to hurt you."

"Hurt me? I'm not hurt," she says stoically taking a seat across from him. "I haven't known you long enough to be hurt by you. Just disappointed. I had the illusion you might be different."

"Please let me explain."

"I'm listening," she says.

"Yes, I am a priest. But the reason I'm here on the Cape is that I'm taking a three-month sabbatical. I took this time away from the church to discern if I felt called to continue being a priest. I'm just not certain anymore, after 25 years in the priesthood. Then I met you on the beach and you were just so wonderfully charming and genuine. I got to know you a little and it felt so good. You were captivating, and a joy just to be with. A friend to talk with, who didn't have any expectations of me as Father Alexander. I was just Seth. I wasn't looking for you Anna. I didn't intend to mislead you and I'm so sorry if I hurt you in any way. I was just enjoying our growing friendship immensely. I've never felt anything like it."

Anna sits across from him in silence listening to every word. Feeling a plethora of emotions, her anger seems to fade away like a receding tide. Compassion takes over, with feelings of sadness, even heartbreak at what might have been. She understands his need to discern the future as she is doing the same. She understands wanting and needing to be accepted just the way you are, with no expectations. To just be.

She has always had great reverence for priests for their commitment to their vocation, to the church, and God. To surrender their lives to God in such a complete way is more than she can comprehend. She knows people leave the church for many reasons as it struggles with social and moral issues in addition to sexual abuse scandals.

"I have questions," she says.

"Ask me anything. Anything at all. I'll do my best to be completely transparent with you Anna."

"How and why were you living on a sailboat? How is it that you drive a 70k car? Don't you take a vow of poverty? How is any of this a priest's lifestyle? It's not like any priest I've ever known."

"Fair enough," he says. "*Synchronicity* is owned by a

very wealthy parishioner and friend. He offered it to me to use while I was here until the guest house at their summer home became available. But when their tenant, a relative, didn't leave as expected, and the boat had to be drydocked for winter, I had to find a place to stay. See, things are not always as they appear.

I am a diocesan priest, as opposed to a priest of a religious order. Therefore, we take vows of celibacy and obedience with some expectation that we live a simple life, leaving vows of poverty to religious orders. Also, diocesan priests receive a salary that varies significantly depending on their role and the size and generosity within the parish they serve. We are generally treated very well by parishioners and the church, leaving us with few living expenses. Expectations are very high and we work hard. I have a desire to lead a simple life, but mine has become very complicated. I hope that it will not always be that way." He pauses to give Anna time to process it all. "Do you have any other questions?"

When she finally spoke again, it was in a whisper, as she asked the last question that was heavy on her heart. "Why are you thinking about leaving the priesthood?"

"That's a great question, Anna. And one I've been struggling with for some time. That's what led me to where I am right now. I love Jesus and my church and I have as long as I can remember. Since I was young. I always knew I would go to seminary right out of high school. There was no question in my mind that I wanted to serve God and his children. I willingly, gladly, committed to this for life. Without hesitancy," he says, shaking his head. "I haven't always agreed with the ways of the church and I'm not entirely certain it follows Jesus's intention for us, at times. But I love working with the people, and the community, being a part of their joys and supporting them in their sorrows." Seth pauses before he continues, searching for the right words, and saying them slowly with great intention.

"I love Jesus so very much, making how I'm feeling incredibly difficult. The older I've gotten, the more I question. But aside from all that, and most importantly... I am not sure that I want to return home every night to an empty room, with only a Bible and Divine Office waiting for me, for the rest of my life. The loneliness is palpable at times. And though I was not actively looking for you, Anna, there you were. A friend who wanted nothing from me but kindness and honesty. I'm sorry I failed you."

As they sat together in silence, Anna absorbed all the information he was sharing and understood how it had not come up sooner. It's not a casual conversation. Her eyes welled up listening to the deep sadness he was conveying. She had all she could do to keep from getting up and going to him. She wanted to in the worst way.

"I guess I'll get going," he says after some silence. "I know this is a lot to take in. If you have any other questions please call me, okay? And Anna, thank you for listening." She nodded, knowing that if she tried to speak, she would burst into tears. He got up and left, closing the door softly behind him.

The next day, back at the Honey-Do Farm, Seth is still unwilling to accept that he signed on to manage an inn, in the owner's absence. He is distracted, to say the least, but has thrown himself into the tasks that need to be done. He recruits help from Emily and Brandon. Emily is the perfect hostess and seems thrilled to keep herself busy baking and contributing to the place where she had found comfort over the years.

Brandon settles into his room and seems more relaxed around the farm, as he helps feed the chickens and talks to the sheep. Seth is still enjoying that little assignment for his friend. The sheep seem to appreciate the attention and he wonders what Brandon talks with them about. He finds it amusing to learn from *the binder* that the sheep are named after the 12 apostles. Peter, Andrew, James, son of Zebedee, John, Philip, Bartholomew, Thomas, Matthew, James, son of Alphaeus, Thaddaeus, Simon, and Judas, the one who betrayed Jesus. He thinks he might advise Brandon to keep an eye on that one. He isn't surprised as Travis appeared to have a great sense of humor.

Just then Brandon walks in carrying the wire basket filled with eggs from the coop. Depending on how many guests are staying, if they have extra eggs, they put them in cartons in a cooler out by the paddock for people to help themselves, offering a donation. But the inn is getting pretty busy, and Emily keeps baking so they use quite a few eggs.

"How's it going?" asks Seth, feeling the need to be a good host. "Getting acclimated, okay? I hope your room is alright."

"Yeah, this place is great. I slept like a baby. When I got up a woman named Emily made me breakfast."

"Yeah, she sort of needs to take care of people right now. It's okay to let her. She loves to bake. You'll gain weight here," says Seth looking at how thin Brandon is. Addiction will do that.

"Hey Seth, thanks for…everything," says Brandon hanging his head in a rare moment of humility.

"No problem. Let me know if you need anything. Take a walk, get some air. Take a look around and explore the property. There are a few small buildings, and some nice foliage this time of year. Make yourself at home. The kitchen is open for whatever you need. And don't forget the sheep. They like company," says Seth smiling as he reaches to answer the wall phone in the kitchen. "Honey-Do Farm how may I help you?"

Seth flips through the binder's reservation section and sees that Henri Dupont is expected to arrive later that afternoon. He is calling to say he'd be arriving early if that is okay. Learning to go with the flow at Honey-Do Farm, Seth encourages him to come whenever he likes. He no sooner hangs up when he hears the door knocker, wondering, "What now?" He opens the door to find a distinguished, well-dressed older gentleman standing there with his suitcase in hand.

"I don't suppose you're Henri?" asks Seth.

"I am indeed," he says with a broad smile.

"Well, come right on in. Welcome to the Honey-Do Farm. Follow me and we'll get you signed in," says Seth leading him to the kitchen. He introduces Henri to Brandon before taking care of the quick business of registration which is mostly done online when people make their reservations. He gives him the rundown on what he could expect for services, and that breakfast is provided, coffee, tea, and snacks are always available, and for lunch and dinner, guests are on their own. It all sounds great to him.

Henri seems in no hurry to get to his room, and Brandon jumps right in offering him coffee and something sweet that Emily had whipped up that morning. He is a hefty guy, maybe six feet tall, sporting a dashing tweed blazer and navy slacks, and about in his mid-70s Seth guessed. He has a ruddy complexion, white hair, bright blue eyes, and a great smile that lit up his face.

"Tell us a little about yourself, Henri. What brings you to the Cape this time of year?" asks Seth. "You've come quite a way."

"Yep, I hail from Bangor, Maine. I'd like to say it is a pleasure trip but I'm here for a funeral. I'm an alcoholic… in recovery. I lost a dear friend who helped me when I was younger. I hadn't seen him in years but the effect he had on me, when my life was out of control, I will never forget. He led a good life, set a good example, and helped a lot of people through recovery, but I guess at 89 he had come to do what he needed to do and was done. He was a good man and I can honestly say, that if it weren't for him, I would probably have drunk myself into an early grave. I just came to pay my respects. The funeral is tomorrow but I thought I'd stay a week to relax, enjoy the foliage, and see what I might see."

Brandon seemed to hang on to every word Henri said, and Seth could tell the story touched him in some way. They engage in lighter discussion and Seth is surprised when Brandon offers to show Henri to his room, as Henri has not stayed there before. It occurs to him he should probably check that binder for upcoming reservations more often. They don't have that many rooms available and now four are occupied. Seth is moved by how well Brandon is settling in, and wonders if there isn't something special about this place he is calling home at the moment. People never cease to surprise him. God never ceases to surprise him.

Emily sails past them on her way to the kitchen, giving both Brandon and Henri a wave. She catches up with Seth to see if he needs anything, as she is going to the store to get ingredients for her next recipe. While listening to Emily, Seth looks up to see a young woman standing in the doorway.

"Can I help you," he asks her. Emily jumps in to introduce Mary, although her bucket of cleaning supplies and grocery bags might have been a giveaway. Seth approaches her to shake her hand but both are full. When she tries to reach out, a bag falls, ripping open and spilling apples, pears, and assorted other groceries on the floor.

"Let me help you with that," he says, scrambling around at her feet chasing apples and Halo oranges. Emily looks on at the chaotic moment and sees Anna behind Mary.

"The door was open, I hope you don't mind me coming in," she says. "I see you're busy." Seth was at Mary's feet. Anna starts to retreat, second-guessing her decision to just drop in. Seth looks up and breathes her name as if to himself. He stands up with an armload of fruit and places it, and Mary's bags on the counter.

"Anna, I'm so glad to see you," he says fumbling around. Emily introduces Mary to Seth and he tries to introduce Anna to both women but she tells him they already met. Seth looks confused. Mary explains to him what she does for Travis and Toni and goes about her business putting away groceries, gathering her cleaning materials, and chatting with Emily about what she is planning to make.

"Please excuse us," he says to them, leading Anna into another room and closing the door for privacy. "I'm so glad to see you," he repeats. "Thank you for coming. How did you know Mary and Emily?" he asks, adding, "Never mind. You're here. That's all that matters. It's a little crazy here today for some reason. Why did you come Anna?"

"Honestly, I don't know." She is silent, trying to collect her thoughts. "It broke my heart to hear you talk about how much you love God, and the church and how difficult a decision you are contemplating. I can't begin to imagine how hard this must be for you. And yesterday, in the cottage, I had all I could do, to keep from going to you. To wrap my arms around you, and just hold you forever," she says getting choked up. "I love God too. And sometimes it's so hard to understand His ways, the reasons for things, the way we are called in one direction or another. I've been thinking about what you've shared, and I can't believe that this infinitely loving God we know so well, would put feelings in our hearts of such extreme loneliness, without it being a sign of some kind, leading to another path."

"Anna, I'm so touched by your words. By you coming here to share them. Would you consider going out with me again? Give me another chance. Just to spend some time together?" asks Seth uncertain how she might respond.

"St. Benedict reminds us, *always we begin again*," says Anna. Seth smiles, hopeful of her response. "I would like that. There are some things you need to know about me as well. I could use a good priest to talk to." He smiles appreciating her humor, knowing their conversation could have gone very differently.

"I'll walk you out Anna, and will pick you up around 7:00?" She smiles at him and nods.

As they step outside, they run into Brandon. "And who have we here?" he asks, giving her the once over.

"Anna, this is my friend Brandon. Brandon, this is Anna." He can see Brandon eyeing her in that way he does. "Don't. Even. Think. About. It." says Seth pronouncing each word with great intention.

Brandon puts up his hands, palms facing Seth, backing away. "Okay man, I hear ya."

"Don't you have some sheep to tend to?" asks Seth, sending Brandon, who decides he will get to the bottom of that later, on his way to the barn to check on the apostles.

Chapter Eighteen

"You were engaged to that guy?"

"The old woman crouched down in the front yard, wedged between the screened-in porch and the yellow and orange mums, hiding out so the neighbor wouldn't see her."

This is a good opening line for her novel, thinks Anna. But as she taps her fingers on the worn blue surface of the desk, she decides, hmm, maybe not. She crumples up the piece of college-ruled looseleaf paper tossing it in the direction of 17 others that didn't make it into the circular file. Taking a deep breath of resignation, she pushes her chair back and heads to the kitchen to make a cup of tea. Her novel is going nowhere fast, despite having what she thinks is a great plot. Her writing process is a hybrid, where she writes initial ideas with paper and pen, then types the material onto the computer, before developing it further. Other times, when she has greater clarity about a story, she bangs out one chapter after another on her laptop.

Space is very important to her creative process and she

finds Gram's old cottage, now her cottage, very inspiring. She has also been known to take a pen and pad, sit on the beach, and bang out a chapter or two. Sometimes a poem. Anna is not one of those coffee klatsch writers. She needs quiet when she writes and could never understand how other writers can pack up their gear and head to Starbucks and get anything done. But she supposes there is something to be said for the dialogue one can overhear in such an environment, assuming the music isn't blaring. As the saying goes, *"I am a writer. Anything you say or do may be used in a story."* You take your chances when you air your private stuff in public.

Anna spent her career as a writer for small-town New England publications, but that was telling other people's stories. That's what she does for a living. She listens really well and then she writes about it. She writes about what they said and what they didn't say. Some of the best material can be found in those microseconds when someone pauses before answering a question. And you just know they are perhaps looking for the answer within themselves before offering it to you. Maybe they're having their own internal epiphany at that moment. Or mindfully curating the information they want to share. She is great at listening between the lines and reporting on events, artists, writers, photographers, communities, and small businesses. Sometimes she writes lifestyle features or less interesting business profiles for financial publications.

But now, as she sits in this precious Cape Cod cottage, with time set aside for one thing, that thing eludes her. As a football fan, she would watch the kicker, often under the pressure of a game-winning act, kick the ball between the goalposts. And when they didn't make it, she would say out loud critically to no one, *"They have ONE job! That's all they had to do. Just that ONE job."* She can be a little critical at times. Especially to herself. Sometimes we kick it through the goalposts. Sometimes not.

She has always wanted to write a book. She knows this is different than writing for magazines and newspapers. Or writing a column. This is *her* story to create. And writing a novel is absolutely, nothing like writing a feature story for a magazine. Or a poem. A feature story might have 500 to 3,000 words, or more, depending on the publication. Writing a book is like a feature on steroids, she thinks. And it's not like a poem, which for Anna is an inspired work, as small as a 5-7-5 syllable Haiku, or something longer, but either way, it doesn't take years to write one. Not usually. But a novel? Good grief. The sheer size of it carries with it a great intimidation factor. She also knows she can overcome it.

Seth creates so much distraction that her muse is nowhere to be found. Although she speculates that her muse might just possibly be wearing a clerical collar. You just never know how they will dress or in what form a muse will show up. Perhaps if I have a priest in one hand and a muse in the other, it seems one has more power, she thinks, holding her hands out and making a weighing gesture. The teapot boils and she pours water into the mysterious *Tuesdays at Ten* mug. She is determined to find out what it means and where it came from. The smell of mint chamomile soothes her senses. She adds honey and returns to the desk to try again.

"The agile old woman crouches down in the front yard,

wedged between the screened-in porch and the yellow and orange mums, hiding out so the neighbor wouldn't see her."

There that's better, thinks Anna, feeling satisfied with her accomplishment. She goes upstairs to get ready for dinner with Seth. She showers, chooses a casual navy polka dot dress to wear, with a short pale pink cardigan, gives herself a spritz of her favorite scent, and is pleased with who she sees in the mirror. Slipping on a pair of burgundy leather loafers she is ready to go.

Looking forward to seeing Seth, she steps outside to catch the sunset. Anna stands in her tiny front yard between the front porch and the colorful potted mums when suddenly, a frog jumps in front of her. Anna is terrified of frogs, primarily because of their unpredictability. You never know what they're going to do. Not unlike men, she thinks. Unpredictable. She runs up onto the front porch gazing out into the distance at Nantucket Sound and hopes the frog will go in the other direction, preferably far, far away.

She breathes in the early evening salt air blowing off the water, when she hears a car turn down her lane, assuming it is Seth. Ethan pulls up in front of the cottage. He gets out of his car and she cringes as he approaches.

"What are you doing here?" she asks abruptly, heading into the house to get away from him. His bony legs catch up with her quickly, and he reaches out to grab her. She turns and shakes him off saying, "Leave me alone! Why are you here? What don't you understand?"

"Anna, Anna," he drawls. "I know you're pissed off, but I've given you some space to get over it. It's time to get your stuff together and come home now."

She can smell alcohol on his breath and she looks at him incredulously. He has an extraordinary audacity and keeps going.

"Why do you want to stay in this shack anyway? We can sell it tomorrow and get good money for it this close to the beach. I looked it up and I can probably get us $1.2 mill, maybe more, just because of the location," he slurs. "Some nice New Yorker will come in, level it, and build something worth having. Where's your suitcase? Let's get you packed up."

"Ethan, you're drunk and you need to leave, now!" Anna says, trying to keep a distance from him.

"Aww, come on honey, you know you don't mean that."

"Actually, I do mean it and if you don't leave, I'm going to call the police."

As he stands up from the couch and approaches her again, he stumbles over the footstool, falling head-on into her, knocking Anna down as she lets out a scream and tries to shove him away.

"Get off of me!"

Before she knows what happened, Seth is hovering over her pulling Ethan to his feet and by the scruff of his neck has him pinned against the cobblestone fireplace. Anna gets to her feet. Shaken, she makes her way to the couch.

"Who the hell are you?" drawls Ethan in his drunken stupor.

"I'm Father Seth Alexander. And who the hell are you?"

"I'm her fiancé and I'm here to take her home," says Ethan. Ignorantly, not the least bit intimidated by Seth's strength or size compared to his scrawny self. Seth looks at Anna still recovering from the fall, shaking her head at him.

"It's not true," says Anna. "Don't believe him." He lets go of Ethan unsure what to do next.

"Tell him, Anna. Tell him we're engaged. We have plans. And you're coming home with me."

"I'm not going anywhere with you, you idiot. Not now. Not ever. You need to leave. If I see you here again, I *will* call the police. I'm not kidding, Ethan. We're done." Ethan stands there not moving.

"I believe Anna has asked you to leave," says Seth. "I suggest you listen to her or I'm happy to help you out the door if you require my assistance."

Unsure of what Seth is capable of, Ethan leaves without a word. He doesn't like to lose and since she was just a trophy for him, tonight's events will not sit well.

"Seth, I can't thank you enough. I don't know what might have happened if you hadn't shown up."

"Are you okay?" he asks, sitting next to her on the couch. Followed by an incredulous, "You were engaged to that guy?"

"Yeah, I was," she says, embarrassed to admit the truth. "I broke it off before I came here, but he didn't take it well, as you can see. He doesn't care about me. He just likes to win."

Seth is a little dumbfounded by this very unexpected situation. "Do you still want to go out for dinner? Or maybe we can order in if you prefer," not wanting to give up time with her.

Anna is grateful to hear those words. She would love some time alone in the cottage with Seth to get to know him better. Just like he had gotten a dose of her just then.

Compliments of Ethan. She knows she has some explaining to do.

"What do you like on your pizza?" he asks her trying to be unphased by the news he just learned.

He orders their pizza and adds chicken soup and salad for delivery. Anna goes upstairs to refresh herself after being attacked by Ethan, hoping to return in better spirits. While he waits for her and their dinner, Seth relaxes in the small, but comfortable space. He is very observant about details and notices the book titles in the bookcase, the Mary Oliver quote on the wall, the nautical touches, and the vintage charm of the whole place. Prayerful signs of a good Catholic are subtle but present everywhere. He wishes he got to meet Anna's grandmother who was so dear to this woman who is rapidly stealing his heart. So engrossed in assessing his surroundings, he didn't hear the car drive up until the delivery guy rang the ship's bell outside. No one could miss that. Just as their dinner arrived Anna came bouncing down the stairs refreshed and feeling a little shy. She wasn't sure how Seth was processing Ethan's proclamation.

She sets a simple table for them, with one of Gram's vintage autumn tablecloths, covering the old enamel top table which can get cool at certain times of the year. She lights a candle in the center and optimistically wonders if this might be the first of many dinners together in the cottage. Or it might be the last, as she realizes she hasn't been fully honest about her past either. Their relationship is complicated, to say the least, and it has just become even more so.

Anna finds that now that the door is open, yet with

some hesitation, it is easier to share with Seth. She tells him all about Ethan and how she doesn't know what she ever saw in him. Anna shares that she caught him with another woman. She can't imagine why she agreed to marry him. But she had. Upon reflection, she can't even remember what attracted her to Ethan. He seemed kind, thoughtful, and loving until he wasn't. They had nothing in common and he clearly didn't care about her. He is great at cultivating his imagined self-importance and manipulating situations to his liking.

"He is the most self-centered individual I've ever met. A narcissist who is all about appearances. All about making more money, and having more things. Whatever he had was never enough. I was never enough," says Anna.

Thoughts of being with Ethan made her stomach churn and her skin crawl. But telling all this to Seth feels freeing, at least to her. She hasn't shared this with anyone else and now wonders what Seth is thinking. He has that very thoughtful, reflective look that she has come to know and love. But it doesn't reveal a whole lot about what his thoughts are. She knows she will have to wait for that. In her mind, there is nothing to come between them and their new friendship now but the church. Just that little ole church. She decides to keep to a safer subject and asks about the inn.

"How are things going at Honey-Do?"

"Well, I can tell you it's not what I signed up for," Seth laughs. "My original idea was to have a house-sitting gig so I'd have a quiet place to stay while I'm on the Cape. Then the house became a farm. And the farm became an inn. And well, you saw the place. It's a little busy at times, but there also seems to be something special about it. I don't know what it is. Maybe you will come again and I'll show you around. It's quite a beautiful property.

"I'd like that very much," says Anna, gazing into the gorgeous blue eyes of Father Seth Alexander. She can't help herself. Can't pull herself away.

Over a candlelight pizza dinner for two, they share a bottle of wine and conversation that continues to reveal more of each other's stories. When they are through with dinner, Seth reaches his hand across the table for hers and somehow knows his life will never be the same. It's hard to say goodbye, and Seth has all he can do to walk out the door.

"Will you be okay Anna? You don't think that guy will be back, do you?"

"I'll be okay. I think you scared the bejesus out of him," Anna laughs at her little joke.

She is trying to make light of the situation but doesn't want him to leave. She also understands why he has to. To be honest, Ethan could be waiting in the shadows, but she can deal with him if he shows up again. Nonetheless, he might come back and next time, Seth might not be there to rescue her. "Rescue" is a funny word, she thinks. She considers herself a strong woman. A smart woman. Not someone in need of, or who has the desire to be *rescued*. And yet, that night, it felt blissfully beautiful to have Seth show up just when she needed him. It doesn't make her weak, but circumstances as they were, Seth was a godsend at that moment. Anna is incredibly grateful for his presence and his reaction to seeing Ethan's violation of her.

Seth reluctantly drives away, the events of the night

making him realize how much he genuinely cares for this woman he has known for such a short time. His reaction when he saw that guy on top of her was like nothing he ever experienced. The pure fury he felt was not like him but came from his very core. Whatever mixed emotions he had before he arrived, have only been magnified. He has much to think about as he heads back to Honey-Do Farm, and he considers what it would be like if he were heading back to church instead. He will know soon enough.

Chapter Nineteen

The Camino de Yarmouthport

The Honey-Do Farm is not much of a farm, a hobby farm maybe, and it is not exactly an inn or B&B either. It has a very informal air to it. The people Seth has encountered so far, staff and guests alike, are less inclined to have specific plans they are committed to, in favor of responding to life's challenges and calling. He has noticed something just a little bit *magical* about the place if he dared use that word. Perhaps *enchanting* is more accurate, because it draws people together just when they need each other most. The Church is a little like that, he thinks. Some people are committed worshippers who attend Mass weekly, sometimes daily, and on holy days, while others feel called to be there only at different times on life's journey. They come and they go. They take what is offered, allow it to nurture, or sometimes crush, their spirits and move on.

Emily arrived because of a transition time in her marriage. Henri is at the inn to attend a funeral for a friend and is in no hurry to leave. Mary took a summer job, cleaning and cooking at the inn, and loved the Cape so much she couldn't bring herself to leave when September rolled around. And Toni and Travis were more than happy to keep her on. Brandon of course had nowhere to go when Seth retrieved him from another drunken encounter with police. Seth is in his own state of discernment, wondering what his second half of life is meant to look like. As he thought about it, even Anna was in a similar place having recently unloaded that obnoxious ex-fiance. Seth can't help but shake his head at the very thought of Anna being attracted to that guy. And yet he can't deny how Anna makes him feel. He needs a good night's sleep to clear his mind if not his heart.

The next morning he awakes to the smell of cinnamon crumb apple muffins fresh from the oven. Walking into the kitchen, Emily carefully transfers them from the muffin pan to a platter and sets them on the table. Others begin to gather as if summoned by the smell of coffee, and a crock filled with sausage and apples. A peppers and cheese scrambled egg creation is in process. Emily is in her element and encourages everyone to grab a plate and help themselves. Honey-Do is a help-yourself kind of place.

Brandon walks in just then, having been out tending to the sheep, and has a fresh supply of eggs from the chickens. "Just let me wash up and I'll be right there. Everything smells delicious," he says.

Seth looks at his friend wondering where that lost and lonely guy he picked up at the police station has gone. He seems to be embracing his new role and his new surroundings.

Emily had purchased fresh apples for the morning's baking and worked with a joy-filled smile on her face, feeling appreciated in a way she hadn't felt in a long while. She thinks about her husband for a moment and realizes she doesn't miss him. She likes being in this warm and welcoming place and enjoys making use of her talents to be a part of something special like she was that morning.

As they all enjoy the atmosphere of the inn, the breakfast, and the camaraderie, they chat about plans for their day. Mary bustles about cleaning up after grabbing coffee and a muffin with the group, followed by a refresh of each of the guest rooms.

One by one they go on their way until Seth finds himself alone. Alone with his thoughts. Although that was his original intention when he accepted this house-sitting position, going deep into reflection and prayer has eluded him. He has kept busy, but today he realizes he has no excuse. Heading over to the Divine Mercy Chapel, just a few minutes away, he wants to spend time with the one who knows him best. Maybe he'll even run into Father Alfred, he thinks. He climbs into the Audi grinning, as he does every time he buckles up. He's amused by the absurdity of the extreme luxury he has come to enjoy while serving such an affluent parish. The Audi is just one of many benefits that have come with his service and he acknowledges, if only to himself, that he is a bit spoiled.

In all fairness, he realizes, too, that he has devoted his entire life to serving God through the Catholic church. As a diocesan priest, a vow of poverty is not one he was expected to take, though they are expected to live a simple life aligned with those to whom they minister. The other vows were challenging enough. Sacred vows of obedience and celibacy were easier when he was younger. But as he turned 50 earlier in the year, both seem to be grating on his spirit and are a constant theme in prayer. He hadn't realized it until coming to the Cape for his sabbatical. So, cruising around in a little ole' Audi isn't too decadent. Or was it?

Standing in the narthex of Divine Mercy, he opens the huge carved wood doors and slips through into the empty sanctuary. At least he thought it was empty. After the requisite blessing with holy water, and genuflecting before stepping into the pew, he kneels down. He closes his eyes and takes a deep breath, uncertain of what might come. Seth has always appreciated silence and contemplation, awaiting with curious anticipation whatever might be revealed during these times with his God. Sometimes nothing came. Sometimes the world. But he always felt the echo of silence, the power of sacred presence, and with it a sacred love. It used to be enough. Now he isn't so sure.

Amidst the scent of incense and candles, looking up in the dimly lit space, he takes in the familiar features of the old chapel. Seth notices someone kneeling far from him on the opposite side of the sanctuary, close to the chancel, and directly in front of a statue of the Blessed Mother. Their forehead is resting on clenched hands as their body shakes with tears. Instinctively Seth thought about going over to them to ask if he could help but held off taking any action. Like him, they too might be discerning direction and he didn't want to interrupt that exchange. For just a moment he thought he should invite the person back to the inn.

The inn has somehow quickly become the place for anyone with no place. The place for those feeling broken and broken-hearted. The place for those seeking community and a safe place where they can feel welcome, no matter what is going on in their lives. The place where you discover who you are when everything else is stripped away, where you might feel broken but never alone. He wonders what all this means. Seth tries to quiet his mind and returns to his prayer, but finds it difficult and when he looks up again, the figure he had seen, is gone, though he never heard them leave.

Returning to the inn, Seth catches Henri and Brandon on their way out the door, heading, of all things, to an AA meeting. Seth is thrilled about the influence Henri is having on his friend who has been noticeably different since they returned from New Hampshire.

You just never know what someone's rock bottom might look like, or what will change their life forever, thought Seth. He knew Brandon had made recovery attempts in the past, but those attempts were short-lived. Some sprite would come along, and steal his attention, or something in life would not go well and his solution was alcohol or drugs, followed by a call to Seth when it got really bad. Seth let those thoughts go as he checked the binder for any upcoming reservations. They were clear for now, but as he has experienced, that can change at any moment. The house is quiet and for that he is grateful. He thinks about calling Anna but decides to give her some space. They both have a lot to think about, but he wants so much to hear her voice. In an effort to let go of that desire, he decides to take a walk around the property and check on the *apostles*, the chickens, and the other buildings he has yet to explore. Travis gave him a quick tour of the house, barn, and paddocks nearby. He was vague about a lot of things, anxious to get Seth locked into the position as inn-sitter and get on the road with Toni. He has forgiven them for their sins of omission.

As sabbaticals go, his has taken some interesting turns. Usually, they are opportunities for spiritual, pastoral, and intellectual enrichment and renewal. In his case, though those things might also be true, it was to discern his vocation in the priesthood. Seth puts on some hiking shoes and a sweater over his jeans to ward off the October chill. He grabs his favorite walking stick which is a very unusual piece of driftwood-worn satin-smooth, that he found on the beach years ago. Grabbing a water bottle and a protein bar just in case, he smiles at his preparation to walk the grounds, as if he were about to walk the Camino de Santiago. The Camino is a 485-mile trek across northern Spain. A sacred pilgrimage that attracts people from all over the world. Some consider it a walking meditation. People walk it for a variety of reasons including nurturing a desire to grow closer to God, for personal discernment, or to connect with their faith. Everyone has their own reason for walking the trail, and Seth had his, as he set out to explore the place he is temporarily calling home.

It is a bright autumn day with just the slightest chill in the air. The leaves have begun to change colors as they do more beautifully in New England than in any other place. As Seth sets out to explore the seven acres that make up Honey-Do Farm, he is reminded of how much he loves New England. He can't imagine living anywhere else. He's been on trips and pilgrimages all over the world, but New

England holds a special place in his heart. He wonders if there is a place there for Anna.

Seven acres isn't enormous, but the property has a few buildings that Seth hasn't seen yet and he needs some fresh air. The property is both wooded and open pasture land. He heads out toward a path leading into the woods following the trail through the pitch pines, white oak, mountain laurel, and dogwood. After a while, he reaches a clearing where he discovers a very neglected small building with a worn and faded sign marked "Chapel." He guesses it is about 400-500 square feet at the most. The building has a peaked roof, a narrow front porch, and a stained-glass window above the door featuring a seastar. A few small windows line the walls. Its white shiplap siding is over-grown and looks like it hasn't been used in a long while but curiosity gets the best of him. Using his walking stick to poke ahead of where he's stepping, Seth tries the knob and the door opens. Stepping inside he finds rows of simple shaker-style pews with an aisle in the center. A makeshift altar sits beneath a second stained-glass window, featuring a radiating heart, at the other end of the structure. It's very simple but charming at the same time. And very neglected. He can't wait to show it to Anna. He is sure she will love it but also wonders why a chapel is in the woods and what it was used for there.

He ventures along the path with his walking stick, a path that is barely maintained and can use some attention. As he continues he leaves the wooded area toward a clearing of open pasture. He notices just how lovely the Honey-Do Farm is. In the distance he comes upon another building, this one not so small. It is an old post-and-beam style outbuilding with a rusty gabled metal roof and a front porch that runs the length of the building. There is natural board and batten siding that has aged gray by the weather and the area around it is overgrown with weeds and tall grass reaching up to the windows. Stepping over the weeds, onto the porch, he looks in one of the windows. The building is empty. He turns the doorknob hoping it might be unlocked as the chapel was. Going inside the building he feels like Honey-Do Farm keeps getting increasingly curious. He ponders all its possibilities, its history, and its future. This building is one big open space with a vaulted ceiling, exposed beams, and a partial hay loft above. The only things breaking up the space are a kitchen and bathroom. What was this place, he wonders. So wonderful and so empty. With nothing more to see, he ventures on.

Continuing his trek, Seth prays as he walks along, thinking about Anna, the church, his love for Jesus, and his future. Not wanting to self-will anything, he prays to hear God's direction for him, for the Holy Spirit to guide him in every way. He comes upon another building which he knows is the last, recalling Travis telling him there were three other buildings on the property in addition to the house and barn. Though he never said what they were for. He sees the roofline in the distance and wonders if it too is empty.

Seth approaches the single-story structure climbing over the growth that has run amuck, and he tries the doorknob. It too is open. He steps inside to find a long hallway leading to several rooms on each side. The outside is worn and weathered like the other building but the inside had a rough coat of white paint. At the end of the hallway, he finds a common bathroom. This structure needs some attention and looks as if it hasn't had any in a long, long, long while. He wonders why it is sitting empty. He hopes Travis can shed some light on the story of the Honey-Do Farm and Inn. It is all so strange.

He continues his walk around the farm checking in on the sheep and chickens and makes his way back to the inn, his mind reeling about what went on there in years past, and why. A ramshackle chapel, two old buildings overgrown and unused, and seven acres of land. Though he just wanted some quiet time to himself on his walk, he returned with a mystery worthy of Oak Island, leaving Seth with plenty to ponder.

Chapter Twenty

Candace, Cannabis, Call of Duty

The big old Victorian is full of people gathering for a fundraiser to support a community art program. Small talk is not something Anna is very good at, and it doesn't come easy to her. She is more inclined to step into her more comfortable interview mode, inviting people to share their stories and hopefully deterring them from asking about her own. She is a very private person after all. With a Highclere Castle Gin and tonic in her hand, she meanders through the different rooms, keeping one eye on Seth, or rather, Father Seth, this evening. She hasn't seen him like this before. He is wearing black pants, a black jacket, and a black shirt. That tiny white of his Roman collar glowing like a full moon. She read once that the collar represents the sacred nature of a priest's calling and their commitment to serve God. The thought makes her feel both reverent and sad.

They each keep circulating as the crowd begins their departures. Each aware of the other at every moment, a certain intentionality to the distance they keep. Until, at last, they are face to face. Anna is unable to take her eyes off the collar. Then she makes the mistake of looking into *his* eyes. Those mesmerizing deep blue and dark as the ocean eyes, and then that smile, like no smile she's ever known. Like it is just for her in all the universe. The room is empty now, but it doesn't even matter. Father Seth Alexander wraps his capable arms around her and she responds. Reaching for him, they are captive in an embrace, holding each other so tight, so completely, as if afraid to let the other go. Until…one of the catering staff clears their throat, apologizes for the interruption, and announces their departure. Anna steps back, reaches up to hold Seth's face in both her trembling hands, and kisses his cheek, saying, "I'm sorry," and runs off in tears, like Cinderella at the ball.

Anna awakes abruptly, sweating and disoriented about where she is. After taking a few deep breaths, she sits up, shaking her head as if to make it all go away. She is in her cottage. Alone.

"What have I done?" she says out loud. "I've fallen in love with a priest." A few more breaths, and she is fully awake. "Well, I don't imagine I'm the first to do that, and I'm guessing I won't be the last. So now what? *Now what?*" She is angry with him, and she is angry with herself. She doesn't know what to do about either. Maybe some space will give her clarity about the whole confusing thing.

The short autumn days never get her down as she loves everything about the season. The smells, the colors, the chill in the air. It is her favorite time of year. Anna lights a small log in the fireplace and curls up on the couch thinking about her future as a storm rages outside. She wonders if it is time to go home. The storm outside is fierce, as shoreline storms often are. She thinks about the time she's been on the Cape and how it has turned out so differently than what she expected. Her mind wanders to the first time she met Seth on the beach. How he rescued her kite from the trappings of a teetering dune fence. And how their time together has been so incredible, making her feel alive in a way she has not felt for a long time, if ever. The practical thing she supposes would be to go home to Mystic, but what is there to go home to? An empty apartment? Ethan is thankfully out of her life now. She gave her notice at the newspaper, deciding not to return to the task of telling everyone else's story while ignoring her own. She has no real reason to leave, and she loves being on Cape Cod. It has always been her second home. It may be time to make it her first. Thunder nearly shakes the little house as the wind howls, and sheets of rain pummel the side of the structure. She pulls the quilt closer to her as she watches the flames do their dance, asking God what she should do.

If only, she thought, if only Seth was honest with her from the start. If only he'd been wearing his black cassock on the beach when they met, ridiculous as that might have been, instead of those khaki shorts and Cape Cod sweatshirt. Not to mention the Coppertone. That didn't help. She smiles at the absurdity of her thought as she reminisces about that day. She was flying her kite on the beach at Sesuit Harbor when it took a nose dive and he came around the bluff having fetched it from the other side of the dune fencing. He asked to give it a try and she was immediately entranced by his smile and charm.

If only she'd refused his dinner invitation as she stood in his boxers and oxford shirt that day after falling overboard on the *Synchronicity*. But he'd just made her speechless with his gleaming toned body fresh out of the water after jumping overboard to *rescue* her.

If only that parishioner hadn't run into them at the theater and shocked her with, "Well, hello Father Seth." If only, he had told her himself. If only…would it have made any difference? It wouldn't have changed a thing. He is still a priest. He will always be a priest.

At the risk of spending too much time with her thoughts, Anna decides some space is definitely what she needs. As the storm settles down, she gathers a few things, battens down the hatches at the cottage, and heads home to Mystic. It's funny, but despite living for years in that seaside village, her short time on the Cape has made Mystic feel less like home. Her small, apartment near the Bascule Bridge overlooking the Mystic River was just what she needed when she found it. But now, she's not so sure. She'll have 2 ½ hours to think about it as the Cape begins to tug at her heart before she's even through Providence. And then she sees signs for Newport, Rhode Island and without hesitation, veers left heading toward her parent's house. She's not sure why. That was not her plan.

Anna grew up in a stately home in Newport with parents who were more concerned with their wealth and stature than with their only child. As she thought about it, she realized Ethan was just like them. How did she not notice that sooner? The clarity was both disturbing and refreshing. Knowledge is power, she reminds herself. She won't make that mistake again.

She pulls into the circular driveway of her childhood home seeing a *For Sale* sign by the road. She rings the doorbell before walking in, not wanting to startle her highly sensitive mother. Anna wanders from room to room, calling out, "Heloooo, heloooo." She takes in the familiar ornate crown molding, the 12-foot ceilings, the gilded fireplace mantel, and the formal furniture, of the home she hasn't visited in over a year. Everything is top of the line, the very best of the best. It is nothing like her beloved cottage with its mish-mosh of old character-filled familiar furnishings.

They also have symbols of their Catholic faith here and there, but she always wondered if their membership at St. Augustine's was as much about appearances as the rest of their life. With 20 Christian churches in Newport, faith is an important part of life. But Anna is unimpressed by the stuffy and pompous nature of the house and thinks about Gram's cottage, so small, warm, and inviting. A cottage that could probably fit in their living room. Their home isn't as big as *The Breakers* or anything, but it is substantial. She never understood why Gram was estranged from her only daughter with neither one of them ever wanting to talk about it. Anna would choose her tiny cottage over a Newport mansion any day.

She expects to find her parents in the dining room, sitting alone at a table for 12, having brunch. Her mother would be in full dress, makeup, and well-coiffed hair, even on a Saturday morning. Her father would be reading the New York Times in a dress shirt and tie. They never relax, Anna thought. Her father would stand to greet her giving her a peck on the cheek and a distant hug. Her Mother would stay seated at the table. But that wasn't what she found. Not at all.

"Well. Hello darling, what brings you here today?" asks her mother, getting up from the chaise lounge in the den. She pauses the TV saying something about not wanting to miss anything the Kardashians are up to and tosses the remote back on the chaise. Sarah Freeborn stands about 5'7" and is all of a size 4, but today Anna can't tell because she is dressed in a vibrant multi-colored flowing caftan and bare feet. She slips on a pair of gold lame Birkenstocks as she gets up to wrap her arms around her daughter, so happy to see her. Anna looks around wondering if she is in the wrong house or perhaps her mother had been kidnapped by aliens. She can't remember her mother ever wrapping her arms around her like that. Not even when she was a child.

In the corner of the room, she sees something move and a cage catches her attention. "What's that?" she asks.

"Oh, don't mind her, that's just Candace, a little hedgehog we rescued. She's a little indifferent to people. Could take us or leave us. But your father and I fell in love with her cute but prickly self."

Anna's mouth gaped open, her eyebrows raised as she listened to the Mother who wouldn't even allow her to have a kitten when she was younger.

"Can I get you some Chamomile tea or coffee? You know we always love having you dear. It's so good to see you. Why don't you go find your father and ask him to join us? He's in his study," added her mother as she bustled off to the kitchen.

Anna seized the moment to look around the den, in a

home where she rarely felt comfortable. She notices the crucifix high over a wall of windows, and the statue of the Blessed Virgin in the corner. She recalls going to church occasionally with them before she was old enough to go by herself or be escorted by their chauffeur, James. She remembers thinking that sometimes there is no one lonelier than an only child with disinterested parents. She wonders if that is why they have taken an interest in the prickly Candace. Kindred spirits.

Anna meanders toward her father's study, concerned about disturbing him. He hated it when she did that and it was common knowledge around their house not to disturb him when he was working. She notices the smell of weed in the air. A repulsive odor she thinks, wrinkling her nose, wondering where it is coming from. Is she imagining it? The door of the study is cracked open a bit and she finds her very steadfast and serious father, playing a game. He's wearing a virtual reality headset. The smell of cannabis was even stronger as she entered the room. She taps him on the shoulder, and realizing he isn't alone, he takes off his headset.

"Sarah, what do you want? I'm playing here." He turns, sees Anna, and jumps up wrapping his arms around her and rocking back and forth. "Oh my gosh, it's you. I'm so happy to see you, sweetie!"

"Hi, Dad. Mom and I are in the den. Will you join us?"

"Uh, sure. Absolutely," he says hesitating a moment. "I'm just finishing a round on Call Of Duty. Reliving my Navy days, you know?"

They return to the den together and Sarah comes in

with a tray of tea, a tower of petite cakes, and chocolates, floating as if she were on air, the caftan swaying in the breeze. Sarah serves them, pouring tea, plating pecan swirls, and offering something she referred to as "special" chocolates. Anna thought they were Belgian. Who doesn't like Belgian chocolates, right? Just as Anna was about to take a bite, her mother explained they were cannabis-infused chocolates. At which point Anna set hers back down. Her Dad pops a couple into his mouth.

"I recently discovered these pecan swirls and they are to die for," says her Mother taking three for her own plate.

"Please, help yourself. Oh Cam, can you just believe she's here? We've missed you so, Anna. What brings you to us today?"

Anna looks at her mother wondering, what did you do with my parents? And Cam? She never heard her mother call her father Cam in her whole life. And what's with all the cannabis? Oh my God!

"You both seem so *different*. I know I haven't been around in a while. Life has been pretty hectic. I just wanted to come and see you. I have something to tell you. But please, tell me what retired life is like. I'd love to hear about it. And why is there a *For Sale* sign out front? I thought you'd be here forever. You love Newport."

"Well, sweetie," began her father, getting up to get Candace out of her cage. "When I retired last year, everything changed," he said patiently stroking Candace's quills as she snuggled in the palm of his hand. "I wasn't working 60-hour weeks anymore, with all the pressure and expectations, all the responsibilities. I started figuring out what was important, and your mom was doing the same thing. We have all the money we need so we might as well enjoy it. We realized we wanted to live more, to have some fun, relax, and enjoy life. So that's what we've been doing. We took a trip down to Key West, you know, where Hemingway went to write *The Old Man and the Sea*. It was so relaxed and chill."

Her mother nodded in agreement, popping a whole pecan swirl into her mouth, affirming him with breathy words, "Yeah, it was chill, really chill."

Did her parents just use the word "chill," thinks Anna.

"We are tired of this rigid lifestyle," her dad continued. "The acquisition of the latest big thing. We just realized we don't need this huge house or all these things in it. We just want to connect with the earth, relax in our retirement years, and have some fun. So, we are. The sign went up and we're going down. As soon as the house sells."

Anna wondered if he'd had too many chocolates but they both seemed to be on the same page, so who was she to judge?

"I hope you'll come down to visit, Anna. People change. Life changes. Life is short, and we don't want to miss one more minute of it," he says.

Anna takes in the familiar space, contemplating her father's words, and watching her mother devour pecan swirls and helps herself to one.

"Life has its seasons darling. So, what did you want to tell us?" asks Sarah.

Anna thinks about it a moment and says, "I just wanted to say I miss you."

She visits a while longer, declines her father's offer to let her hold Candace, and says her goodbyes, leaving with lots to digest. She drives away knowing she has just minutes to decide. Does she want to head north and pick up 1-95 in Fall River crossing the Braga Bridge toward the Cape? Or does she want to head west, over the Newport Pell Bridge, the longest suspension bridge in New England, and head toward Mystic? The bridges offered such powerful symbolism for her journey. She's crossing a bridge, on the road, and in her life. But which one will take her home?

Chapter Twenty-One

"I'd like to tell you a story."

Standing in the kitchen Seth answers his cell phone on the first ring.

"Hello, Honey-Do Farm, Seth speaking, how may I help you?"

"Hey, my man. I thought that was your familiar voice. What's the Honey-Do Farm? And why are you answering your phone like that?"

"Hey, Father Harold, how are you? Sorry about that. I was preoccupied, and um...well it's a long story. How are things going in New Canaan?"

"I'm well Seth, though we miss having you around here for sure. A refreshing young seminarian is filling in where he can, but no one can replace you, of course. Our parishioners are getting antsy in your absence. Which is why I'm calling. I hate to disturb you when you're on sabbatical, that is a sacred time for sure. But we have something of a problem. One of your favorite and very generous parishioners, Millicent Wright, reached out to Bishop Hanrahan, with an issue of grave concern to her. And now his excellency would like a word with you."

"Seriously? Are you kidding me? Fine, fine, I can give him a call tomorrow," says Seth.

"Actually Seth, he wants to see you in person. I know, I know, we shouldn't be bothering you at all. But Ms. Wright seems concerned about your fitness to continue being her priest."

"I'm not *her* priest," Seth corrects him, trying not to sound as irritated as he felt.

"It seems she ran into you in a movie theater out there on the Cape. She says you were holding a woman's hand. It looked a little *cozy*. You know she's got eyes for you and if she can't have you, she doesn't want anyone else to either."

"Good grief, the woman must be 90. I was with a friend. That's all. Fine, I'll come back, and meet with the bishop, but then I'm leaving at the earliest opportunity. I shouldn't have to be back there at all until after Thanksgiving. Three months, remember? I'm supposed to have three months. I can be there by 1:00 tomorrow. Okay?"

"I wouldn't lose any sleep over this, Seth. It isn't the first time Millicent created a little havoc. You know she loves the attention. The bishop will be here at the rectory on other business, so I'll see you then."

"You got it." Seth hung up frustrated that his sabbatical was being interrupted. It was supposed to be his personal time. It's precious time that he gets very little of. A time to discern his calling. Having it interrupted over church nonsense only pushed him closer to a decision that was becoming increasingly less complicated.

Seth put a few things in an overnight bag, and made

arrangements with Emily to tend to the inn, grateful for her joy in everything she did there. It was a little contagious he thought. He had plenty of time to think the next morning with a three-hour ride ahead of him. Too long to make a quick return trip so he'd have to stay overnight, which he did not want to do. Next thing he knew they'd be asking him to celebrate Mass before he left. Or God help him, sit in on a committee meeting. But he planned to head out early before they had a chance to put him to work. Not that he didn't love the Mass, but he is feeling compelled to stand firm on his conviction about this time being his own. Only the bishop's summons could pry him off the Cape. A parish of 850 people, as much as he cares about them, are not the people he wants to spend time with right now.

His drive flies by quickly as he plays his favorite radio stations, thinks about Anna, and prays, and prays, and prays. "Talk to me," says Seth. "Tell me what to do," he pleads. Before he knew it, he was pulling up to the rectory at St. Ignatius. The place he called home for the past 12 years. He is grateful to arrive early enough to have time to go to his room and freshen up before he meets with the bishop. He stops in the sanctuary before their meeting and kneels in prayer surrendering the outcome to Jesus, thy will be done.

"Jesus, why don't you ever listen to me?" He knows he isn't being fair to ask that. But it is how he feels at that moment. Seth puts his head in his hands and goes silent. He breathes in the incensed atmosphere of the sanctuary and looks up at the life-sized crucifix looking down at him.

Sitting back in the pew he closes his eyes waiting expectantly for some guidance, some wisdom that he knows can only come to him there. The sanctuary at St. Ignatius Church has been a place of comfort and solace since he first arrived there so many Sundays ago. He looked around at the stained-glass windows, the statues of Mary and Joseph, the saints, the images of the stations of the cross, and the candles lit for prayer. He wants, in the worst way, to do the right thing. But what does that mean? What does his God want from him at this time in his life? He wants to know. He listens, trying to still his mind, but thoughts of Anna keep rushing in. The day they first met on the beach in Brewster. The way she seemed so carefree and joyful flying her kite. And later that day when he picked her up for dinner in that little cottage. That unforgettable day when they had dinner on the beach and watched the sunset together. And then that fateful day at the movies. The irony is that St. Ignatius of Loyola is the patron saint of helping people discern God's will. "I'm waiting," he says quietly.

He knocks on the partially open door to Father Harold's office, where he knows they will gather, and enters the space that some find stuffy. But Seth finds it comforting. There is a bookcase-lined wall full of not only spiritual texts of the East and West traditions but also all 50 Best-Selling John Grisham novels. Father Harold was a big Grisham fan and he always had the latest title as soon as it was released. On occasion, he'd even pre-order on Amazon. And the day it arrived everyone knew not to bother him. Even Cora the housekeeper would set his tray of lunch and sometimes dinner, on his leather-topped desk, careful not to interrupt his mystery-induced stupor.

Today isn't one of those days though, and as Seth

settles into one of the three burgundy leather chairs, he looks at the older priest and wonders how long this will take. He is anxious to get back to the Cape. In the middle of Seth's 25th year of ordination, he is hoping Harold isn't planning another party. He loves parties and Seth thinks that just maybe those gatherings make Harold feel just a little less lonely. Being a priest is a very isolating and lonely lifestyle in many ways. It's a busy lifestyle with more people in need than there are enough hours in the day to go around. It is a call that reaches the absolute depths of the soul. No one knows that better than him. But he is there to meet with the Bishop because of one lonely and disgruntled parishioner. He hopes to make this quick.

With all required reverence he greets Bishop Hanrahan with *Your Excellency*, as he takes a seat. Harold initiates the meeting suggesting they begin with a prayer, and it feels as if he is the intermediary before they even begin. Then he turns it over to the bishop who wastes no time, confronting Seth about Millicent's claims.

She says you were, "flagrantly flirting about with a young woman in Hyannis."

Young woman? He wonders how old Anna is, but realizes that compared to the many decades Millicent has under her belt, Methuselah might seem young.

Bishop Hanrahan is in good shape for his years, tall and thin, with kind eyes. He looks very serious as he sits there wearing his cassock, a large cross hanging from his neck, and round wire-rimmed glasses. Seth imagines he must be about 70 or so and he always appreciated the way he communicated. He is serious, tough when he has to be, intuitive, and insightful about his priests, but also has a humorous side. Seth wonders if he'll be laughing today.

"Thank you for meeting with me today, Father Seth," said the bishop with a particular emphasis on *Father*. "Harold, would you mind if I have a few minutes alone with Seth?" Harold excuses himself, happy not to be needed.

"As you know the church is in a difficult time right now with a shortage of priests, and many having to straddle two, sometimes three parishes at once. An injustice to both the priests and the parishes. They struggle to do it all well as one might expect. And the call to attend seminary is not necessarily high on today's list of vocations being chosen by our young men. We've lost many priests due to indiscretions in their actions creating church scandals, and many are just plain getting older and are done serving actively. You're well aware of all this, I know, Seth.

"I realize there is an immediate and meaningful solution to this problem with our sisters who would relish the opportunity to become ordained priests. But even their numbers are declining. Did you know that in America, we have fewer than 42,000 nuns as of a couple of years ago? And the average age is 80 years old. But opening that window of opportunity to be a priest could draw more women to the vocation. But our Holy Father just isn't ready to do that and I'm not sure it's the right move myself. So, I understand and support his decision. The life of a priest is not always an easy one as you know Seth. But it is also filled with unfathomable gifts and blessings as we serve our Lord. The call to the priesthood is a wonderful gift reserved for very few."

Seth shifts in his seat wondering where this is going. If he is going to get blasted, he wishes the bishop would get on with it.

"I'd like to tell you a story, that I'd like kept between us," the bishop says. "I was about your age Seth. And much like you I had discerned a vocation to the priesthood fresh out of high school. I embraced it wholeheartedly. I knew I wanted to be a priest. I wanted to serve God in every way. I went to seminary, got ordained, and was eventually assigned to a busy parish, not unlike this one right here at St. Ignatius. Fast forward, I think it was my assignment at the third or fourth church, about 20 years into my service, that I began to question whether I was going to be in it for the long haul, or if my tour of duty had run its course." Seth raised his eyebrows, interested in where this was going.

"I know we commit to God for life Seth, but we're also, first and foremost, human. *Never forget that.* A new sister arrived at my church and for reasons I can't even explain, she made me question everything. We worked on fundraisers together. She had a beautiful spirit and great devotion to the Blessed Mother. I was completely enamored with her. Perhaps even in love. I felt like I was at a crossroads. I had to make a decision, to continue serving God as I vowed to so many years earlier, or move on. My heart belonged to Jesus. There was no question. But it had also been captured by Sister Meagan.

"Now, I'm here today as you can see. And I can tell you with all honesty, that although my work in the church is fulfilling beyond measure, as I know yours has been, a day does not go by when I don't think about Meagan and wonder, *what if?*"

Sitting in silence for a few moments he added, "So my dear Seth, if your heart is calling you to other places, consider the possibility that perhaps Jesus has placed that calling there. Only you can know. But don't spend the rest of your life wondering, w*hat if?*"

The bishop stood up, placed his hand on Seth's shoulder, and walked out of the room.

With Seth dismissed, and after seeing the bishop off, Harold returns to his office. He opens the bottom right-hand drawer of his substantial antique mahogany desk and takes out the three-quarter empty bottle of a Remy Martin XO Cognac. He removes one of the two tulip glasses he prefers for an enhanced appreciation of the aroma. A very thoughtful, very wealthy parishioner gave it to him as a special gift knowing his penchant for fine things, especially 10-year-old barrel-aged cognac. He leaves one glass in the drawer as he usually does, reluctant to share the experience with anyone. He pours the coveted liquid and sets the exquisite bottle back in the drawer. Liking it neat, Harold picks up the glass, takes a sip, savoring the taste, and wonders about Seth's future at St. Ignatius. He slowly takes another sip and keeps going, emptying the glass.

The rectory is an old house built in the early 1900s filled with the charm and character of many New England homes from that era. It is kept immaculate, including the mud room and large kitchen. Father Harold usually sits at a small oak table in the kitchen and prefers taking his meals there rather than in the large formal dining area. But for this meal, they hadn't shared in a while, they sat in the dining room. Seth pulls up a chair and looks around, asking if Cora is still there. Cora has worked at the rectory since before Seth arrived, cleaning, cooking, and keeping its priests, seminarians, and guests, well-fed. He likes her. She is a spunky five-foot-tall African American woman, who is great at what she does and doesn't take any nonsense from Harold. For that reason, Harold enjoys teasing her by calling her Corabelle, just to get a rise out of her.

Seth and Harold enjoy dinner together, neither one bringing up their time with the bishop. They catch up on what's been going on at St. Ignatius and life off-season on Cape Cod. Cora is happy to see Father Seth back in the rectory and he is happy to remind her he isn't staying. That he will be leaving first thing in the morning, but is expected back after Thanksgiving. She ran in and out serving their meal and cleaning up afterward until they parted for the evening with Harold saying, "Thank you, Corabelle." She feigned annoyance but smiled at him.

He lay in his bed in the rectory and for the first time ever, his thoughts were not on his next homily, an upcoming fundraiser, or the most recent crisis one of his parishioners is going through. His thoughts were not even on prayer. Instead, they were on Anna, and in that space that was sacred for him and God alone, entered an angel he was certain, was sent from above.

Seth is an early riser and went right into his usual routine where he recited morning prayer, put on his shorts and one of his threadbare seminary t-shirts, and made his way to the third-floor attic where he had set up a workout area. He hadn't worked out in weeks since he arrived on the Cape, so he seized the opportunity to get a little exercise in before breakfast. After a shower, packing his bag, and dressing in black with his Roman collar out of respect for his environment, he went to the kitchen. Without thinking, Seth poured two cups of coffee. He'd been doing it for over a decade, the whole time he'd been at St, Ignatius. Twelve years getting up before the sun, dressing in the same black clothes, reciting those familiar prayers. For twelve years he came downstairs in the old rectory to greet Father Harold at the kitchen table, pouring their coffee and sitting down in silence. Harold was a man of few words unless he was in the pulpit. Then you couldn't shut him up. He was like a father to Seth, who is 18 years his junior. Harold had taken Seth under his wing fresh out of seminary, as a mentor before he was ever serving at his church. It was a time when Seth wanted nothing more than to become a parish priest. He needed guidance at the time, as they all did. But Harold had taken a special interest in Seth, a very, very special interest. Harold realized his calling to the priesthood late in life, so attending Holy Apostles Seminary seemed like a given, as it was one of few seminaries that embraced older second-career seminarians. Some people who knew him well said he was running away from something. Harold liked to think he was running toward something.

They said their goodbyes, Seth grabbed his bag and a dish of leftovers from the night before that Cora insisted he take with him, and he was on his way back to the Cape.

Notice that autumn is more the season of the soul than of nature. Seth thought of this line from the Nietzsche poem that had been one of Anna's favorites. She shared it with him one night at her cottage after they first met. It stuck in his mind for some reason and he thought that the image somehow resembled his life right now. His life, like autumn, is full of change, a season of the soul. He has a decision to make, and he wants to get it right. We tend in life to want a guarantee, a sign that we are doing the right thing, he thought. But the reality is, there are no guarantees. We can only make what seems to be the right decision at the time and hope for the best. If it doesn't work out, we take what we've learned, perhaps grow from it, and move on. He wished it were that simple.

He thought about his life edging near its slippery slope and realized it could be the biggest mistake of his life. Or, the best thing that's ever happened to him. If he left the church, what would he do? What would his life look like? Would Anna want to be a part of it? He doesn't even know how she feels about him, he realizes. But he is becoming pretty clear about how he feels about her. Perhaps he should tell her. To take his mind away from his thoughts he turns the radio on. As he draws closer to the Bourne Bridge he looks out at the horizon over the Cape Cod Canal and knows change is in the air. Just then *Ace of Base* comes on the radio with their hit song, *I Saw the Sign*. He grins at God's humor and sings along.

Getting closer to Hyannis, Seth stops to get gas at the only full-service 7-Eleven he knows of. He hates to pump gas and considers having it pumped for him, just a little bit indulgent but well worth it. The attendant comes out as the bells sound off announcing a customer.

"Whoa, how ya doin' Dude? Look at this Audi! I'll bet it's a nice ride. What can I do you for?" says the young man with frizzy red hair.

"Fill it with premium please," says Seth, handing him his credit card.

"Father Seth Alexander," he reads. "Wow. Pretty cool. My Dad's a father, too. You know we have a new Slurpee flavor today, check this out... Tropical brain freeze, oh my God it's epic. We've got a special inside. You want one? I can get you one. We have some buzzin' new vape carts in there too if you want to try it....take your spirit to a whole new level."

"I'll pass on the vape carts and brain freeze, but a receipt would be great," says Seth, in a hurry to get on his way. He's pretty sure the guy has indulged in a little too much of both the vape carts and the brain freeze. He offers a silent prayer for Red, and heads toward Route 6A anxious to get back to the Honey-Do Farm.

Arriving back at the inn, he finds everyone in the kitchen sharing a mid-morning meal. As he walks through the door the room goes silent, all eyes are on him, eyebrows raised. For just a moment, he doesn't know why. Until he remembers, anxious to return to the Cape and with thoughts of Anna on his mind, he hadn't changed clothes before he left the rectory. His Roman collar shone like a beacon of light from the Sandy Neck Lighthouse on a foggy day.

Chapter Twenty-Two

"So now you're a painter too?"

Anna pulls into the gravel driveway of her Magic Cottage by the sea. Each time she does this, she can't help but think of Gram and how much joy the cottage gave her. With Anna having much of her second half of life ahead of her, her best life she liked to think of it, she embraces every moment now to call it home. Back in Newport, her parents were discovering the path to living their best life, with reckless abandon. She was impressed. While she was there, she took a moment to ask her mother about the estranged relationship she had with Anna's grandmother. Anna was curious how anyone, especially her mother, could have a problem with her sweeter than a Snickers bar grandmother. She just couldn't see it. As Sarah had always done in the past, she chose not to talk about it. She encouraged Anna to let it go and enjoy the happy memories she held so dear. That was not her usual response regarding Anna's grandmother. It was kinder and gentler, and Anna suspected those *special* chocolates and cannabis-infused snacks, might be the reason. If those made her mother a kinder, gentler spirit then God bless her. *Eat up*, thought Anna.

She grabs her things from the car, takes a deep breath of that familiar salt air, and goes into the cottage. As if on cue, her phone rings. She instantly recognizes the number and wrestles for a moment about whether to answer. Difficult as it was, she sent Seth to voice mail. She is conflicted about him and wants to send him packing even further away. But for now, voicemail will do. They have a lot to talk about, but she isn't ready.

Unpacking her bags she begins to settle into her new home. It is late and she has much to think about. For starters, she wants to make her cottage feel more like her own. She has been a visitor and reluctant to change anything, for fear of losing her memories of Gram. But she knows better. Her memories are deeply embedded in her love and perhaps even in her grief.

Feeling like she had one foot in Mystic and one on the Cape, she felt free from commitment in either place, but at the same time wants something more permanent. It is confusing. If she is going to live on the Cape full-time, she needs to let go of her apartment in Mystic and commit to living on the Cape. Commit. Hmm...., thought Anna. That's a powerful word. She was committed to Ethan and where did that get her? Now she's considering another commitment. And what about Seth? What is he committed to? The answer is obvious. She wonders if she could ever be enough for him.

Anna thought about her apartment in Mystic with its exposed brick wall, high ceilings, and tall windows overlooking the Mystic River. She loved sitting on the thick tufted floor cushion in the corner of her loft, with a rice paper and pine shoji screen creating a dedicated space for her meditation and prayer. A small altar covered with one of her grandmother's white lace doilies softened the sound of the Tibetan brass bowl that cleared the air with one tap of the wooden mallet.

She locates the bowl in a yet-to-be-unpacked box at the cottage and chooses a spot in the corner of her bedroom that might be ideal for prayer. She positions the purple cushion on top of one of her grandmother's folded quilts on the floor and arranges a small stool to serve as an altar. Anna carefully places a pottery cross on it, with a design of a chalice and Eucharist that she treasures. She locates a sandalwood votive candle from Gram's stash, reminding herself to get more when she goes shopping. She finds her incense holder and favorite Jasmine sticks and wooden matches with *"Let your light shine"* on the cover. Minus the shoji screen, it feels just like the prayer space in her apartment. With everything in its place, Anna strikes the bowl with the mallet and thinks about Seth as she lights the incense and candle, setting them on the chipped clamshell that holds both. She runs her finger over the chip and remembers the day she found the shell. It was the first day she arrived in South Yarmouth with plans to stay for one month, without a thought of making it her permanent home. Funny how things change. She wondered back then, what her time on the Cape might reveal to her. How might a month away from everything and everyone, shape her future? If she only knew…

As she finally begins settling into the cottage to make it

home, she walks around with eyes wide open, a fresh experience, noticing the details of the cottage and its furnishings. It feels like she is seeing it differently. It is hers. She doesn't plan to make any drastic changes at this point, just a little tweak here and there. The enclosed front porch has a small café sized white wrought iron table, two chairs, and a couple of classic New England porch rockers facing the direction of the water. A sisal rug covers the painted floor and nautical-style lanterns flank the periwinkle front door. It is perfect. No changes to make there.

Her stomach lets out a slow rumble and she knows it's time to head to the kitchen. It is fully equipped and Anna has stocked it with some essentials since she arrived. She rummages around for a saucepan and warms up a container of beef barley soup from the Bass River Food Emporium. It is a local take-out eatery that she stopped at on her way home earlier that day. Some crusty French bread, a little Brie, and soup will be perfect for dinner. The pan she finds is an old vintage enamel pot with a thin red stripe around the edge. There are others like it of varying sizes. She knows it isn't Cuisinart but neither is she Jacques Pepin. So the vintage pot will do just fine. Creating something of a rustic experience familiar to her camping days. She loves the simplicity of it. Sitting at the table, still covered with the vintage tablecloth with the autumn design, she savors the soup and bread. Closing her eyes, Anna takes a deep breath to calm herself and says a prayer for the abundant blessings in her life and God's continued guidance. As she tears off another chunk of French bread and dips it in her bowl, she is overwhelmed with gratitude.

Anna slept well that night and the next morning

continued her quest to make the cottage her own, one little nook at a time. She knows she has to go slow and is in no hurry. She believes she will learn what her home wants to be in God's perfect time. It will tell her, she is certain. That's what spaces do. Her creative process is that way with her writing as well as in life. Patience is needed and is not her greatest strength. After pulling on some jeans, a long-sleeve chartreuse T-shirt with *Perfectly Imperfect* printed in bold letters, and a pair of thick socks that Gram had knit for her, she explores further. With her decision to live there, she finally feels like the cottage is her own and she isn't violating Gram's privacy to poke around. So, she did. It is a strange feeling like Gram is watching her, and she probably is. Anna embraced it, opening drawers and checking out the few closets that were there, just looking at first, like a bystander. She took an in-depth look at the built-in book-shelves next to the cobblestone fireplace. She didn't reach out to touch anything but rather just explored with her eyes, waiting for something to speak to her.

The house was still full of Grandma Iris's things and she is learning more about her grandmother with each discovery. She has always had a curious nature and wants to understand what makes people the way they are. But more often than not, people are a mystery. No matter how hard she tries to understand them. She wonders if she will ever have the opportunity to understand Seth.

When Anna was young and visited the Cape, she wasn't interested in what filled Gram's closets and drawers, but more interested in time at the beach with her friends. Yet with each visit, she remembers some little discovery that she now suspects Gram arranged on purpose. Her findings always led to some colorful stories about Gram's past. She was a fabulous storyteller, and always made Anna's time there something special, so much so that she didn't want to leave. Now she doesn't have to. As she thinks about those times, she grabs a tissue to wipe her tears, missing her grandmother so much at that moment. "Thanks, Gram," she says out loud, confident that her spirit is still there. Anna reaches out for Mary Oliver's book *Swan: Poems and Prose* from the bookcase. She gets a chill. She randomly, if anything can be random, opens the book to a poem called, *Don't Hesitate*. It read,

"If you suddenly and unexpectedly feel joy, don't hesitate … very likely you notice it in the instant when love begins… Joy is not made to be a crumb."

Anna reads it again and again and then gently closes the book, placing it mindfully back in its spot. She walks over to her favorite comfy chair, lifts the patchwork quilt that was thrown over the back, and sits down, wrapping it around her. *"Joy is not meant to be a crumb."* That's kind of all Anna has known. Most of her relationships all her adult life have been built on crumbs. She hates to admit it, even to herself. She wants more. And she won't settle for less ever again. She wants it all. She deserves it all. Anna spends time with the poem in her mind, trying to figure out what she needs to do. It doesn't take long.

Grabbing her keys and a light jacket, she hops in her Volvo and heads across the Cape to 6A and the Honey-Do Farm. She doesn't know why. Traffic is light in the off-season and she appreciates the opportunity to collect her thoughts without the necessity of dodging wayward tourists. She gets there in no time, uses the anchor door knocker, and lets herself in when no one answers. She finds Emily in the kitchen putting away groceries and asks if Seth is around.

"You mean Father Seth?" Emily asks with a mischievous grin. Laughing, she says, "I just saw him a short while ago with some tools, and paint and he was headed toward the barn I think."

"Great Emily, thank you," and off she went, back outside. Anna starts walking toward the barn but then notices Seth in the distance near a path leading into the woods. She heads toward him. He is facing away from her, scrunched down completely engaged in painting something. As Anna draws closer, she realizes he is working on a sign.

"So now you're a painter too?" she asks. "Is there anything else I should know about you?"

Seth turns his head and looks up at her with a slow, perhaps guilty grin, almost as if he was expecting her. Proud of his handiwork he holds up the sign and nails it back on the tree where it hung for years, but this time with fresh paint. Anna reads the sign, *Chapel.* Her heart is pounding.

"Hi, Seth. Can we talk?"

"Yes, of course." With the excitement of a little kid, he says, "But first please come with me. I want to show you something."

He takes her hand leading her along the trail of scrub pines and mountain laurel through the woods until they come to the tiny white chapel. Since his initial discovery, he returned and began clearing away some of the overgrowth and brush. He even cleaned the windows, taking great care, especially with the stained glass. Anna stands back looking at the lilliputian-sized structure shaped like a tiny church. Seth watches Anna's expression. She appears as taken with the discovery as he was when he first came upon it.

"Anna, I'm so happy to see you. Thank you for coming. I tried to reach you but my call went to your voicemail."

"I know," says Anna. "I just returned from seeing my parents in Newport and I just needed some time. To think. I don't know what to make of this, this thing" she says, wiggling her finger back and forth between the two of them. "Honestly, I'm a little confused."

She silently reminds herself he is a priest. But without the collar, it is easy to forget. He is just a man. A sexy, kind, charming, compassionate, too handsome for his own good, kinda guy. But she can't let herself forget. She *won't* let herself forget.

"I understand. Come inside. I've cleaned up the chapel and it's relatively useable. We can sit down and talk."

Anna is so enchanted by the little place, that any reservations she has about Seth, are rapidly melting away. She can't help herself. What kind of guy goes to such lengths to clean up an old unused chapel in the middle of the woods?

"Well, first, what is this and why is it here?" she asks.

"I know, right? I wondered the same thing. So, I did some research and learned that this property used to be a summer camp. We've got seven acres here and several outbuildings that were used back then in addition to what is now the inn."

"We??? When did *we* happen?" she asks. "You are getting very comfortable here at the Honey-Do Farm."

"It is a special place. I guess I am getting comfortable.

I'm here 'til the end of November...at least. And what about you Anna? When are you going back home?" he asks with a concerned look.

"Well, I'd love to tell you about that. Are you free for dinner? Come to the cottage tomorrow night and I'll cook for you. I'm not a gourmet chef or anything but I can cook a few things. And if it doesn't work out, there is always pizza."

"That sounds perfect. I'll walk you out," he says, reaching for her hand as they traverse the trail. Confusion takes over at his touch, and her feelings for him are too much given the uncertainty of it all. She pulls her hand away and runs off to her car, yelling, "I'll see you tomorrow night Seth. Bye." She isn't taking any chances that her heart wouldn't melt into a puddle at his feet.

Chapter Twenty-Three

"Perhaps ice cream was not the best idea."

Seth looks forward to dinner with Anna and is dreamily contemplating what that might be like when Brandon appears at the open door to the study. He sees the look on Seth's face and wonders if they need to have *the talk*. The talk, would not be unlike many that Seth has had with him over the years when he was on the precipice of destroying his life for the umpteenth time. He knew Seth always had his best interest in mind, but his brotherly, or *fatherly* talks were irritating nonetheless. Maybe Seth needs one of those now himself.

"Hey, come in, have a seat. How are things going with you? We haven't had much chance to talk," says Seth, giving Brandon his undivided attention. Sitting in one of two nautical navy wingback chairs he sips a short glass of apricot brandy. "I'd offer you some but…"

"No thanks. I'm good," affirms Brandon making himself comfortable in the other chair. "I have to admit, the inn is very warm and welcoming. I've been going to meetings just about every day. Sometimes I call an Uber and go myself, but sometimes I go with Henri. He's really great and it's been fun getting to know him. There is something about those meetings that gives me a feeling I haven't known in a long time."

"Like what?" asks Seth, encouraging his friend to continue.

"Well, every time I get there, there is a cup of free coffee, and somebody says to me, *"We've saved a seat for you."* They say that every time. And nothing is expected of me. Especially not perfection. I just show up in all my brokenness," he says honestly. "We say the Serenity Prayer. Someone shares their story. You can talk or just listen. There is a sense of belonging. Kind of the same way I feel here at the inn. It isn't anything I was looking for but here I am, feeling a part of something bigger than myself. It's like something I've been looking for but never knew it, Seth."

"Wow, that's pretty powerful. I'm really happy that you've made some connections. Henri seems like a genuinely nice guy," says Seth.

"He is, he is." Brandon lost his parents in a car accident early in life and he never had a father figure around to guide him. So, he strayed. And he strayed far. "I've learned a lot in the short time Henri has been here. I'm glad he doesn't seem to be in any hurry to leave."

"This place has that effect on people," says Seth laughing. "How are things going with the apostles and chickens?"

"We're actually getting along great. They give me someone to talk to and they listen pretty well," he says, laughing. "I wanted to mention that I've noticed a few things around here that look like they need repair. Want me to take a look and see what I can do? I used to do a lot of maintenance at the ski resorts. Maybe I could earn my keep. Ya know? Give a little something back."

Seth looks at his friend and thinks just possibly, that might be the first time, in a long time, that he witnessed Brandon thinking about others. It nearly brings tears to his eyes. He remembers that night at the police station when he went to his cell and Brandon's legs were dangling from the ceiling HVAC vent as he tried to hoist his drunken self into an escape route. He's come a long way. He has hope for his dear friend who seemed to have lost hope. There he was, appreciating a flock of sheep, gathering eggs for breakfast with a group of strangers every morning, offering to help keep the place up and just maybe, taking his recovery seriously. Taking his life seriously. Healing comes in so many different ways thinks Seth, wondering about his own.

"Speaking of things in need of repair, what's up with you and Anna? I thought you were lying low and then you walk into a crowded kitchen like you're ready to do confessions. What were ya thinking? What gives? Spill it." Brandon sat back and waited patiently, still remembering a few things he learned in seminary.

Seth looks at him and tries to hold back a smile, unsuccessfully, as he thinks about Anna. He can't help himself. But he also isn't sure how much he wants to share with Brandon. He takes a sip of the apricot liquid savoring its warmth, avoids looking directly at his friend, and says, "I'm thinking of, leaving the priesthood."

"No shit!!! You think I don't know that? Showing up

dressed like a priest didn't help. What are you gonna do?" asks Brandon.

"I don't know. I came here to be alone, to figure it out. I never expected to meet Anna. But there she was. Never expected to find myself inn-sitting with a pack of beautiful people who don't want to leave. Never expected, to not want to leave myself. Yet here I am. And I don't know what to do. Bishop Hanrahan basically gave me his blessing and told me if my heart was calling me other places, perhaps Jesus had placed that calling there. He cautioned me about not spending the rest of my life wondering, *What if?* And to be honest, I don't know how Anna feels about me. I know she was pretty angry. I don't blame her. But I also can't deny how I feel about her. Our time together has been nothing short of magical. She makes me feel like a kid again. I can't stop thinking about her. She may not want anything to do with me. I just don't know. But she did invite me to dinner so we could talk. I just want to be with her."

"Wow, you've got it bad," says Brandon shaking his head. "And you also love the church. Right? You *do* love the church, right? You have devoted your entire adult life to serving God, to serving the church. Are you prepared to live without the only life you have ever known?"

"I don't know Bran, I just don't know. There are many ways to serve God. I know that. I just have to discern mine. I thought I knew my forever purpose. I did not become a priest to take those vows lightly. But at this time in my life, I'm just not sure about it anymore. I definitely want to continue serving God, just maybe not the way I have been. Maybe God has other things in mind for me, something beyond my imagination. He's creative like that. And I'll bet he's got something special in mind for you as well."

"Well, for now, I think I'll make myself useful and make a list of some of the issues that need attention and we can talk about it. Enjoy your dinner with Anna. I can't wait to hear all about it."

"Just worry about your list," said Seth, shutting down any plans Brandon has to *hear all about it*. "and Brandon... thanks." They parted ways and Seth jumped in the shower to get ready for dinner, a dinner he is a little nervous about.

Seth arrives at Anna's cottage right on time, carrying a bottle of her favorite Ballet of Angels wine, and with his usual attention to detail, it is already chilled. He is used to being prompt when an entire congregation is waiting for his arrival. She answers the door as soon as he rings that blasted ship's bell. It is loud and he wonders if the entire neighborhood is conscious of his arrival. Though he knows that many homes would be empty by now, with many folks leaving by Labor Day or soon after. He can't contain his smile when he sets eyes on her, presenting his gift.

Anna feels a little reserved about the whole thing and questions what she was thinking when she invited him for dinner. Not only is she not a very good cook, but she doesn't even enjoy cooking. She also didn't want to feed him a bad meal and thought, ever so briefly, of going to the Emporium to buy a prepared something. But she wanted to be authentic with him, and that meant making him aware that she was a limited, if not a lousy cook. She decides to suck it up and cook the man a meal. He's used to being cooked for, cared for, she imagined, since he is, after all, a priest. So, this is okay as she is just hosting a friend for dinner who happens to be a parish priest. People do this, she told herself. Not anyone she knows, but she is pretty sure some people do this.

Seth hesitates to give her a hug for fear of scaring her off but decides to give in to it as he would have greeted any parishioner, he is close to. Taking a seat on the couch, he realizes he should offer to help. He opens the wine, while Anna begins grilling two sumptuous tenderloin filets on the back deck. She already has salad prepared and stuck a container of Bob Evans mashed potatoes in the microwave, hoping Seth won't hear it going. Three minutes, a stir, and three minutes more and she relocates the creation to a bowl and sets it in the oven to stay warm. The steaks won't take long. She joins Seth in the living room with their wine and a small charcuterie board. See, she knows how to entertain, she thinks, proud of herself. Sitting next to him on the couch, she grabs a cracker and attempts to spread brie on it, breaking the cracker and sending crumbs flying. It was a Triscuit. She was just trying to keep her hands busy while Seth did the same. And she was happy to jump up when the timer went off letting her know to flip the filets. "I'll help you," he says getting up to follow her as she flies out the kitchen door. Seth joins her on the deck that is barely big enough to hold Gram's grill and a yoga mat. Anna feels compelled to stay busy, uncertain of what might happen if she doesn't.

Seth watches over her shoulder to assess their dinner and catches a whiff of her coconut shampoo. "Hmmm… delicious," he says quietly.

"I know. I've impressed myself," she says flipping the steaks. Oblivious to the real reason for his response. And off she goes back into the kitchen, setting out the rest of the dinner while Seth stands on the deck looking up at the sky and asking… "Why?"

A flickering candle brightens the kitchen space. She has fixed their plates with mashed potatoes and steak, with salad in a large pottery bowl. Seth helps himself to salad filling his bowl. He knows she is nervous about cooking for him and wants to ease her mind.

"It looks delicious," he tells her.

"Does it? I'm not really a very good cook," she confesses, "but I can cook these steaks. I don't eat steak too often but when I do, this is what I get. It's something special. If you cook them right, they practically melt in your mouth." Anna was rambling but then got poetic about how food should be a celebration. "So often though we just whoof it down in a hurry, much like we do with life, without thinking. But this…this should be an experience for the senses."

Seth hangs on her every word and is having his own full-on sensory experience. Anna seems oblivious to that fact, which is probably a good thing. She continues chatting away, hoping to keep things light fearing anything else might create a problem.

"Seth,?" Anna asks.

"Yes?"

"Would you say grace?" she asks shyly.

"Of course." He takes her hand offering a heartfelt prayer and she is touched when he asks Jesus for guidance for both of them as they get to know each other better. In the silence, he holds on to her just a few moments longer, reluctant to let go.

Then they dig into their meal, savoring this precious time together. The mashed potatoes were infallible really. You just can't kill delicious Bob Evans potatoes, and the salad was direct from God, so she couldn't go wrong there. Those pricey filet mignons are a bit finicky to get just right. She did her best, hoping not to disappoint Father Seth by serving him hockey pucks for dinner. *Father Seth*, she repeated in her mind. *Father Seth*. As if it were a delayed epiphany, creating even greater confusion within her, she realizes there is something very sexy and very forbidden about this. Not about having dinner, but her feelings for him. Lost in thought about what could be, she realizes Seth is talking to her. She literally has to shake her head to clear any impure thoughts about the holy one sitting across from her.

"So how does that sound,?" he asks.

"I'm sorry, what, what did you say?"

"I just wondered if you would like to get ice cream after dinner. At that place, you told me about, down the road. Are they still open this time of year? I know it gets kind of quiet here in autumn. I love the stillness of it. Such a beautiful time of year though. It's my favorite season," says Seth.

"It is? It's mine too," she says, unable to hold back her smile or her enthusiasm. "I just love it, the colors of the leaves changing and then falling, a crackling fire, the cranberry harvest, and the smell in the crisp cool air is …magical. The events are fun. I love it, and yes, they are still open, at least well into November. We can walk over later."

Anna is grateful for the idea as she uncharacteristically forgot to think about dessert. Watching him, Anna notices Seth chewing quite laboriously and struggling to choke down, the melt-in-your-mouth creation she had promised, but not delivered. They are supposed to be savoring their shared meal and their discovery that they have more in common and more to celebrate. Instead, she overcooked the steaks, by a long shot, and is disappointed with herself and embarrassed for letting that happen. Barely edible, Seth continues chewing and making an effort to assure her it is delicious. Whenever she looks away, he graciously wipes his mouth with his napkin and extricates the tough wad of beef from his mouth. After they ate and cleaned up the dishes together, they sat next to each other on the couch for a short time, until it was evident that was no longer a good idea. She suggests they take a walk and get that ice cream. By then the sun had set and the night sky was lit with a nearly full moon.

Anna seized the opportunity to share what she knew about moons from Zoe, trying to keep the conversation casual. "Did you know that full moons can represent heightened emotions, spiritual enlightenment, and new beginnings?" Anna asks immediately wondering what she was thinking. That is not casual conversation. That is stirring up things that should not be stirred.

"I did not know that," says Seth looking up at the sky. "I guess I'm not surprised," tuning into how he is feeling at the moment. His emotions are most definitely heightened, his spirit is alive and well, and as for new beginnings, he doesn't know how things can ever stay the same. He can't imagine it.

They arrive at the ice cream shop, where they each order an ice cream cone, coffee flavor for Seth, and vanilla for Anna, and walk across the street to the waterfront.

Sitting on a bench overlooking Nantucket Sound, the moon shone a streak of light onto the water, and it felt like they were alone in the world. Embracing the art of food as a celebration, Anna enjoys her ice cream cone, licking away as it runs down her chin. He watches in rapt astonishment before reaching out with one bent finger to catch the drips while she holds his gaze. And then hands her a napkin from his pocket, noticing his heart is racing, he whispers, "Perhaps ice cream was not the best idea."

"I think it was the perfect idea," she says, refusing to think beyond that moment, and trying to restrain a grin.

Chapter Twenty-Four

"Could be a devastating situation... or a heavenly one."

Laicization is a process whereby a priest is returned to a lay state and can no longer administer the sacraments. A priest is considered a priest for life, having been permanently changed with an indelible mark on his soul, through the sacrament of Holy Orders or Ordination. In some cases, they may receive a dispensation from the sacred vow of celibacy. This allows a man to marry and still be in good standing with the Catholic church, though no longer performing clerical duties. One must jump through many hoops and the time required to obtain both laicization and dispensation can be considerable, with no guarantee of the latter. If a priest marries without permission they may be excommunicated and barred from receiving the sacraments.

Anna is speechless. She is in full Anderson Cooper mode, investigative reporting at its finest. She wants answers and she wants them now. And she doesn't like what she's finding. After Seth left the night before, she had another date…this time with Google. She wanted and needed the facts about this situation that appeared to be getting increasingly complex. She researched until 3 a.m. before finally crashing on the couch, too tired to even go up to her loft for bed.

And in the way only Zoe can do, the ship's bell sounded around 8:30 the next morning rousing Anna from her research-induced sleep. Twisted up in the quilt on the couch she fell on the floor trying to get up. She pulled back the curtains to see Zoe standing there like she was the day after Anna arrived, with another glorious creamsicle-colored box from *Tokens of My Confections*. Amen for Zoe.

"What are you doing here? I'm so happy to see you. Come in, come in, I'll put some coffee right on." Following Anna to the kitchen, Zoe sets the box of deli-cate pastries down while Anna starts the coffee. "You always show up when I need you most," says Anna. "You have no idea. Do you mind if we sit on the porch? I need to see the water and smell the salt air. Perhaps a cleansing."

"Uh oh. What did you do? This ought to be good," says Zoe. "But you know you do the same thing, sweetie. You know just when to show up. It's an energy thing."

With coffee in hand, they grab a couple of plates, napkins, and the bright box of miniature pastries and head to the porch where the white wrought iron table and chairs await. They can see the water at the end of the lane.

"So…what's going on with Father what's his name?"

"It's Seth. His name is Seth. And like so many things in life…it's complicated."

"Oh, bullshit! Spill it. What's going on?" says Zoe.

Anna takes a deep breath and fills Zoe in on last night's joys and fiascos.

"Every time I see Seth I get deeper into the muck and mire of what could be a devastating situation… or a heavenly one. Devastating for me. Or extraordinary for me… for us. And I'm not sure I'm up for another relationship nightmare. Not to compare him with Ethan in any way. I realized Ethan was an extreme narcissist way too long into our relationship and by then it was hard to get out. His abuse ran rampant and I'm embarrassed that I put up with it for so long. And although that is not a concern regarding Seth, there are plenty of other red flags. No that's not fair. There's one great big flag. Just the one. And I'm scared to death of getting my heart broken again.

"But when I'm with him, this writer cannot even find the words to articulate how he makes me feel. I don't know what to do to save myself, Zoe. I like him so much. I was up all night, researching what the deal was. I mean if he decides to stop being a priest. But I realize none of it matters. I don't even know how he feels about me."

"Are you kidding? Are you serious?" asks Zoe.

"I know we have not shared specific words of interest, but the chemistry and attraction are beyond me, so much so that I want to run away. But I can't run away, don't want to run away. Yet, I'm risking my heart staying. It's so confusing. And he is a flight risk I suppose. And then there's Jesus. He made a commitment to him for life. He's been a priest his whole adult life. How can I come between Seth and our God? It would break my heart. I know we need to talk honestly and openly. I know this. We just haven't …yet. The last time I was over at the farm, Seth showed me this tiny little chapel in the woods. It was so precious…like holy ground. You could feel the spirit of it. We have seven acres there with all kinds of buildings and animals and interesting people. It's quirky and fascinating and everyone is so nice."

"*We*? When did you all become *we?*" asks Zoe.

"I meant *he* has, or *they* have, err maybe *it* has, seven acres," says Anna correcting herself. "It's just that, it's a special place for some reason. People show up there with wounds, with heartbreak, or seeking direction, and they don't leave. They help each other, take care of the place, and contribute in whatever way they can. Seth didn't know or expect any of this. He was just hired basically as a house sitter while the owners were away. They'll be back right after Thanksgiving. But the place has such wonderful spiritual energy. It reminds me of places I've been on retreat. A place to get quiet, get still, and connect with nature. A place to create. Maybe even a place to heal."

"That's all well and good, but what about you?" asks Zoe, concerned about her friend. "What are you going to do about Father Seth?"

"I don't know, I just served him microwave potatoes and overcooked steak and he still wanted to go get ice cream. He's forgiving if nothing else," says Anna.

"He was probably still hungry," said Zoe munching on a pastry.

"Hmm, maybe. He did eat a lot of salad. Anyway, I'm going to go there. I'll talk to him. I could be misunderstanding kind, thoughtful behavior. Nothing more than he would do with any parishioner. Yes, that's probably it, and

I'm just overreacting as someone just out of a terrible relationship. Yes, that's what I'll do."

Zoe looked skeptically at her friend knowing the potential for heartbreak was high. But she also knew Anna would have to learn for herself. She pushed the bright orange box toward her friend saying, "Here, have a pastry. Pastry makes everything better."

Anna helps herself to a tiny apple tart, but she can't help but think about the feeling of Seth's finger touching her chin last night.

Zoe left after cautioning Anna about giving her heart away and they planned to go out for dinner one night soon. Anna cleans up from the serendipitous and most welcome visit and decides to take a walk on the beach to clear her mind and maybe find some direction. Wrapping herself in a warm jacket and light scarf, she sets off, hoping time along the water might be just what she needs. Her hands deep in her pockets and at a meandering pace, she looks alternately between the horizon and the shoreline for shells, sea glass, and stones that catch her attention. She loves finding heart-shaped rocks. Sea glass is scarce on her beach so it is a special delight when she does find a piece.

She remembers a story she heard about a woman walking a labyrinth on the beach. The labyrinth is a spiritual walk toward the center, physically and metaphorically, and then out again representing our journey of life. It was a seven-circuit path constructed of driftwood and mostly beach stones. The woman had a recent tragedy in her life and went to walk this sacred path and surrender her pain to God. The story goes, with her head down as she walked mindfully through the labyrinth, one slow step at a time, she noticed numerous heart-shaped rocks lining the path, all along the way. After she had walked to the center and back out again, she mentioned the rocks to the woman who built the labyrinth.

"How did you ever find so many heart-shaped rocks?" she asked the builder. "I saw them everywhere."

"What heart-shaped rocks? There are no heart-shaped rocks in this labyrinth," the builder responded.

Healing comes in many ways. The story gives Anna chills every time she thinks of it. Anna walks for quite a ways toward the breakwater, hardly seeing another soul. There is an occasional power-walker getting in their morning workout, or someone walking their dog, but that was about it. She loves the Cape off-season for that very reason. The opportunity for quiet and solitude. As she walks along the water's edge, looking out at the horizon, she feels such gratitude for her life. It is evolving in ways she never imagined. The journey to get here hasn't been easy but she feels so grateful for how far she's come. The life of a writer on Cape Cod is her dream come true. She wonders if sharing it with someone might be a part of that dream.

Just as she was having that thought, she looked down to find a piece of translucent sea glass. She almost missed it as it was mixed in with sand, stones, and shells. Anna picks it up to add to the others she found. She looks closer realizing it is shaped like a heart. She lifts it to her own heart and keeps it in her hand the rest of the way home. She is getting used to the realization that this is her home now, and the very thought brings her joy.

She returns to her cottage, gathers a few things, and

still holding that piece of sea glass, she drives to the Adoration Chapel in Harwich. It is calling her name. Anna sat in silence in one of only a handful of pews and prayed. She talked with God as a friend, Father, creator, healer, and endlessly forgiving, infinitely loving God. He is easy to talk to. Anna often wondered over the years if she was meant to serve him as a nun, living in an abbey, or some other religious or retreat setting. But she thought a vow of obedience might have been a challenge for her. She does love having a beautiful relationship with God and having him a part of everything she does. She wonders what Jesus is thinking about her and Seth. It's like the holy grail of relationships. To have someone come into your life who loves God the same way you do. That's rare. She looks at the piece of sea glass in her hand and knows what she needs to do.

Back in her Volvo, she texts Seth to see if she can stop by. He is at the Divine Mercy Chapel and is on his way back to the farm. He will meet her there.

Coming from opposite directions, they both pull in about the same time, excited to see each other. Anna can't wait to show him her treasure.

He's dressed in black and doesn't want to keep Anna waiting while he changes.

"Is there someplace where we can talk privately?" she asks, surprised by what he's wearing. There's that blasted white collar, and now she's uncertain about what she has to say.

"Yes," he says taking her hand and leading her toward the trail and ultimately, the tiny chapel.

"This is perfect. I have something I want to show you,"

she says as they sit in a pew awkwardly facing each other. "What were you doing over at Divine Mercy?"

"Oh, they needed me to fill in over there because Father Alfred, a dear mentor of mine from way back, has taken a little vacation and they're short-handed. I said I would help out 'til he gets back."

"You are celebrating Mass?" she asks, noticing how this news feels to her. It kinda makes his priest thing real. As if that collar left any doubt.

"Yes. Are you okay?" he asks her, feeling the energy shift.

"Just kind of caught me off guard," says Anna. "Maybe I should go."

"Oh no, please stay. It's so good to see you. And you said you have something to show me. What is it?"

Anna eyes the chapel door and debates about whether she wants to bolt or do what she came to do, which is have a heart-to-heart talk with Seth. She doesn't know if she can now. She doesn't know what to say and can't take her eyes off that collar and everything it represents.

Seeing her staring at it, Seth reaches up to unsnap the collar where it is secured and removes it from his shirt. He carefully sets it on the pew behind him with Anna watching his every move. She's still here, he thinks. A good sign.

Taking her hand, he says, "So what is it you wanted to show me, Anna?"

In her other hand is the heart-shaped sea glass. With her fist closed around it, she lifts her hand to him and opens it like the slow-motion blooming of a lotus flower.

"I was walking on the beach and talking with God and

asking if I was meant to have someone special in this dream life he has given me, …and I looked down and saw this. It's sea glass, shaped like a heart."

"Yes, I see that," says Seth, realizing how much he loves her innocence that she could be so excited by a piece of sea glass. And that she talks with God like a friend. She loves simplicity. And she tried so hard to cook him dinner. And she makes an absolute mess when eating an ice cream cone, and doesn't even care. He loves it all. He's just not sure what to do with this knowledge.

"Extraordinary," he says about the treasure and about her. "You know, John Lennon said, "A dream you dream alone is only a dream. A dream you dream together is reality."

"Seth, I came here to talk with you…about us. I'm a little confused. Okay, I'm a lot confused. Umm…."

Seth's cell phone rings with a tone he has set up for calls forwarded from the inn. It plays a snippet of *Love Is Still The Answer* by Jason Mraz, reminding him of his reality.

"I'm so sorry Anna, I need to take this," and he steps outside the chapel. "Hello, Honey-Do Farm, how may I help you?"

"Hi. I'm calling to see if you have any rooms available for three nights. Just for one person, arriving tonight if you have space," says the throaty voice reminding him of Sharon Stone or Marilyn Monroe. "We do have one room left and you're welcome to it. The rate includes house-keeping service and a community breakfast. For other meals you are on your own but there are plenty of places nearby. You can complete your registration online. What was your name? And when can we expect you?"

"I'm driving in from the city so I should be there around seven tonight."

"Very good. We'll be waiting for you. And your name is?"

"Vanessa," she says disconnecting the call.

He looks at his phone finding the whole call very odd. They don't get many inquiries as the farm is not widely publicized. It's more like guest referrals. But he knew they still had one room empty so it's good to get it booked. He sees Anna watching him from the doorway of the chapel. She looks angelic.

"I'm going to go now. I can see you're busy. We can talk another time."

"Anna, don't go. I just needed to deal with some farm business. Someone wanted to book a room for a few nights. When will I see you again?" he asks.

"When do you want to see me again?"

His first thought was, "How about every moment of every day for the rest of my life?" But he didn't say that. Instead, he said, "Would you let me take you out for dinner? Someplace nice? Do you have a favorite place? I'll take you wherever you want to go."

She looks at him, evaluating the situation, and shakes her head, hardly able to believe this thing she is getting deeper, and deeper into. He thought she was going to say, " No."

"What am I doing?" Anna asks herself. Unable to walk away, wanting to be with him more than anything, she smiles and says, "I'd love that." He is so worth the risk.

On her way home, she pulls up *Love Is Still the Answer* on her phone and sings along.

Chapter Twenty-Five

"Do not hesitate to love and to
love deeply."

U nsure where he might take Anna for dinner, and
needing someone to talk with since Father
Alfred is on vacation, Seth heads to Jacob's
house. Since it's a weekend he's hopeful he might catch him
at home. He pulls the Audi into the familiar driveway and
has a flashback of the days when his mother dropped them
both off Memorial Day Weekend. As their summer
getaway with their grandparents, it was great fun, but he
missed his mom. As he got older, he was grateful for that
time away from her.

"Hey you came back," says Jacob greeting him at the
door. I didn't think we'd see you again for another decade,"
reaching out to greet his brother.

"Hi Jacob, are you busy?"

"No, actually, Grace and the kids went to a matinee at
the Cape Cinema, and I've got a little time to myself. Let
me get you some coffee and we can sit on the back deck.

Gracie made some peanut butter cookies this morning. I'll get some."

Jacob is the perfect host. They sat on the deck reveling in the glorious autumn day, and Seth reflected on his relationship with their mother and wondered if Jacob's experience was the same.

"Do you remember our summers here?" asks Seth. "Like Mom dropping us off? Did you ever wonder what she did while we were gone? Or why she did that? I mean I loved it, the freedom we had and everything. But have you ever thought about why?"

"I think she was doing the best she could Seth, and being a single Mom and raising us alone, especially back then, it was a lot for her. Our summers here gave her a break, I guess. I mean she had to work so what would we have done? I don't think I would have had it any other way. I loved it here and still do. I think those summers created a true love for the area that's never left me. I'm grateful for it. I know you've always been curious about her."

Seth's thoughts wandered to one visit that stood out, when she had made it to their cottage, one of the few times she came to see them over the summer. Trying to sleep in the twin bed next to the wall, he could hear everything going on in the next room. He wished he hadn't, and pulled his pillow over his 12-year-old head. Seth usually shared their cottage bedroom with Jacob, but he had gone to Liam Hurley's house for a sleepover. Jacob and Liam were inseparable from the time they arrived in Brewster, until Labor Day weekend when they packed their bags and returned home. Seth didn't mind having the room to himself that night, appreciating the solitude even back then. Until…he heard his mother in the next room. She wasn't alone. There was arguing and he finally determined that she was arguing with his grandfather. He was curious about why they were yelling, but couldn't understand much of it through the wall.

"He's old enough now. He has a right to know," said Seth's grandfather.

"Never! I'm not discussing this." was his mother's response.

More yelling and a door slamming shut. He didn't like this one bit. He hated conflict and that was a big one, whatever it was about.

Jacob suggested they relocate to his office and went to refresh their coffees. Seth looks around at the blue and green plaid, overstuffed chair in the small room where Jacob corrects papers for school. It has the smell of an open candle on Jacob's desk that he guesses may have come from one of his students. The jar reads "Benevolence." It has a musky, jasmine scent that is not unpleasant, though Seth disputes Jacob's *benevolent* qualities sometimes.

He didn't know his mother well. They were not as close as Jacob was with her. She worked a lot, showed up when she could at school events, and provided for them in a minimalist way. She favored Jacob in nearly every way and Seth never understood why or how a mother could do that. Being a good human being is no easy task. Being a good parent is an even more insurmountable one he imagines. They didn't starve or anything. She showed her love as best she could, he reminded himself, wondering if that was enough.

He hopes opening a conversation with Jacob might give

him some insight into his mother who he wished he'd known better, understood more, perhaps forgiven more. He wonders if she is worthy of his forgiveness, which he questions. He is thinking about God's infinite forgiveness through the sacrament of reconciliation when Jacob returns with their coffee. Seth has more questions but they'll have to wait.

"Oh, Father Seth?" says Grace sticking her head into the office. Their home is a busy place. "Can you join us for dinner? We just got back and I'm about to put a meatloaf in the oven."

"I'd love to Gracie but I have to get back to the farm to get a new guest settled who's arriving shortly," says Seth looking at his watch. "I better get going."

"Promise you'll come by again soon and spend time with us."

"I will. I promise. Oh Gracie, can you recommend a particularly nice restaurant around here? You know, sometimes the guests want suggestions about where to eat."

"Uh-huh…" says Grace skeptically. "If you really want to wow someone, try *Epicurean Encounters*, *if* you can get a table. Their food is spectacular, and it overlooks the water."

"Thanks a bunch. I'll remember that. By the way Gracie… I can *always* get a table," he says with a big grin.

"I'll bet you can," she counters. Saying his goodbyes, he promises to return soon and drives off, letting go of his thoughts about his mother… for now. He has to meet the new guest who is arriving soon.

He had no sooner parked and gone inside when a polished black Cadillac Escalade pulls in. The driver gets out to open the door for his passenger, who reaches her manicured hand for his and steps down from the huge SUV. The driver proceeds to unload her bags which he piles near the front door. Waving him off, Vanessa bangs the door knocker impatiently, but Seth is already on his way to greet her. He is his usual cordial self, welcoming her to the inn.

"Please be careful with my bags, they're Gucci. And I'd like a cup of tea in my room as soon as you can. Ginger Lemongrass will be fine," she demands.

Vanessa waltzes past him leaving a trail of pungent perfume as if she owns the place. Seth gives her a quick tour of the kitchen where she can help herself to a cup of tea as there is no room service. He retrieves all six of her Gucci bags before showing her to her room on the second floor.

"I'd like to see the innkeeper to discuss my dietary, as well as transportation needs."

Seth looks at the woman who arrived at this simple inn wearing a tight red dress and stilettos to match.

"I'll get him for you," he says stepping out of her room and closing the door. He turns around and knocks "Hello, my name is Seth and I'm the innkeeper here. Nice to meet you. I understand you wanted to speak with me. How can I help you?"

"Oh, I didn't realize," she says. "Umm, I just wanted to inquire about breakfast. I'm vegan, so I don't eat meat, fish, poultry, eggs, dairy, honey, or other animal products."

"Well, this is a farm and you might find some fresh fruit down there in the morning but the menu is a hearty one filled with meat, fish, poultry, eggs, dairy, honey, or other animal products. And, of course, coffee and tea are always available. You'll find some wonderful folks to chat with," says Seth. "There are also many restaurants in the area and small shops where you might find something to your liking."

Not looking too pleased, she says, "That leads me to my other issue. How do people get around out here? I feel like I'm in the middle of the woods. Perhaps you'd like to give me a ride?" she asks looking him up and down, liking what she sees.

Feeling like a piece of meat, Seth gets chilled just looking at her and says, "Most folks arrive here with a vehicle, and those who don't, call an Uber to get around. You have to plan ahead as they don't have many drivers at certain hours, especially off-season. But if you need a ride close by, I can probably take you. Are you here for an event or something special?"

"Don't you know who I am?" she asks finding it inconceivable that he might not.

"I'm sorry Vanessa, but no. Perhaps you can tell me."

"I'm Vanessa Stein. You know…" She lists off several Broadway performances where surely, he would have recognized her. He shrugs to her dismay. "Anyway, I'm a last-minute addition to a play at the Performing Arts Center," she says looking put out that she has to explain who she is.

"Very nice," says Seth, unimpressed. "So, let me know if you need anything and make yourself at home."

Over breakfast the next morning, Vanessa makes herself comfortable in the kitchen, charming everyone with her tales of Broadway. The group listens attentively as she regales them with her stage adventures and accolades. Brandon seems to have a particular interest in her, though she appears older than his usual playmates. He doesn't need a Vanessa in his life right now. Henri is heading out to an AA meeting and asks Brandon if he wants to join him, and off they go. Fortunately, Brandon has the attention span of a gnat.

Settling into the simplicity of the place, Vanessa changes into more reasonable clothing for mucking around a farm. Only Emily has heard of her. Afterward, she coaxes Seth to give her a tour of the farm, cringing just saying the word. He introduces her to the sheep and as they come near, he invites her to touch them, and she practically jumps into his arms. Being the actress that she is, he wonders if the drama was intentional, as he pries her off of him. They move on to the chickens. That was not much better. He avoids showing her the chapel that has become something special to him. Walking quickly around the grounds he tries to wrap up their "tour." The woman can't seem to keep her distance or her hands off of him. She keeps rubbing up against him, or rubbing his back as they walk and finally, she links her arm around his and that is enough. He deposits her back at the entrance to the inn and returns to the barn briefly where he knows she won't venture again.

As he often does when he wants to connect with God in ways other than through church, he goes to the water. Much like Anna, he thought. They are alike in many ways. He drives to Gray's Beach Boardwalk, a quarter-mile-long stretch reaching out over a tidal marsh and creek. He walks to the very end, far away from the beach, looking over the rails at various sea life, and then sits on a bench. He is silent, listening only to the gentle movement of the water.

Occasionally someone else walks to the end, takes a quick look, and returns down the boardwalk. But his thoughts are on two things. What is Anna doing? And how soon will he be with her again?

A line from the prolific Dutch-born Catholic Priest, Henri Nouwen, from his book, *The Inner Voice of Love* came to mind. *"Do not hesitate to love and to love deeply."* Seth contemplates these words as he immerses himself in the moment, sitting on a bench over marsh and tidal pools, alone with his God…and thoughts of Anna.

Chapter Twenty-Six

That little piece of white plastic. How could
something so simple hold so much power,
she wonders.

Anna stands in front of her closet wondering what she should wear to a *nice* restaurant. Seth said he wanted to take her somewhere *nice*. She doesn't want to disappoint him but she has very simple tastes and menus at those fancy places are sometimes over-the-top gourmet, ie. weird. It is important to him. I get it, she says to herself, still unsure what to wear. An Egg McMuffin would sound good to me, as long as they make it with a folded egg and regular bacon instead of Canadian bacon. See? I'm easy. Or even Heart and Home. They make great breakfast though you have to ask for half cheese in the omelet or it will be sliding off the plate. Or pizza! Pizza is always a good idea. It's never a bad day for pizza.

When she is done speculating about the horrors of fine dining, and the joys of fast food, she chooses a simple taupe linen jumper with a white T-shirt underneath and a navy cable knit cardigan. Her black patent leather Birkenstocks will be fine. She knew Gram would have critiqued that outfit but she is trying to get better at celebrating who she is, not apologize for it. No one else's opinion matters. Except for Seth's maybe, and he needs to appreciate her for her simple, elegant, fabulous self. If being with Ethan taught her anything, it was that she owed it to herself, to be authentic. She didn't recognize who she was with him. She lost herself trying to be something she wasn't and didn't want to be. It was a lesson she didn't plan to repeat. She looks through Gram's jewelry box to add a short beaded necklace and matching bracelet. Just a little sparkle. It will feel good to have Gram with her in spirit.

If he shows up in a suit, looking more handsome than ever, they may not get out the door. The thought stirred up Anna's anxiety not to mention her other parts. "Could he *be* any more handsome?" she asks out loud to the empty room. She doesn't know if it is possible. Then she remembers sitting in the chapel with him. She knew they weren't alone with that collar next to him on the pew. That little piece of white plastic. How could something so simple hold so much power, she wonders. And yet it does.

With a little time before Seth is expected, Anna feels inspired to write a poem about where she lives now. So many feelings are getting stirred up by everything that is going on in her life, surely a poem must be ready to be born. Her poetry and her writing in general are inspired works. That is the only way she can write. She knows that isn't every writer's path but it sure is hers, without a doubt. Often something would happen in her life, or she would see something at the beach, or in the woods, and a poem was just waiting to come alive. If she didn't pay attention, and give it life when it was ready, she would lose it. She published a couple of poems but is rather shy about sharing her work. Maybe she would share one with Seth, she thought. One day.

A Yarmouth Poem

Walking beneath a canopy of trees
Pinecones everywhere
Some have fallen to the earth
Others on branches in the air

Seeds of something greater
Yet beautiful as they are
Unique in their simplicity
Nature's treasures by far

Scrub pines all around me
Golden needles blanket the ground
Creating a bed for the fallen
Softening their sound

Breathing in the salty air
Of this wondrous little place
Seaside, sunrise, sacred
An experience to embrace

Wondering if healing
Is happening in all the ways I need
My face, my spirit, my sadness

In some ways my greed

There is much I want from this life
Yet aching to be true
To all God has in store for me
I surrender it, I do.

Satisfied with what she wrote, and hearing the ship's
bell ring, Anna gets up and smoothes the wrinkles out of
her linen jumper. She recalls something she read about
entering a room as if God sent you there. So she stands as
tall as she can, summons an indifferent attitude, while
shaking in her Birkis, and answers the door. Seth stands
there wearing a navy Italian Canali suit, which she only
recognizes because Ethan shopped at Saks Fifth Avenue to
buy them. And it fit Seth like a glove. She notices the playfulness of the Vineyard Vines tie with a whale pattern in
direct contrast to the serious sexiness of the suit. It makes
her smile and she can't stop. *So much for indifference.* She
isn't sure, but she might have gasped, softly of course. She
continues staring at him.

"May I come in?" not sure if she was going to let him.

"Of course, come in," she says stepping aside,
wondering where the collar is, as if it were an entity unto
itself.

"Uh, what are your plans for tonight? Am I dressed
okay?"

"You're perfect," he says looking not at her clothes but
in her eyes. "I've reserved a table at *Epicurean Encounters* in
Chatham. It overlooks the water and I hear the food is
incredible. Does that sound okay?"

Anna thought about it a minute, ruminating about her egg McMuffin idea earlier. She decides she doesn't want to waste a night with this gorgeous man at McDonald's. That would have been a sacrilege. Tragic even.

"That sounds lovely," she says, trying to mean it but cringing at the thought. She would get through it. Surely there will be something she can eat, and if not, she will just gaze at him all night and that might be all she needs to satisfy her.

Seth is in full-on gentlemen mode and opens the door for her as she gets into his car. He keeps looking at her and she at him. In some way, it is as if they are seeing each other for the first time. Or don't want to forget what the other looks like. They arrive at the Epicurean and are welcomed as if they are royalty, and seated at a table in a quiet corner with a most spectacular view of the water. The sky is lit up with stars over Nantucket Sound. Anna just keeps smiling unsure what to do with this level of pure joy. It is unfamiliar.

"Would you like a glass of wine Anna, or something else to drink?'

"Wine would be nice," she says hoping it might calm her nerves. "And ice water with lemon please." Seth orders the wine, having requested her favorite in advance to make sure they had it on hand. He is well-versed in fine dining as his wealthy parishioners are very gracious and enjoy having him be part of their celebrations, which they do often.

The waitress returns.

"Ballet of Angels as you requested Sir," she says filling their glasses and placing the bottle into an ice bucket by their table.

Oh my God! Anna thinks. A man who presupposes a need. Priceless. The atmosphere is transcendent as the candle at their table flickers. Twinkle lights around the room add to the ambiance and the stars lit up the ocean casting a glow in their direction.

"Well, let's look at the menu Anna. What sounds good to you?" he asks.

Well…Hearing you say my name, thinks Anna. That sounds very good to me. Opening the menu, she scans it, seeing one gourmet creation after another, looking for something she might find palatable. Lemon Herb Lamb Loin, Steak Tartare, Coq Au Vain, Seared Scallops with garlic butter, Truffle Risotto, Lobster Bisque. Ugh! She couldn't choke down any of these things if Bobby Flay himself cooked and delivered it to their table. She also didn't want to offend Seth who had gone to such trouble to take her to this beautiful place.

Then she spotted it. Her saving grace. Her simple option, hidden in a sea of haute cuisine.

"Oh Yes! Thank you, Jesus!" she thinks. She hardly ever orders anything straight off a menu without giving it her own twist, and that night is no exception.

The waitress returns to take their order and Seth invites Anna to go first.

"I see you have the Mediterranean Swordfish and I wondered if I could have that just grilled with butter and lemon? And a small salad with extra balsamic dressing on the side." She threw in the salad, not because she wanted a plate of tasteless greens, but rather to give the illusion of better adulting. Her parents have always taken her to fancy restaurants since she was young, and she hated it even then, just liking things simple. She never developed a taste for gourmet cooking. She learned to adapt by simplifying whatever the menus offered. And she loved swordfish. Though Anna was less impressed with the menu, the atmosphere was spectacular.

"Oh, Anna that sounds delicious. I think I'll have the Diver Scallops. And we'll start with an order of the shrimp cocktail to share. Thank you so much."

The waitress returns with a basket of sliced sourdough baguette with a thin wedge of Brie and their shrimp. Seth reaches for her hand bowing his head to say a prayer of thanks, for the meal and Anna's company, and then encourages her to help herself to the shrimp. But watching him pray, transports her to somewhere else and she sees his collar in her mind. To make matters worse, he says, "Oh my gosh this is so good," after tasting the bread. "Here Anna, try it," he says, tearing off a small piece and holding it up to her mouth to taste." She opens her mouth to receive it wondering how to separate the man from the priest.

"It *is* good," she affirms after tasting it.

Seth remembers that Anna doesn't like seafood much except for shrimp cocktail and swordfish. They enjoy the meal. Their conversation flows effortlessly as they eat, and Anna tells him all about her grandmother and her recent trip to see her parents. That was a trip all right. He tells her about his recent albeit brief, conversation with Jacob about his mother. He wouldn't have shared that with just anyone but he easily shares with Anna. He trusts her.

They order the Black Forest Cheesecake with two forks for dessert. It has layers of chocolate cake, cheesecake, cherry filling, and frosting, topped with cherries, and is to die for.

"Oh my God," says Anna with her eyes closed at first bite, savoring its heavenly deliciousness.

"Oh, sorry," she says when she opens her eyes and sees him watching her. He is mesmerized as she enjoys each bite. He tries it and feels the same.

"Oh my God," he agrees.

There is something very sensual about sharing that uber-decadent dessert with him, and she wonders if he feels it too.

He hopes that Anna enjoyed the experience and when they step outside, it is unseasonably cool. They walk to the car and their ride home is quiet, each lost in their own thoughts, maybe the same, maybe very different. This time *she* reaches out for *his* hand, and holds it all the way home. She aches for that connection with him. When they arrive at her cottage, uncertainty is in the air. He walks her to the door and she doesn't want the night to end.

"Thank you for dinner, Seth. It was just lovely. Would you like to come in?" she asks in barely a whisper. Seth is facing her, holding both her hands in his now. He reaches up to tuck a few stray hairs behind her ear, resting the palm of his hand on the back of her head. He closes his eyes, kisses the top of her head, and takes his hand down.

"I would love to come in Anna," he says, taking a deep breath. "Very much. More than you can possibly know." Mustering all the God-given strength within him, he adds, "But I better not."

"Are you sure? I can make coffee or tea if you like," she says hopefully, just wanting more time with him.

Looking into her very soul he whispers, "It's not coffee or tea that I want Anna."

She watches him drive away from the porch window. Going into the cottage she turns on one dim light and sits on the couch, still feeling the warmth of his hands that just left hers, the emptiness in her heart, palpable.

Chapter Twenty-Seven

"I will always be a priest," he says, making
Anna wince with the realization.

S eth awoke to the pungent odor of Vanessa's
perfume in the next room, surprised that the smell
carried as it did. He took an extra-long shower
trying to wash away the smell, and as he did most mornings, he drove over to the Divine Mercy Chapel for Mass.
Sometimes he was scheduled to celebrate Mass himself. He
also began each day as priests do, reciting Morning Prayer,
called Lauds, and later, Evening Prayer, called Vespers, from
the *Liturgy of the Hours*. He has been doing this for so long,
that he couldn't imagine beginning and ending his day any
other way. It is a connection to the Divine and one he
would love to share with Anna. He thought about how
difficult it was to walk away from her the night before and
wondered what life might be like waking up next to her
each morning and seeing her next to him as he closed his
eyes at night.

Returning from the DMC he joins Brandon, Henri,
Emily, and Vanessa in the kitchen for breakfast.

"How is everyone doing this morning?" he asks, helping himself to coffee and some of Emily's morning offerings of cinnamon French toast and bacon. She keeps them all well fed and he is grateful for the budget that allows for everything the inn needs to operate.

"I have that list we can go over whenever you have a minute, Seth," says Brandon. "I'll need to gather the materials and I'd like to get to work on it next week. I've pinpointed several items that can use some attention."

"I could use some attention too," says Vanessa, batting her eyes at Seth who turns his attention to Brandon.

"I'd be happy to give you a tour of the grounds, Vanessa," says Brandon.

"Oh that's okay," she says. "Seth was already sweet enough to do that when I arrived. Maybe you'd like to have dinner later?" she asks looking directly at him.

"Gee, that sounds great, why don't we all go?" Henri suggests. "My treat."

"Well, that's awfully nice of you Henri. Let's do it," says Vanessa eyeing Seth. "Are you coming?"

"I have plans," says Seth putting the kibosh on that idea. "But that's great that you all want to get together outside of the inn. There are several restaurants close by to choose from. You might want to try Monk's Tavern. Monk and Roni are a husband and wife who own the place, and they have live music some nights."

He notices the sense of community that has developed there and wonders what it was like so many years ago as a summer camp. There must have been many friendships that blossomed on these very grounds. It had that kind of energy to it.

With plans made for dinner, Vanessa gets up to leave them, without clearing her place. As she passes behind Seth, she runs her hands over his shoulders and upper arms, squeezing his biceps. As she stands behind him, she whispers something in his ear he can't quite make out, but it makes his skin crawl, feeling her breath so close. The group looks on, and thankfully for Seth, off she went.

They all disperse and Brandon and Seth gather in the study to go over Brandon's suggestions for repairs and maintenance.

"The chicken coop roof needs patching, and the fencing in the paddock area where the apostles spend much of their time needs mending in several places. Vanessa reported a leaky faucet in her bathroom. And the mailbox near the front door is hanging by a thread. I noticed a crack in the glass of the storm door off the kitchen. There's more but that's a place to start."

"That sounds good Brandon. Whatever you can do is appreciated. We have a budget for maintenance so you can get paid."

"Oh, I didn't expect that as I'm staying here for free, but that would be amazing. I figured I would need to find some work eventually," says Brandon. "But with no car at the moment, my options are limited. And I really don't want to touch my inheritance. I've been living off the investments of those funds and my needs are simple."

"It sounds like we have a solution then. You maintain things around here and earn a little income, and we get to keep the place in great shape for when Travis and Toni return. And Brandon, be cautious around Vanessa."

"I'm not worried," says Brandon, laughing as he heads for the door, "but you ought to be."

Vanessa left in an Uber for rehearsal at the Performing Arts Center and Seth was relieved to see her go. Honestly, she creeped him out. She returned dressed all LuLuLemon in time to get ready for dinner with the gang. Seth hoped they would have something for her fussy appetite at Monk's, guessing they probably have at least a veggie burger on the menu.

Looking forward to having quiet at the inn for at least a few hours, he thought about inviting Anna over. Hmmm, Anna and him alone at the inn. Maybe not the best idea. So naturally he picked up the phone and asked her to come over. He knew it was a risk. He knew he wasn't playing it safe. But he didn't care. He just wanted to be with her. Anna didn't hesitate and after a quick shower and change of clothes, she was clanging the door knocker, as anxious to see him as he was to see her. He had done the same and came bounding down the stairs, hair still damp, to greet her.

They sat down in the living room filled with cozy over-stuffed upholstered furnishings and farmhouse antiques and talked and talked. They learned a lot about each other, about their past and present as well as talking about their dreams. At forty-five and fifty, they both lived full lives but also had dreams for their second half of life. Anna asked all kinds of questions about the challenges of being a priest and what it would mean to give that up.

"I've been questioning my vocation for some time, Anna. Then this opportunity came up for a sabbatical and time for genuine discernment unencumbered by anything else. My Bishop told me a story about his life that opened my mind further about what I want and need. I have loved being a priest more than I can say. It has been everything to me. My life and breath. When I think about giving up the priesthood, well, this is huge, and not something I consider lightly. I will always be a priest," he says, making Anna wince with the realization. "But I've realized there are other ways to serve God. So many other ways. Like what I'm doing here, right now. Providing this safe space for people to re-envision their lives, a place to heal.

The day I met you on the beach, I thought I'd made up my mind to leave. I wasn't looking for you, but there you were. I didn't know what to do with what I was feeling as we got to know each other. I didn't know how you felt. I'm so sorry I didn't tell you sooner that I was a priest. I honestly didn't think it would matter. It's just who I am. And you were just someone I met on the beach. But then I got to know you. My feelings for you Anna, have overwhelmed me. So unexpected."

Anna just listened to him and wondered if it was humanly possible to love anyone as much as she loved him at that moment. She got up from the rocking chair and joined him on the couch, facing him. Without saying a word, she wrapped her arms around him and rested her head on his chest, wanting more than anything not to let him go. They held each other, eyes closed, feeling God's love for them permeating their embrace.

Lifting her head and immersing her very soul in the depth of his gaze, she reached up and ran her fingers, lingering, through the dark waves of his hair.

"Anna, what have you done to me?" he whispered

barely able to find his voice. He lowered his mouth toward hers, when the front door burst open, with everyone returning from dinner. Seth stood up quickly looking achingly and apologetically at Anna.

Everyone appeared to have had a good time, but Vanessa seemed to have had enough to drink for all of them. She made a bee-line in his direction.

"There's my man," Vanessa says, tripping in her red patent leather stilettos, and falling into his arms. Her alcohol breath nearly knocking him over, if her body hadn't.

"Anna, I'll be right back. Vanessa, let's get you upstairs. Brandon, could I have some help here?" says Seth.

"Oh, I think you're doing fine," says Brandon, until Seth gives him a look that tells him he better help or else. The two men get her upstairs and Emily follows to make her comfortable as she passes out on the bed. When Seth returns, Anna is gone. He feels his heart plummet, missing her already.

The next morning Seth is scheduled to celebrate Mass. He has come to love the Divine Mercy Chapel and its dark wood, marble details, cathedral ceiling, and stained-glass windows. It is a small church, which he appreciates in contrast to the huge church he serves back in Connecticut. But his favorite thing is the life-sized Sacred Heart of Jesus statue with his arms open wide, high in the chancel across from the Blessed Mother. Mass begins and people stand as they do when the priest enters.

Anna slips into a pew in the back of the church when everyone is standing. She wants to see him. To see what he loves about being a priest. She wants to see him in action.

And she does. She is immersed in the Holy Mass being celebrated by the man she loves. The church is packed. It is so small that isn't too difficult to imagine. He says a beautiful homily about how important it is for all of us to find ways to serve God in unexpected places. Then it is time to receive communion, the Body of Christ. A deacon stands next to him offering the sacrament to a second line of people. Anna is approaching Seth. He doesn't notice her yet. A few people ahead of her, then two, then one, and then she is standing directly in front of him. He looks up, frozen. He has seen a lot over his 25 years as a priest, but seeing Anna stand before him felt like nothing else.

"Body of Christ," he finally managed to say, looking into her eyes, his heart racing. "Amen," she says, opening her mouth to receive the Blessed Sacrament. He places it on her tongue and his finger gently brushes her bottom lip for a microsecond. She makes the sign of the cross never losing eye contact with him until she begins walking back to her pew. She kneels in prayer as a flood of tears runs down her cheeks, knowing she can never come between Seth and their God. Just before the benediction, she slips away, rushing to her car.

After recovering from her dinner at Monk's with the gang the night before, Vanessa comes down late for breakfast. She joins Henri, Mary, and Brandon enjoying that day's creation by Emily, a broccoli cheddar quiche and blueberry scones. It was Vanessa's last day at the inn so she invited everyone to her show that night at the Performing Arts Center. She is taking her first bite of the quiche, having relaxed her dietary requirements during her stay. She reaches for a glass of fresh squeezed orange juice and nearly chokes on it, as Seth walks in the door. He is fresh from celebrating Mass at the DMC, all dressed in black with that little white collar glowing. He greets everyone, sits down to have breakfast, and looks directly at Vanessa who is turning several shades of crimson, mortified by her behavior.

"Good morning, Vanessa. Feeling better today?"

"Are you really a priest?" she asks, thinking it might be a Halloween costume. It is late October after all.

"I sure am," says Seth, loving every moment of this. She excuses herself, tells everyone she isn't feeling well, and goes upstairs to pack her bags. She is making a quick exit, at least as quick as she can with six bags. She orders an Uber and calls for Brandon to help her with the bags and she is gone, with the same flurry as when she arrived.

With that breath of fresh air out of the way, thought Seth, he went upstairs to change his clothes and reflect on what to do about Anna.

Chapter Twenty-Eight

"There are some things that leave a man no choice."

Seth can feel changes in the air, seasonally as well as spiritually, as the days draw closer to Travis and Toni's return to the inn, and his return to Connecticut and full-time pastoral duties. He receives a most unexpected call from Travis to say they aren't returning to the Cape and are selling the property.

"Do you know what you're putting it on the market for yet?" asks Seth.

"We've been approached several times in recent years with offers of 1.2 and 1.3 million. But it's not about the money for us. We want to know that the whole estate is in good hands and not going to be used to build condos or a parking lot. We love the place and it's been part of our lives for 40 years. Our kids grew up there. We never planned to leave, but San Diego weather and being near the kids, and grands, is hard to beat. That's the only reason Toni and I are willing to let it go."

"I know it used to be a summer camp and you have the

inn now. Would you find its use as a retreat center appropriate?" asked Seth.

"That would be the perfect use for it. Toni and I had talked about creating something like that in our younger days, but life got in the way as it often does. We never got around to it. Do you know someone who might be interested?"

"Well, I might be for the right price," says Seth. "Let me think about this and I'll get back to you. Thanks, Travis."

With Seth finding a rare minute to himself, he heads out to the chapel in the woods to think about his recent conversation with Jacob. What was his mother's story? Did she have a relationship with God? Why did she dump them on the Cape every summer and not return 'til Labor Day? *Was he that difficult to love?* He may never know any of this. However, he might gain some insight about his mother from his conversations with Jacob, which would be valuable to him. He struggles with her humanity as he struggles with his own. He acknowledges if only to himself, that he is quite judgmental for a man who administers the sacrament of reconciliation, the ultimate forgiveness. But mothers are supposed to sacrifice. Make time for their children, love them, and make them a priority. She's gone now so he may never understand.

The challenge to understand his current situation feels inconceivable, as well he considers. Giving up the priesthood feels as impossible as it would be to give up Anna. An unfair contest between religion and romance, and yet in some ways, they are the same. True love can and perhaps does come from the Divine. A gift from God. Knowing that truth, how could he see his love for Anna as anything other than Divine intervention? And that means surrendering the only life he has ever known in the church. Perhaps it's time.

He also recognizes both he and Anna have a love and passion for Jesus and the church. And despite the spectacular loss to the church, when, or if, they lose him, he will never not love the church in all its idiosyncrasies. He knows that people are fallible, filled with imperfections and so is the church. He has accepted that. And he doesn't believe that Anna could ever give it up either. She doesn't agree with all its practices and beliefs but loves the rituals and symbolism. She loves the Eucharist and above all she loves Jesus and Mary. She loves the incense and candles, high ceilings, and stained glass. She has an incredibly deep reverence for priests and their calling to serve God in such a complete way. It amazes her as she has articulated to Seth. Yet here they are. Completely in love with each other. Against all odds. So now what?

He remembers a line from a song by Luke Combs, *"There are some things that leave a man no choice."* Seth reflects in the silence a while longer hoping to hear some response from his God, toward the most difficult decision he has ever had to make. He doesn't know how he could bear the loss of either the church or Anna. But he realizes now, that while leaving the church is a sacrifice, being with Anna is a joy that makes him feel alive in a way he never imagined possible. And considering other ways to serve God is its own beautiful call.

～

Back at the inn, an occasional new guest came and went. They were always in some kind of transition, not tourists, although as it got closer to the holidays, things did get busier at the inn and on the Cape in general. It is a festive place as the calendar inches its way toward Thanksgiving and Christmas. Anna and Seth see each other often, taking bike rides, enjoying intimate dinners at the cottage, taking walks around the cranberry bogs, sharing their stories, and learning more about each other. Seth labors over a decision he has to make sooner rather than later. However, he has known what he has to do in his heart for some time. Taking action is another story. His sabbatical will be ending and he is expected back in Connecticut for Advent, the busiest of the church seasons. Anna is falling deeper and deeper for someone she knew better than to think she could have. It didn't keep her from falling though, falling, falling, falling. Such is the way of true love.

She still can't get the image of Seth out of her mind. Seeing him at the altar, celebrating Mass, sharing a thought-provoking homily, and then those words that mean so much to her, and Catholics all over the world. "The Body of Christ." They aren't just words. They mean something. They mean a lot to her. And his words earlier, "I will always be a priest." What did that mean? Dare she even think about it? She can't imagine coming between him and God. She just can't. And she also can't imagine life without him. She loves him more than she ever thought was possible.

❧

Anna set aside her novel in favor of writing poetry during the holiday season, which she always enjoys. The inspired nature and immediate gratification of poetry appeal to her, in contrast to the seemingly never-ending work of her novel. Her feelings for Seth created a need within her to express them through poetry. One day while cleaning out one of the few closets in the cottage, she found a hidden nook revealing an old Royal typewriter and a fireproof document box. She took both out and sat in Gram's favorite chair placing the typewriter carefully at her feet. Trying to open the box, she finds it locked. Gram clearly did not want anyone to know what was in it. It couldn't be end-of-life planning documents she speculated because Gram's attorney had all that paperwork. This was just another of several curiosities since she arrived in September. Just as she had that thought, she remembered the key she'd found in Grams' purse. She still hadn't figured out what it was for. It's a long shot, she thought, but is there a chance it will open this box? She fetched the key and put it in the lock. It opened.

Her jaw dropped as she discovered pages and pages of poetry with Gram's name on each, and a note on top that read,

"Dear Anna,

I want to tell you about my secret passion. I know you aren't aware but I used to attend a writing group every Tuesday for years. During those sessions, these poems evolved. Though I'm not very reserved as a rule, I find that I've always been a little shy about sharing my writing so I've kept it under lock and key as you will have found if you're reading this. Forgive me. I'm not the best writer, but I always enjoyed that group and found it nurtured my creativity in a way nothing else had back then. Do whatever you like with it. It would make a fine tinder for the fireplace.

Our gathering was called Tuesdays at Ten and had a delightful assortment of beautiful, talented women writers who came and went over the years. The group was led by a brilliant author and weaver who guided us on a very affirming journey toward manifesting our writing lives. I hope and pray you find ways to explore your own passion for writing which I know is deep within you. As well as whatever other passions stir your soul. Life is short, dear Anna. Celebrate it with reckless abandon. Don't be afraid to get hurt. Take risks and above all, trust your heart and Jesus will guide you.

All My Love, Gram"

The poems were typed with her Royal typewriter on onion skin paper. Anna couldn't believe it. She had no idea her grandmother wrote anything, much less poetry. She had that quote by Mary Oliver on the wall and a few poetry books on the shelf, but aside from that she had no idea she was a poet. She sat and read one after another. In tears, she realized she may well be the only person to ever see Gram's work. And it was good. The idea came to her to publish some of it with her own poetry, although given that it was so hidden, she wonders how Gram might feel about that. "She did say I could do what I want with it, though. I've no plan to use it for tinder. I'll pray about it," she says to herself.

She sits on the couch in her cottage wrapped in a quilt as usual, the comfort helping with the discomfort of her thoughts. November is just around the corner and it feels like it. This time of year, being near the ocean can feel frigid. Though they don't get a lot of snow traditionally, they do get some. In New England anything is possible. Knowing she needs to shake off these thoughts about Seth, she bundles up to take a walk on the beach. It is brisk out but the sun is shining. She stuck her hands in her coat pocket and found the heart-shaped sea glass she discovered earlier. She held it as she walked, feeling sad and scared and a little lost. She can't believe she has fallen in love so quickly, so deeply. She knows better. The heart wants what the heart wants though. She never expected to meet someone like Seth. Never in a million years.

On her walk, she imagines what life might look like if Seth decides to give up the priesthood. If he does, it will have to be for himself, not for her. She knows she can't be the reason. She could never be. He might resent her for it later on. And where will they live? What would their second half of life together look like? They both still love Jesus and still love the church. That will never change, right? Will they live in her tiny cottage? It warms her heart to think of waking each morning next to him and she can't hold back a smile just thinking about it. But she is afraid to think of what she knows she can't have and bends over at the edge of the Sound to touch the ice-cold water to bring herself back to reality.

Chapter Twenty-Nine

"I don't understand," she says, looking into his eyes.

O ne day when the leaves were still in spectacular autumn colors and just beginning to let go, Seth asked Anna to meet him at the inn. They had been spending a lot of time together and they took a long walk around the grounds. Taking in the New England charm that they both appreciated so much, they eventually ended up in the chapel. It had become a special place for them, where they often had some of their most meaningful talks.

"I received a call from Travis this week. He called to say he and Toni aren't coming back to the Cape," he told her, pausing to see her reaction. "They love it so much in San Diego, being near their kids and grandchildren, they've decided not to return. At least not to live. They are selling the inn, the whole property, all seven acres. They'll be back before it's sold to pack up their personal items but they're selling it furnished."

"Well, that's interesting," she says looking puzzled, wondering why he is telling her this.

"Anna, I've been wrestling with the future of my vocation as you know. I *need* to continue serving God and the church in some way." Her heart fell, listening to his words. "I was thinking about this when I received Travis' call. I took a long, prayerful walk around the property. Anna, this used to be a summer camp, and now it's an inn and farm. As I walked around taking in the natural beauty of it, the buildings and surroundings, I realized that it could be something really special."

"It would make an amazing retreat center," says Anna. "A place for people to come and get quiet, recharge, and maybe take spiritual or creative programs. Those two buildings you showed me on the far side of the property, with a few renovations, could be a space for small groups, programs, and accommodations. I think there is a need for something like that. In fact, when I first came here it reminded me of places I'd been on retreat over the years."

"I've seen the need in the people who have come to the inn," says Seth. "And it would be a way to continue serving God... even if I'm no longer actively serving as a priest."

"But Seth... are you absolutely sure you want to give up the priesthood? It has been your life."

"Anna, I've spent the last two and a half months thinking about it every single day. And for several months before I arrived here. Wondering what my life could look like and how I could continue to serve God, but not through the church. To be a part of the community and give something back in a spiritual way. This is one way.

And I've thought about what my life would be like with you in it, Anna. I've thought about that a lot."

"Oh Seth, I've thought about that too," says Anna trying to hold back tears. "I can't get you out of my mind...or my heart...as much as I've tried. And I have tried."

"So, I guess you like the idea?" he asks.

"Absolutely! I love the idea! You could facilitate spiritual retreats and offer spiritual direction. I could offer poetry programs if you want, or writing workshops. And Zoe could do some kind of creative program. It could be a safe space for people to come and relax and get quiet. Maybe heal and connect with God. Imagine what you could do with this place? The possibilities are endless."

"I have imagined it, Anna. Perhaps we can imagine together."

"But how would you do it?" she asks. "This property must be very valuable."

"Yes, it is," he admits, laughing. "I plan to talk with Travis and explore some options. But first, I wanted to get your thoughts about it. We'll talk more, but will you come with me tomorrow? There's something I want to show you," he says wanting to get away from the inn.

"Of course," she says, unable to keep from smiling.

"Great. Dress warm, it's a little cool out. I'll pick you up around 11:00."

"Okay." She continues ruminating about everything he shared as she drives away from the inn, promising to talk with him later, her thoughts laying heavily on his words.

The next morning right at 11:00 Seth was clanging that ship's bell on the porch and he wondered if maybe Anna would like a normal doorbell. He made a mental note to ask her. She answered the door right away, trying to restrain her beaming smile at the sight of him. Dressed in jeans, a black turtleneck, and sneakers she decided to keep it simple and refrain from stressing herself out every time she saw him. She is determined to embrace her quirky self. Getting her jacket on with a scarf and mittens in her bag, just in case, they walk to the car as she asks where they are going.

Opening the door for her he whispers in her ear as she gets in, "It's a secret." Feeling his breath that close to her gave her chills and she wrapped herself in her blue and white plaid cashmere scarf before he was even in the driver's seat.

"Oh, I'll put the heat on," he says as soon as he sees she is cold, not realizing her chill wasn't from the autumn air.

From South Yarmouth, he drove about 30 minutes heading toward Chatham, an area Anna hadn't spent a whole lot of time in during her Cape Cod trips. He made several turns off the main road and her curiosity was piqued as he pulled the Audi into Chase Park. All she could see were trees, some flowers, a huge sprawling green lawn, and a paved path leading up the sloping hill.

"You wanted to show me a park?" she asks him.

"Patience, dear Anna," was his response as he opened her door, offering his hand as she got out. They followed the sidewalk toward the top of the hill where there was a historic wind-powered gristmill built in 1797.

They read about its significance on a posted sign.

"You wanted to show me a windmill?" she asks.

He places his hands on her shoulders and turns her around facing the opposite direction and she gasps at the sight of a spectacular labyrinth made of stone pavers. They walk down the other side of the hill toward it and Anna is awestruck by its beauty.

"I thought you might be familiar with labyrinths, Anna, and this one is particularly special, isn't it? It's the Chatham Labyrinth and is a replica of the 11-circuit labyrinth in Chartres Cathedral in France. I've actually been there. I've been here many times and I've been blessed to have it to myself on most occasions. It seems to be a best-kept secret," he says, noticing there isn't another soul in sight.

"Have you really?" She asked, eyes wide open. She couldn't get the words out fast enough. "I've never been to Chartres Cathedral but have always wondered about it. I love labyrinths, they are a magnificent tool for prayer, like a walking meditation, a way to process grief, and a way to process joy. A way to grow closer to God. How did you know? How did you know I would love this?"

"I just had a feeling. Shall we?" he says inviting her to begin her walk.

Giving her some space before he begins as appropriate, they follow the path with all its twists and turns. So much like life thinks Anna. Back and forth they follow the path leading toward the sacred center. She tries to still her mind as she walks, trying to empty herself of any expectations. To be open to whatever God has in mind for her on this journey, on the labyrinth, and in life. She doesn't know it but Seth's prayer is the same. As she reaches the center, Seth joins her. Standing facing each other, looking into each other's eyes, into each other's souls, they savor the moment. He reaches for Anna's hands and they stand for the longest time just being present to each other. When he can't restrain himself any longer, and is inches from Anna's lips, he hears someone walking over the crest of the hill toward the labyrinth. They are no longer alone. Pulling themselves away, they walk the path leading out of the labyrinth and walk hand in hand, back to the car. They don't say a word until they are settled in and Seth starts the engine.

Reluctantly breaking the silence, Seth asks if Anna is hungry. Anna is always hungry. At that moment she was starving... for him. He knows of a place in West Chatham that has a vintage feel, like an old-fashioned diner.

"That sounds perfect," says Anna, lost in her thoughts of what might have been. Soon they were pulling into *Larry's PX* for lunch. Anna thought it looked familiar but she wasn't sure why until they got inside and sat down. As she looked around, she realized it was a filming location for one of her favorite movies, *Year By the Sea*. It was an adaptation of Joan Anderson's, memoir *A Year By the Sea*, one of Anna's absolute favorite books of all time. She's read it over and over.

"Why did you choose this restaurant?" asks Anna, explaining to him about its significance.

"I walk the labyrinth often when I'm in the area," says Seth, "and that led me to discover this place. I liked its simplicity and vintage flair," he said laughing. "I thought you might too."

They order lunch and talk more, sharing details about themselves. It seems they never run out of things to talk about. When Seth drops her off back at the cottage, she is filled with gratitude for the day, and hope for her future. Whatever that might look like.

Thanksgiving was special this year as they worked together at the Inn to cook and share a meal with assignments given to her being the simplest of things. Word must have gotten out, she thought. Everyone pitched in where they could with Emily cooking the turkey; their shared meal was a feast for the senses. Then they worked together all weekend to put up the Christmas tree and decorate the inn for the holiday.

Brandon caught up with Anna when they were done decorating and asked if she had a minute to talk with him. They hadn't had much opportunity to get to know each other except through Seth. They went into the study where they could have some privacy and sat down across from each other.

"Anna, I just wanted to talk with you a minute about Seth," said Brandon, choosing his words very carefully. "Seth and I go way back. He's like family to me as you probably know. I care about him very, very much. Now I know he's head over heels for you. I've never seen him so happy. And I know you love him too," he said pausing. "I don't know how much you are aware of regarding this process, but what he is about to do for you, cannot be easily undone. I just wanted you to know that. And to ask you... Please be certain about what you're doing. And please don't hurt my friend."

Brandon got up and left without giving Anna a chance to say a word. But she didn't need to. She understood.

Seth had to be at church for the first Sunday of Advent and he'd been disappearing a lot lately between work at the inn, and having to be back in New Canaan for all the holiday commitments as well as his regular responsibilities there. Anna knew Seth came out to the Cape as often as he could, and they talked on the phone for hours. Still, she missed him terribly. He promised to be back late Christmas day for them to celebrate together and she couldn't wait to see him. He called her Christmas Eve and they talked for over an hour and neither one wanted to end their call.

Christmas day arrived and Anna was waiting to greet him at her cottage. She had put up a small Christmas tree from a local tree farm and had tiny white fairy lights strung everywhere. She made a wreath for her front door and strung fresh pine garland over the fireplace mantel. A few of Gram's vintage Christmas decorations finished the simple look. Anna had found a Swedish Angel Chime at a local gift shop that she remembered from her childhood and put that out. It was made of very thin gold tin and had three angels hanging from it. This always brought her joy as a child and still did today. She can't wait to show Seth.

She is ready and full of anticipation when he finally pulls up in front of the cottage around 8:00 p.m. It was dark and she ran out into the cold and into his arms. They went inside and sat together on the couch by the Christmas tree listening to the crackling fire she had ready for them. She was glad she thought to have him come there instead of the inn, so they could have time alone. He'd had a long drive and she knew he must be tired. They sit together on the couch both overjoyed to be together again. Anna can't get close enough to him and he feels the same way as they sit talking, holding hands, and drinking in each other's eyes. She has long since forgiven him for his original sin of omission. And has moved on to head over heels in love with someone who was already spoken for. But he is worth whatever time they can have together. She tells Seth about discovering Gram's poetry. Anna thought of the wisdom of her grandmother's words now, "*Life is short dear Anna. Celebrate it with reckless abandon. Don't be afraid to get hurt. Take risks. And trust your heart and Jesus will guide you.*"

With childlike enthusiasm, she shares with him the story about the angel chimes as they spin around in front of them, a soft ringing of the chimes with candles glowing, and one angel on top with a horn, heralding Christmas.

She can't wait to give him his Christmas gifts and he can't wait to give her his. Once they settle in, she hands him a large package, which he opens to find a vibrant patchwork quilt and a poem.

"Anna, it's beautiful! Did you make this?" he asks, surprised.

"I did. So that wherever you are, you might remember me, and feel me close, even when we're not together." And there's a poem I wrote for you.

The Christmas Gift

I never knew I could love someone
The way that I love you
Miraculous, unending
Eyes of Nantucket blue

Kind beyond imagining
Oh so handsome, hard to leave
Always ready to listen
To every want and need

I never thought I would love again
Wounded, to say the least
But you have healed my trust within
A brave, courageous feat

I look at you and see our God
And all is as it should be
Longing to be in your loving arms
Today, tomorrow, and always

At first, he says nothing, so moved as he is by her thoughtfulness. He just takes her hands and looks at her, struggling to find the words to tell her how incredibly blessed he feels to have found her.

"I'm so moved by this Anna. And I'm so sorry I hurt you. I hope you give me a chance to make it up to you. I love both of your gifts. They are just beautiful and I'm so touched that you created these for me."

He gives Anna a large package with a little box on top,

which she sets on her lap and doesn't rush to open. "I'm so happy to be with you right now Seth. I love you so much. I don't need anything else."

"Open it anyway," he says. "Open the little one first."

She carefully opens the tiny package and finds a white linen box with a satin ribbon tab and holds it in the palm of her hand. She can't imagine what it could be and looks up at him.

"Go ahead. Open it."

She pulls on the ribbon, sliding out a little drawer with a white velvet drawstring pouch. The mystery continues as she opens the pouch to find a set of keys.

"Keys?" she asks, puzzled.

"Yes. Those are keys to our retreat center," he says. "I bought it. Well, we'll actually close on it next month."

She is speechless and wraps her arms around him even though she has a thousand questions. They can wait. She just wants to be with him…forever. He is her holy grail.

"Are you certain that's what you want to do?" she asks in disbelief.

"Geez, I don't know… " he teased. "Why don't you open the next package and you'll find out."

She carefully opens the gift, first removing the Christmas wrapping, lifting the lid off the box, and unfolding the tissue paper. There on her lap, she finds his clerical collar. She can't touch it as if it might burn her hands.

"I don't understand," she says looking into his eyes.

"It's official Anna. I'm no longer a practicing priest, though my laicization and dispensation can take a long while. But that's the church's problem, not ours. I love you,

Anna. I have loved you since the day I first set eyes on you. It took me a while to realize just how much, as I wrestled with my vocation. I'm sorry for that. But I know with absolute certainty, I don't want to spend another day without you. I want to wake up every morning next to you and be the last thing you see at night."

"Oh Seth, I love you too, and it has scared me half to death. To love you so much and know I couldn't have you."

"You can have me now Anna. I would give up the world for you. You are the one I want to spend the rest of my life with. If you'll have me, I'm all yours."

Anna wraps her arms around the only one she could imagine being with. The one who can share her love of God. The one who brings her joy, makes her heart swell and makes her feel safe. She holds his handsome face in her hands and looks into those eyes that hold her captive as no one else can. And with tears running down her face, he wipes them away and brings his lips to hers. They savor that long-awaited moment. One that could only come from the synchronicity of two hearts, held apart by forbidden love, for way too long. Anna bites her bottom lip as she thinks for a moment. And without further hesitation, she takes his hand leading him to the stairs, as they retreat to the cottage loft.

Amen ~ The End

Dear Readers

Thank you for your interest in *Synchronicity - Two Hearts, One Spirit, a Forbidden Love*. I hope you have enjoyed the story of Seth and Anna and perhaps even fallen in love with them as I have. Of course, we've spent much more time together. That's because I began writing about them over a decade ago.

They initially came to be, one 20-minute writing prompt at a time. I was attending a fabulous writing group in Rhode Island off and on for years. Led by a beautiful spirit who gathered different women and inspired us to write. So I wrote there and I wrote at home, and anywhere else I had a minute, developing this story while I also worked as a reporter and columnist for a local newspaper. I led Creating A Writing Life Retreats for about 10 years and I later served a church as its community minister where I used my skills as an expressive arts educator and spiritual director. But my roots were Catholic. Perhaps we always find our way home.

Two years ago, I asked a couple of friends if they wanted to gather with me to work on our novels. I got out my substantial pile of hand-written work about Seth and Anna and transcribed it all into the computer, somehow giving it a shape that turned into a story. It was no easy task. Once most of the original material was woven together, I finished the story...for now, because I knew there was so much more to tell. So just about two years and a decade later, I published Synchronicity. Writing it has stirred my heart and brought me joy beyond my imagining. I hope reading it has brought you some as well. I've already started the sequel.

I'm not a huge fan of social media but I'll do my best to keep up. I welcome your comments and communication via email, my website, and Facebook. You can sign up for my newsletter at www.PatriciaAnnChaffee.com and check in for the latest blog posts.

Lastly, if you enjoyed Synchronicity, please take a moment to post a quick review on Amazon. Those thoughts you share mean so much.

God Bless & Peace to You,
Patty

Reach out to me at:
www.PatriciaAnnChaffee.com
Seastar1013@gmail.com
https://www.facebook.com/patriciaann.chaffee

About the Author

Patricia Ann Chaffee is an award-winning writer and published poet from the Connecticut shoreline who considers Cape Cod her second home. She has worked with writers and creative souls for several decades. She lives and celebrates life near the ocean, loves all things simple, spiritual, quiet, and creative, and is now working diligently on the sequel to Synchronicity. Watch for it to see what happens next in the lives of Seth and Anna.